the
farming of
bones

the
farming of
bones

• a novel •

edwidge danticat

Portions of this novel appeared in altered form in *Granta* 54,
Best of Young American Novelists (Summer 1996) as "The
Revenant" and in *Conjunctions* 27, The Archipelago: New
Caribbean Writing (1996) as "Condolences".

Published by

Soho Press, Inc.
853 Broadway
New York, NY 10003

Library of Congress Cataloging-in-Publication Data
Danticat, Edwidge, 1969–
     The farming of bones: a novel / Edwidge Danticat.
          p.   cm.
     ISBN 1-56947-126-6 (alk. paper)
     I. Title.
PS3554.A5815F37   1998   98-3655
813'.54—dc21   CIP

10 9 8 7 6 5 4 3 2 1

Jephthah called together the men of Gilead and fought against Ephraim. The Gileadites captured the fords of the Jordan leading to Ephraim, and whenever a survivor of Ephraim said, "Let me cross over," the men of Gilead asked him, "Are you an Ephraimite?" If he replied, "No," they said, "All right, say 'Shibboleth.'" If he said, "Sibboleth," because he could not pronounce the word correctly, they seized and killed him at the fords of the Jordan. Forty-thousand were killed at the time.

Judges 12:4–6

In confidence to you, Metrès Dlo, Mother of the Rivers

Amabelle Désir

1

His name is Sebastien Onius.

He comes most nights to put an end to my nightmare, the one I have all the time, of my parents drowning. While my body is struggling against sleep, fighting itself to awaken, he whispers for me to "lie still while I take you back."

"Back where?" I ask without feeling my lips moving.

He says, "I will take you back into the cave across the river."

I lurch at him and stumble, trying to rise. He levels my balance with the tips of his long but curled fingers, each of them alive on its own as they crawl towards me. I grab his body, my head barely reaching the center of his chest. He is lavishly handsome by the dim light of my castor oil lamp, even though the cane stalks have ripped apart most of the skin on his shiny black face, leaving him with crisscrossed trails of furrowed scars. His arms are as wide as one of my bare thighs. They are steel, hardened by four years of sugarcane harvests.

"Look at you," he says, taking my face into one of his spacious bowl-shaped hands, where the palms have lost their lifelines to the machetes that cut the cane. "You are glowing like a Christmas lantern, even with this skin that is the color of driftwood ashes in the rain."

"Do not say those things to me," I mumble, the shadows of sleep fighting me still. "This type of talk makes me feel naked."

He runs his hand up and down my back. His rough callused palms nip and chafe my skin, while the string of yellow coffee beans on his bracelet rolls over and caresses the tender places along my spine.

"Take off your nightdress," he suggests, "and be naked for true. When you are uncovered, you will know that you are fully awake and I can simply look at you and be happy." Then he slips across to the other side of the room and watches every movement of flesh as I shed my clothes. He is in a corner, away from the lamp, a shadowed place where he sees me better than I see him. "It is good for you to learn and trust that I am near you even when you can't place the balls of your eyes on me," he says.

This makes me laugh and laugh loud, too loud for the middle of the night. Now I am fully disrobed and fully awake. I stumble quickly into his arms with my nightdress at my ankles. Thin as he says I am, I am afraid to fold in two and disappear. I'm afraid to be shy, distant, and cold. I am afraid I cease to exist when he's not there. I'm like one of those sea stones that sucks its colors inside and loses its translucence once it's taken out into the sun, out of the froth of the waves. When he's not there, I'm afraid I know no one and no one knows me.

"Your clothes cover more than your skin," he says. "You become this uniform they make for you. Now you are only you, just the flesh."

It's either be in a nightmare or be nowhere at all. Or otherwise simply float inside these remembrances, grieving for who I was, and even more for what I've become. But all this when he's not there.

"Look at your perfect little face," he says, "your perfect little shape, your perfect little body, a woman child with deep black skin, all the shades of black in you, what we see and what we don't see, the good and the bad."

He touches me like one brush of a single feather, perhaps fearing, too, that I might vanish.

"Everything in your face is as it should be," he says, "your nose where it should be."

"Oh, wi, it would have been sad," I say, "if my nose had been placed at the bottom of my feet."

This time he is the one who laughs. Up close, his laughter crumples his face, his shoulders rise and fall in an uneven rhythm. I'm never sure whether he is only laughing or also crying at the same time, even though I have never seen him cry.

I fall back asleep, draped over him. In the morning, before the first lemongrass-scented ray of sunlight, he is gone. But I can still feel his presence there, in the small square of my room. I can smell his sweat, which is as thick as sugarcane juice when he's worked too much. I can still feel his lips, the eggplant-violet gums that taste of greasy goat milk boiled to candied sweetness with mustard-colored potatoes. I feel my cheeks rising to his dense-as-toenails fingernails, the hollow beneath my cheekbones, where the bracelet nicked me and left a perfectly crescent-moon-shaped drop of dried blood. I feel the wet lines in my back where his tongue gently traced the life-giving veins to the chine, the faint handprints on my waist where he held on too tight, perhaps during some moment when he felt me slipping. And I can still count his breaths and how sometimes they raced much faster than the beating of his heart.

When I was a child, I used to spend hours playing with my

shadow, something that my father warned could give me night-mares, nightmares like seeing voices twirl in a hurricane of rain-bow colors and hearing the odd shapes of things rise up and speak to define themselves. Playing with my shadow made me, an only child, feel less alone. Whenever I had playmates, they were never quite real or present for me. I considered them only replacements for my shadow. There were many shadows, too, in the life I had beyond childhood. At times Sebastien Onius guarded me from the shadows. At other times he was one of them.

2

Births and deaths were my parents' work. I never thought I would help at a birth myself until the screams rang through the valley that morning, one voice like a thousand glasses breaking. I was sitting in the yard, on the grass, sewing the last button on a new indigo-colored shirt I was making for Sebastien when I heard. Dropping the sewing basket, I ran through the house, to the señora's bedroom.

Señora Valencia was lying on her bed, her skin raining sweat and the bottom part of her dress soaking in baby fluid.

Her waters had broken.

As I lifted her legs to remove the sheets, Don Ignacio, Señora Valencia's father—we called him Papi—charged into the room. Standing over her, he tugged at his butterfly-shaped mustache with one age-mottled hand and patted her damp forehead with the other.

"¡Ay, no!" the señora shouted through her clenched grinding teeth. "It's too soon. Not for two months yet."

Papi and I both took a few steps away when we saw the blood-speckled flow streaming from between his daughter's legs.

"I will go fetch the doctor," he said. His hidelike skin instantly paled to the color of warm eggshells.

As he rushed out the door, he shoved me back towards the señora's bed, as if to say with that abrupt gesture that the situation being what it was, he had no other choice but to trust his only child's life to my inept hands.

Thankfully, after Papi left, the señora was still for a moment. Her pain seemed to have subsided a bit. Drowning in the depths of the mattress, she took a few breaths of relief.

We sat for a while with her fingers clinging to mine, like when we were girls and we both slept in the same room. Even though she was supposed to sleep in her own canopy bed and I was to sleep on a smaller cot across from hers, she would invite me onto her bed after her father had gone to sleep and the two of us would jump up and down on the mattress, play with our shadows, and pretend we were four happy girls, forcing the housemaid—Juana—to come in and threaten to wake Papi who would give us a deeper desire for slumber with a spanking.

"Amabelle, is the baby's bed ready?" With her hand still grasping mine, Señora Valencia glanced at the cradle, squeezed between the louvered patio doors and her favorite armoire deeply carved with giant orchids and hummingbirds in flight.

"Everything is prepared, Señora," I said.

Even though I wasn't used to praying, I whispered a few words to La Virgen de la Carmen that the doctor would come before the señora was in agony again.

"I want my husband." The señora clamped her eyes shut, quietly forcing the tears down her face.

"We will send for him," I said. "Tell me how your body feels."

"The pain is less now, but when it comes on strong, it feels like someone shoves a knife into my back."

The baby could be leaning on her back, I thought, remembering one of my father's favorite expressions when he and my mother were gathering leaves to cram into rum and firewater bottles before rushing off to a birthing. Without remembering what those leaves were, I couldn't lessen the señora's pain. Yes, there was plenty of rum and firewater in the house, but I didn't want to leave her alone and go to the pantry to fetch them. Anything could happen in my absence, the worst of it being if a lady of her stature had to push that child out alone, like a field hand suddenly feeling her labor pains beneath a tent of cane.

"Amabelle, I am not going to die, am I?" She was shouting at the top of the soft murmuring voice she'd had since childhood, panting with renewed distress between her words.

We were alone in the house now. I had to calm her, to help her, as she had always counted on me to do, as her father had always counted on me to do.

"Before this, the most pain I ever felt was when a wasp bit the back of my hand and made it swell," she declared.

"This will pain you more, but not so much more," I said.

A soft breeze drifted in through the small gaps in the patio doors. She reached for the mosquito netting tied above her head, seized it, and twisted the cloth.

Gooseflesh sprouted all over her arms. She grabbed my wrist so tight that my fingers became numb. "If Doctor Javier doesn't come, you'll have to be the one to do this for me!" she yelled.

I yanked my hands from hers and massaged her arms and

taut shoulders to help prepare her body for the birth. "Brace yourself," I said. "Save your strength for the baby."

"Virgencita!" she shouted at the ceiling as I dragged her housedress above her head. "I'm going to think of nothing but you, Virgencita, until this pain becomes a child."

"Let the air enter and leave your mouth freely," I suggested. I remembered my mother saying that it was important that the women breathe normally if they wanted to feel less pain.

"I feel a kind of vertigo," she said, twitching like live flesh on fire. Thrashing on the bed, she gulped desperate mouthfuls of air, even though her face was swelling, the veins throbbing like a drumbeat along her temples.

"I will not have my baby like this," she said, trying to pin herself to a sunken spot in the middle of the bed. "I will not permit anyone to walk in and see me bare, naked."

"Please, Señora, give this all your attention."

"At least you'll cover my legs if they come?" She grabbed her belly with both hands to greet another surge of pain.

I felt the contents of my stomach rise and settle in the middle of my chest when the baby's head entered her canal. Still I felt some relief, even though I know she did not. I told myself, Now I can see a child will truly come of this agony; this is not entirely impossible.

In spite of my hopefulness, the baby stopped coming forward and lay at the near end of her birth canal, as though it had suddenly changed its mind and decided not to leave. Numbed by the pain, the señora did not move, either.

"Señora, it is time," I said.

"Time for what?" she asked, her small rounded teeth hammering her lower lip.

"It's time to push out your child. I see the head. The hair is dark and soft, in ringlets like yours."

She pushed with all her might, like an ant trying to move a tree. The head slipped down, filling my open hand.

"Señora, this child will be yours," I said to soothe her. "You will be its mother for the rest of your days. It will be yours like watercress belongs to water and river lilies belong to the river."

"Like I belonged to my mother," she chimed in, catching her breath.

"Now you will know for yourself why they say children are the prize of life."

"Be quick!" she commanded. "I want to see it. I want to hold it. I want to know if it is a girl or a boy."

Her forehead creased with anticipation. She tightened every muscle and propelled the child's shoulders forward. The infant's body fell into my arms, covering my house apron with blood.

"You have a son." I proudly raised the child from between her legs and held him up so she could see.

The umbilical cord stretched from inside her as I cradled the boy child against my chest. I wiped him clean with an embroidered towel that I'd cut and stitched myself soon after I'd learned of the conception. I rapped twice on his bottom but he did not cry. It was Señora Valencia who cried instead.

"I always thought it would be a girl," she said. "Every Sunday when I came out of Mass, all the little boys would crowd around my belly as though they were in love with her."

Like Señora Valencia, her son was coconut-cream colored, his cheeks and forehead the blush pink of water lilies.

"Is he handsome? Are all his fingers and toes there?" she asked. "I don't think I heard him cry."

"I thought I would leave it to you to strike him again."

I felt a sense of great accomplishment as I tore a white ribbon from one of the cradle pillows, wrapped it around the umbilical cord, then used one of the señora's husband's shaving blades to sever the boy from his mother. Señora Valencia was opening her arms to take him when a yell came. Not from him, but from her. A pained squawk from the back of her throat.

"It starts again!" she screamed.

"What do you feel, Señora?"

"The birth pains again."

"It is your baby's old nest, forcing its way out," I said, remembering one of my mother's favorite expressions. *The baby's old nest took its time coming out. It was like another child altogether.* "You have to push once more to be certain it all leaves you."

She pushed even harder than before. Another head of curly black hair slid down between her legs, swimming out with the afterbirth.

I hurried to put her son down in the cradle and went back to fetch the other child. I was feeling more experienced now. Reaching in the same way, I pulled out the head. The tiny shoulders emerged easily, then the scraggly legs.

The firstborn wailed as I drew another infant from between Señora Valencia's thighs. A little girl gasped for breath, a thin brown veil, like layers of spiderwebs, covering her face. The umbilical cord had curled itself in a bloody wreath around her neck, encircling every inch between her chin and shoulders.

Señora Valencia tore the caul from her daughter's face with her fingers. I used the blade to snip the umbilical cord from around her neck and soon the little girl cried, falling into a chorus with her brother.

"It's a curse, isn't it?" the señora said, taking her daughter into her arms. "A caul, and the umbilical cord too."

She gently blew her breath over her daughter's closed eyes, encouraging the child to open them. I took the little boy out of the cradle now and brought him over to the bed to be near his mother and sister. The two babies stopped crying when we rubbed the soles of their feet together.

Señora Valencia used the clean end of a bedsheet to wipe the blood off her daughter's skin. The girl appeared much smaller than her twin, less than half his already small size. Even in her mother's arms, she lay on her side with her tiny legs pulled up to her belly. Her skin was a deep bronze, between the colors of tan Brazil nut shells and black salsify.

Señora Valencia motioned for me to move even closer with her son.

"They differ in appearance." She wanted another opinion.

"Your son favors your cherimoya milk color," I said.

"And my daughter favors you," she said. "My daughter is a chameleon. She's taken your color from the mere sight of your face."

Her fingers still trembling, she made the sign of the holy cross from her forehead down to the sweaty cave between her swollen breasts. It was an especially hot morning. The air was heavy with the scent of lemongrass and flame trees losing their morning dew to the sun and with the smell of all the blood the señora had lost to her children. I refastened the closed patio doors, completely shutting out the outside air.

"Will you light a candle to La Virgencita, Amabelle? I promised her I would do this after I gave birth."

I lit a white candle and set it on the layette chest beside the cradle that had been the señora's own as a child.

"Do you think the children will love me?" she asked.

"Don't you already love them?"

"I feel as if they've always been here."

"Do you know what you will name them?"

"I think I'll name my daughter Rosalinda Teresa to honor my mother. I'll leave it to my husband to name our son. Amabelle, I'm so happy today. You and me. Look at what we have done."

"It was you, Señora. You did this."

"How does my daughter look? How do you find my dusky rose? Does she please you? Do they please you? She's so small. Take her, please, and let me hold my son now."

We exchanged children. For a moment Rosalinda seemed to be floating between our hands, in danger of falling. I looked into her tiny face, still streaked with her mother's blood, and I cradled her more tightly in my arms.

"Amabelle do you think my daughter will always be the color she is now?" Señora Valencia asked. "My poor love, what if she's mistaken for one of your people?"

3

In the awakened dark, Sebastien says, if we are not touching, then we must be talking. We must talk to remind each other that we are not yet in the slumbering dark, which is an endless death, like a darkened cave.

I tell him that I would rather he touch me, stroke me in all the same places, in all the same ways. He is too tired, he says, so we must talk. Silence to him is like sleep, a close second to death.

He asks about my family, what my parents were like when they were alive.

"What was it you admired most about your mother?"

At times I like it when he is just a deep echo, one utterance after another filling every crevice of the room, a voice that sounds like it's never been an infant's whimper, a boy's whisper, a young man's mumble, a voice that speaks as if every word it has ever uttered has always been and will always be for me.

"Tell me what you liked most about your mother?" he asks again, when I spend too much time admiring the voice and not answering.

"I liked her tranquility," I say. "She was a woman who did everything slowly, in her own time, as my father liked to say. She was a woman of few words. When she did speak, her words were direct and precise. 'The baby's old nest took its time coming out. It was like another child altogether.' She was a stern-faced woman with a half gourd for a forehead, that is to say, her forehead was big, high and wide, like mine, a sign of a good mind, some say. She didn't show a lot of affection to me. I think she believed this was not a good way to raise a girl, who might not have affection the rest of her life. She also didn't smile often."

"You don't smile often."

"She was a thin woman like me. I think I look like her, but I do smile more."

"Are you smiling now?" I can hear him smiling in the dark. The smile blends into his voice, slightly halting his speech now and then.

His fingers slice the air towards me. Before his hands land on either side of my waist, I'm already squealing and cackling like a sick hen, already feeling as if I'm being tickled.

"Tell me something more of your mother," he says, once the tickling and more squealing have stopped. "Tell me what her name was."

"Her name was Irelle Pradelle," I say, "and after she died, when I dreamt of her, she was always smiling. Except of course when she and my papa were drowning."

4

Doctor Javier dashed straight to Señora Valencia's bed as soon as he arrived. When he walked into the room, she quickly announced, "Amabelle and I have done it, Javier. We have given birth to the children, twins."

Doctor Javier was a remarkably tall man who seemed to be looking down at everyone around him. His squinting eyes appeared dangerous and fierce as he examined the children, clipping their umbilical cords closer to their bellies.

"How long was it, your labor?" he asked Señora Valencia.

"It began last night," she answered.

"Why didn't you send for me then?"

"Remember the way we'd counted? I thought it could not be time yet."

"We misjudged things perhaps."

"The children and me, we are lucky Amabelle knew how to birth babies," she said. "I could never have done it by myself."

"We are all grateful to Amabelle." Doctor Javier smiled at me as he brushed aside his wiry auburn hair, which extended in a widow's peak to the middle of his forehead. A small wooden carving of cane leaves was pinned to the collar of his embroidered shirt. It was a charm, like the amulets the cane cutters here in Alegría wore around their necks to protect them from evil spells.

"Amabelle, boil some water, please," the doctor said. "The little ones will need a wash."

The house stood at the top of a hill with a view of the azure-green mountains in the back and a wide road in front. I went out the back door, where the pantry opened onto the grounds. Rushing to my room, I took off my blood-drenched apron and blouse, and piled them both in a corner near the latrines.

Far down the hill, I could see the housemaid, Juana, returning from the stream with a bucket full of clothes on her head. Juana and her man, Luis, had worked for Papi even before Señora Valencia was born. Juana stopped at their house, whose peaked roof lay half buried in the grassy hill.

I put the pot of water to boil on a bed of charcoal in my own outdoor cooking shed and waited for Juana to come up. From the yard I also saw the tightly closed shutters of Señora Valencia's room. They were painted indigo blue like most of the main house except for the wraparound veran-dah, which was the crimson red of Alegría's flame trees at high bloom.

Juana did not climb up, so I returned to Señora Valencia's room with two enameled basins full of warm water, carrying one on the crown of my head and the other one in my hands. Señora Valencia was fully covered from chin to toe, the bloody sheets mounded in a pile in the corner. Papi had removed the mattresses from her bed, replacing them with the clean ones from her mother's old bed in the sewing room.

Doctor Javier helped me put the containers down on the layette chest. He poured some medicine in the water with which to bathe the children. Señora Valencia handed him her son.

"Amabelle, do you remember precisely what time the children were born?" Papi asked. He had a notebook on his lap in which to inscribe the details for the birth certificates.

"It was still morning." Señora Valencia looked up at an old clock set in a mahogany case that Papi had been sent from Spain by his father some twenty years before.

I looked over Papi's shoulder as he wrote ceremoniously in his best script the time and place of the births, noting that it was on the thirtieth of August, the year 1937, the ninety-third year of independence, in the seventh year of the Era of Generalissimo Rafael Leonidas Trujillo Molina, Supreme Commander-in-Chief, President of the Republic.

"And how long apart were the children born, Amabelle?" asked Papi. "Do you remember?"

"The second one was a surprise. I don't know," I said.

"Not more than a quarter of an hour later," offered Señora Valencia.

When it was her turn to be bathed, Doctor Javier took Rosalinda and dipped her in the water. She remained still as the water met her skin.

"She has a little charcoal behind the ears, that one," Doctor Javier boldly told Señora Valencia as he lifted her daughter from the water.

"It must be from her father's family," Papi interjected, his fingertips caressing the skin of his sun-scorched white face. "My daughter was born in the capital of this country. Her mother was of pure Spanish blood. She can trace her family to the Conquistadores, the line of El Almirante, Cristobal Colón. And I, myself, was born near a seaport in Valencia, Spain."

We swaddled the babies in the white bands that I had hemmed during Señora Valencia's pregnancy when she thought she would only have a girl. She took her daughter in her arms while Papi stared down at his grandson, rocking him back and forth across his chest.

"You make a very impolite assertion," Papi scolded Doctor Javier in a low voice when he thought his daughter wasn't listening. "We don't want to hear anything more of the kind."

"Amabelle, could I trouble you for un cafecito?" Doctor Javier thought it best to escape from Papi's presence.

"Give him anything he wants," Papi said without looking up from his grandson's face.

Doctor Javier followed me to the pantry. As he passed through the doorway, a suspended bundle of dried parsley leaves brushed his scalp, leaving behind a few tiny stems in his hair. I reached up to flick them away but stopped myself in time. It would be too forward of me to touch him; he might misunderstand. Working for others, you must always be on your guard. Doctor Javier always addressed me kindly, but I could not presume that he would enjoy the feel of my hand wandering through his hair.

"Amabelle, were you a midwife all this time and you never told us?" he asked.

"I don't think myself a midwife, Doctor." Some of the coffee spilled as I poured it into a red orchid-patterned cup, set on its saucer, on a silver tray in front of him.

"How did you know how to birth those children?"

"My mother and father were herb healers in Haiti. When it was called for, they birthed a child," I said, wanting to be modest on behalf of my parents, who had always been modest themselves.

"Valencia tells me the little girl had a struggle," he said.

"She had a caul over her face and the umbilical cord was badly placed, yes."

"Badly placed, around her neck? It's as if the other one tried to strangle her."

"If you will permit me, Doctor, I would rather not condemn these little children by speaking such things."

"Many of us start out as twins in the belly and do away with the other," he persisted. "When I was a medical student, one time we found the two small legs of a baby separately lodged in the back of a grown male cadaver. No other manner to explain this, save that these legs had been lodged in the man since before he was born."

I thought perhaps he told me this to unnerve me. Many people who considered themselves clever found pleasure in frightening the household workers with marvelous tales of the outside world, a world they supposed we would never see for ourselves.

"On the other hand," he continued, "sometimes you have two children born at the same time; one is stillborn but the other one alive and healthy because the dead one gave the other a life transfusion in the womb and in essence sacrificed itself."

"I am thankful ours both survived," I said.

"Aside from medicine, my passions are language and lineage," he said. "That little Rosalinda teaches me something when I look at her."

Was he showing off more of his knowledge for my sake?

"Now that our old friend, the señora's husband, is an officer, I never know what to call him," he said. "His rank changes so often. If I remember, he was last a colonel. I have not seen him for some time."

"He returns from the barracks often enough," I said, trying to make my way out of the conversation. "When he's at home you're always elsewhere. You should ask Señora Valencia your questions, Doctor."

"I'm weary of military men," he said, not discouraged by my lack of interest. "They don't often like me, those men of the Guardia, even those like Pico who are old acquaintances. But let us put this thought aside for a moment. Amabelle, what I wish to tell you is this: I'm quite anxious about the little girl."

"Isn't she healthy?" I asked.

"If Valencia feeds her well, she could become robust in a few weeks. But she is so small. Can you make certain that she nurses her often? Please tell Juana too. She may also be looking after the children."

"And the boy?"

"He looks healthy. It's little Rosalinda who makes me anxious." He turned his empty cup upside down on the saucer, a signal that he didn't want any more coffee. "Let me also say this to you, Amabelle. You should leave here and become a midwife in Haiti."

I felt my eyebrows shoot up, my mouth forming a grimace that might be interpreted as a smile.

"I am not a midwife," I said. "And I haven't been across the border since I was a child of eight years."

"You can be trained," he said. "Valencia once told me that you can read and write. People like you are needed at the small clinic I sometimes visit across the river. We have only two Haitian doctors for a large area. I cannot go there all the time, and I know of only one or two midwives in that region of the border. You are greatly needed."

"You're kind to think so highly of me, Doctor."

"Would you like to go?"

"There is much to consider—"

"Consider all of it, then," he said as he left me.

I was still feeling pleased by the doctor's proposal when Juana walked into the pantry with the house linen folded in a basket.

"I received some coffee from my sisters today," Juana said. Juana's two younger sisters, Ana and María, were both nuns living in a convent orphanage in a mountain village close to the border.

Juana pulled a ripe yellow mango out of her pocket and handed it to me. "I know you would have picked that one if you passed it on the tree," she said.

I immediately sank my teeth into the mango, letting the thick, heavy juices fill my mouth.

"How is the señora?" she asked.

"Didn't you hear the screams?"

"What screams?"

"The señora in labor."

"Baby?"

"Babies!"

She dropped the linen basket on the floor, then bent down and picked up all the scattered sheets. Juana was a heavy woman whose every movement was exaggerated by the expanse of her flesh. Her pale hands were large but fragile looking, as though they would explode if you stuck a needle in them.

"How many babies?" she asked, her head bobbing with excitement.

"How many could it be? She's not a hen."

"Two?"

"One boy and one girl."

"Twin babies in this house," she said, crossing herself. "This is for certain the doing of Santas Felicitas and Perpetua. Where's the señora now?"

"In her room, with Doctor Javier."

"Oh! It was Santa Mónica's doing, bringing Doctor Javier on time."

"He came too late," I said, neglecting the modesty I had been taught in childhood by my parents. "I birthed the babies myself. It happened so quickly, you would call it a miracle."

"Miracles always happen in my absence," she said. "I have to tell Luis." She rushed out of the pantry, then came running back in. "First I must see the señora and the babies for myself."

I put my mango down. We walked to Señora Valencia's room. Juana burst into tears as soon as she saw the children: Rosalinda in her mother's arms and the little boy undergoing another close examination by Doctor Javier.

Señora Valencia held Rosalinda out towards Juana.

"Take her," she said. "Wouldn't you like to hold my daughter, Juana?"

"I'm afraid I will cry," Juana sobbed.

"You're already crying," Señora Valencia observed.

Peeking at the little boy, Juana approached the bed.

"I've named my daughter Rosalinda Teresa," Señora Valencia said.

"For your mami!" Juana sobbed louder now. "Oh, had your mother lived to see this day, she would have been so joyful."

"Then, why are you crying?" Señora Valencia said. "It's a happy day."

"Your mother would have been crying, too, more tears of joy than tears of sadness."

"I will go to the barracks to fetch Pico," Papi said. "I want to come back before dark."

"Don't go alone, Don Ignacio." Juana stepped in front of him with Rosalinda resting in her arms.

"No need to worry, I'll go with God," Papi said, a trace of impatience in his voice.

"Yes, please go with God. But also take Luis with you," Juana urged. "He's in the banana grove cutting a few bananas for me. I don't know how he missed hearing all of this."

"We'll try to return tonight," Papi said, kissing his daughter's hand.

"Señora, you rest," Juana said. "Amabelle and me, we'll look after everything."

"Don't spoil her too much," Doctor Javier cautioned.

"Valencia, don't let the kindness of these good women spoil you."

"Pobrecita, this is her time of risk," said Juana. "She must spend the necessary number of days lying in, resting, both for herself and for the children."

5

Sebastien—who is from the north of Haiti like I am, though we did not know each other when we lived there—feels haunted by the crooning of pigeons. Their cry, he says, sounds like it's not meant for others to hear, but like each howling pigeon is trying to bury its head deep inside itself. He imagines that the way pigeons moan is the same way ghosts cry when they are too lonely or too sad, when they have been dead so long that they have forgotten how to speak their own names.

Sebastien's father was killed in the great hurricane that struck the whole island—both Haiti and the Dominican Republic—in 1930. He lost his father and almost everything else. This is why he left Haiti. This is why I have him. A sweep of winds that destroyed so many houses and killed so many people brought him to me.

Sebastien's mother is still alive in Haiti. Sometimes, when we are almost asleep together, Sebastien will hear a pigeon; the pigeons he hears—and I don't always hear them—tend to go on moaning night after night with their mysterious calls in their mysterious language.

The pigeons always make him draw in his breath, suck his teeth, and say, "Ay, pobrecita manman mwen." My poor mother.

6

Doctor Javier went off to see a young man who was bedridden with chills and a fever. He promised to return to visit the children once more before nightfall.

Juana was in the pantry preparing chicken soup for the señora, a soup made from the meat of an old hen, and a stew for the rest of the household. The children were sleeping in their cradle as Señora Valencia lay in her bed, everything but her face covered by several blankets.

I walked over to look at the babies. Dwarfed by her brother, Rosalinda lay completely still. I reached in and picked her up. Señora Valencia turned over on her side and saw me holding her daughter.

"Amabelle, put her face on your breast," she said.

Rosalinda remained asleep while I unbuttoned my blouse and placed her tiny cheek between my breasts and collarbone. I could instantly feel the air streaming in and out of her nose, her breathing falling into step with the beating of my heart.

"Isn't it miraculous?" Señora Valencia's eyes traveled back between her daughter and her son as though there was nothing else in the world she could see. "Javier says that they can't see anything except the light and the dark for the first days. I don't believe him. They're too perfect."

Señora Valencia motioned for me to come sit on the bed next to her. I put Rosalinda back in her cradle and walked towards her mother.

"Amabelle, I must confess something," she said. "When I had you light the candle to La Virgencita after the children were born, it was really for my mother. I promised her I'd light her a candle after I gave birth. Last night when my first pains began, I felt like my mother was with me. I'd been having more than my usual number of dreams since I became with child, but last night did not feel like a dream. My mother sat here next to me, in this bed. She put her arms around me and touched my stomach. This is why I did not scream until the last moment. I never felt alone."

She turned to look at the white candle on the layette chest, the wick half buried in a mass of melted paraffin, the flame long since extinguished by all the movements in the room.

"I wish you had known Mami, Amabelle," she said.

"I wish I had known her as well, Señora." But her mother had died even before my parents had drowned, leaving us both to parent all our childhood dreams out of ourselves.

Juana walked in with a tray of steaming soup and a sweet tea brew and placed them on the bed, in front of Señora Valencia.

"Eat well, Señora," she said. "Remember, the children feed from you."

Tears began to stream down Juana's face again. She turned to me and said, "See that the señora eats," and then she ran out of the room.

"Juana was at Mami's side both times Mami was pregnant," Señora Valencia explained.

I placed an embroidered shawl around the señora's neck and handed her a spoon. After the señora had eaten a few spoonfuls, Rosalinda began to whimper. I picked her up and brought her to her mother.

"My tiny little one, she must grow strong, or how will she defend herself when her brother wants to tussle?" Señora Valencia said as she took her from my hands. "I can't wait for Pico to see the children. I hope he and Papi will return tonight."

"I know the señor will want to come," I said.

"My Pico is so full of ambition. He told me that he's dreamed since he was a boy of advancing in the army and one day becoming president of this country."

"And you the wife of the president, Señora?"

"I wouldn't like it," she said, wrinkling her nose, as though smelling something sour. "When Pico procures everything he wants, he might not want me anymore. As a boy, he was so poor. Now he can't accept that he has a bit of comfort and he doesn't have to fight to make the sun rise every morning."

"The señor's work is important." I told her what I knew she also believed.

"I wish I could see him more," she said. "I miss the dark taste of cigars in his mouth."

Señora Valencia raised the little girl up to her shoulder as if she had already been doing it all her life.

"I've thought of everything I want to tell the children," she said, "things they might need to know and other things as well, where I may have to hold my tongue."

"You know what best to do, Señora."

"What you did for me today, Amabelle, Mami should have been here to do, except she was like me and would have been screaming in agony, too." She threw her head back and laughed at the pain linking her with her mother. "Amabelle, after my mami died, Juana told me that in our faith if there is a choice between a baby and a mother during a birth, you must choose the baby."

"I am glad we never had to choose, Señora."

"If you'd had to make this choice, I'd want you to look after my children. See what we've brought forth together, my Spanish prince and my Indian princess."

"Wouldn't you like to be a princess?" Señora Valencia murmured into her daughter's face. "She will steal many hearts, my Rosalinda. Look at that profile. The profile of Anacaona, a true Indian queen."

"Juana and I will sleep in the house with you tonight," I offered to the señora.

"Juana will only drown us in more of her tears," she chuckled.

"I will ask her to call on the patron saint of tears to stop hers."

"I think it best if she sleeps in her own house and you in your room."

"One of us must stay with you, even if Señor Pico returns."

I left the señora to the care of one of her husband's girl cousins, who had come from the village with more old hen soup, eggs, nutmeg, money, and dog's teeth for the babies' protection, and went down to the pantry to find Juana.

Juana was sitting at the table, stirring a wooden spoon around the plate of stew in front of her. Her eyes were red from all the crying she had done. She got up and ladled out a bowl of stew from the pot for me.

"I think a tear or two might have fallen in the stew while you were cooking," I said as I sat at the table next to her.

I didn't realize how hungry I was until I saw the chunks of cabbage, yucca and manioc floating in my bowl.

"There are no tears in your bowl," Juana said. "I was careful. Nothing but what is meant to be there ever enters my stew."

"I was not serious," I said, patting the cushion of flesh on her back.

"Don't tease. What if the señora heard you?"

"Why are you crying so, Juana? I don't believe they're all for joy, your tears."

"It's a grand day in this house," she said, "a day that comes to remind me how quickly time passes by. A woman like me grows old while more and more children arrive in this world."

"Are you jealous, Juana? Do you want your own babies?"

"Jealous? Santa Ana, the Holy Mother who gives life, what if she heard you?" She rapped her knuckles on the four corners of the table, as though to test the strength of the wood, and then picked up a rag and wiped the already clean table legs.

"If she has ears, then Santa Ana, she's already heard everything I said."

"The sin's on your head, then," she said. "But you're not a believer."

"How do you know I'm not a believer?"

"Do you believe in anything?"

Juana rubbed her closed hands together as though washing in the stream. After years of working as a housemaid, it was hard for her to remain still.

"I remember when Señora Valencia's mother became pregnant with her," she said. "One day, she had no menstrual rags for me to wash. I said to her, 'Señora Rosalinda, could you be with child?' She said to me, 'Juana, I dare not even dream it.' I said, 'Why?' She said, 'It would be too miraculous.' She was with child indeed, and during the first and second months her body became so uneasy. She grew larger and larger until she was too wide for most passageways in this house. If anyone looked like they were going to have twin babies, it was Señora Rosalinda."

Juana stood up and poured another bowl of stew for herself. She'd had an enormous appetite over these past few months and had grown even broader, especially around her face.

"Now Señora Valencia has children of her own." She pondered the event out loud. "Look how quick the time has passed. It's not the time itself, but what it does to us."

"You're far from old," I said. She was at least fifty, twice my and Señora Valencia's age, but her body looked hardy and capable, like it could still bear many children.

"You don't know how long I prayed for a child myself," she said.

"I have no child, but even I know you must do more than pray."

"Sinner!" She laughed and playfully slapped the back of my hand.

"So you've wanted babies?" I asked.

"Babies always lead us to talk of more babies. Don't you want to have your own?"

I shook my head no. Perhaps because my parents both had died young, I never imagined myself getting older than I was, much less living long enough to bear my own children. Before Sebastien, all my dreams had been of the past: of the old country, of places and people I might never see again.

"I was close to becoming a mother once," Juana said. "My stomach grew for three months and nine days, then all at once it was gone. ¡Adiós bebé! This child was never born. It never had a sex. Never had a name. My Luis, he loves children. If they could grow out of the ground, he would have grown one for me long ago. At this moment in life, a woman asks herself: What good is all this flesh? Why did I have this body?"

Juana and her sisters had been raised in a convent school where their mother was the cook. She was going to be a nun like her two sisters until she met Luis. She and Luis left together and settled in the valley. Juana thought she couldn't have children because she had abandoned her calling. Even her lost pregnancy must have seemed like a deserved punishment from a God she had defied.

"Look at me," she said, rotating her arms as though she were ironing. "I have no need to cry for myself. I must cry for Doña Rosalinda, who died in the attempt to bring a second child into the family. And I must cry for Señora Valencia, who's without her mother on this day."

7

One night, in the awakened dark, when he is missing his father, Sebastien asks, "What was it that you admired most about your father?"

I pretend that I cannot remember, but he insists. "Please tell me, Amabelle, I wish to know this."

"My father's name was Antoine Désir," I say because I know he will ask it again. "I always heard people call him Frè Antoine, Brother Antoine, like they called my mother Man Irelle, Mother Irelle. My mother was older than him, I believe, and some say she looked it."

"Tell me what you liked most about him, your father." Sebastien's voice is more hesitant than usual, it's as though he really does not want to know, like he would rather I say I never had a father, but he knows I had one, whom I lost like he lost his.

"My father was joyful, contrary to my mother's quietly unhappy ways," I admit. "He used to pick me up and try to throw me up in the air, even when I became too heavy to be carried, even when everything he did ceased to seem like a miracle to me. He liked to make like he was going to eat my food if he finished his plate before I finished mine. He spent a lot of time doing the birthing and healing work. He was always looking for some new way to heal others, searching for cures for illnesses that he had not yet even encountered. Aside from the birthing and healing work he and my mother did together, he spent a lot of time outside the house trying to help other people plow their fields and dig waterways to their land. I was always very jealous of the time he spent on other people's land."

I can tell, he is ready. He wants me to ask about his dead father. I can tell by the endless pause after I'm done speaking, the way he opens his mouth now and again and then only sighs as if to ask himself where he could possibly make himself begin.

"How did the hurricane find your father?" I end up saying. It is not the gentlest or most deft way to ask, but I believe it will help him speak.

He opens his mouth a few more times and moans.

"If you let yourself," he says finally, "you can see it before your eyes, a boy carrying his dead father from the road, wobbling, swaying, stumbling under the weight. The boy with the wind in his ears and pieces of the tin roofs that opened the father's throat blowing around him. The boy trying not to drop the father, not crying or screaming like you'd think, but praying that more of the father's blood will stay in the father's throat and not go into the muddy flood, going no one knows where. If you let yourself, you can see it before your eyes."

8

Señor Pico Duarte bore the name of one of the fathers of Dominican independence, a name that he had shared with the tallest mountain on the island until recently, when it was rechristened Pico Trujillo after the Generalissimo. Yet, at thirty-six years of age, Señor Pico Duarte was still shorter than the average man, even in his military boots, which seemed to add height to the other officers. With his honey-almond skin and charcoal eyes, he was the one that baby Rosalinda resembled most.

The floor thundered under his boots as he ran from Papi's automobile into the house to find his wife and new-born children, looking for hints of their presence in the parlor and all the different rooms in the house. Juana and I both followed him blindly, instinctively, to his wife's room, thinking perhaps he might need something we could bring for him, or his wife, or their new children. Working for others, you learn to be present and invisible at the same time, nearby when they needed you, far off when they didn't, but still close enough in case they changed their minds.

Juana was more herself now. She watched with a reserved

smile as Señor Pico rushed to the bed where his wife lay and kissed her hair and forehead.

"Pico, let me see your face," she said, her fingers pulling at his bristly tar-black hair.

"Go look at the children," Papi urged him with a hearty laugh.

As he stood over his children's cradle, Señor Pico's body shook as though he wanted to scream; he held his fist to his mouth to contain his joy. His eyes lingered on his son, his heir. Raising the sheet covering the child's body, he peeked beneath his diaper to check the boy's testicles.

"I will name him Rafael, for the Generalissimo," he said as Juana reswaddled the children even more securely than before. The señora agreed to this name with a coy nod. And so the boy became Rafael like the Generalissimo, the president of the republic. Rafi for intimates.

As he contemplated the splendor and uncommon elegance of his new son's name, Señor Pico peeled off his cap and tunic, which formed a pile of khaki on the floor, where he dropped them. Juana walked over to collect them. This was precisely why we had followed him here, to perform the incidental tasks so he wouldn't have to think about them at the peak of his joy.

I glanced over at Juana's man, Luis, who stood alone in the doorway, looking as though he were going to cry. Luis was still dressed in his daily gardening clothes, a mud-streaked shirt and a roomy pair of pants hanging like an opened parasol around his narrow frame. He held a straw hat reverently against his chest. His face showed the ache of wanting that I had seen in Juana's eyes earlier. Because of his shyness, Luis hid all emotion behind his careful gestures of courtesy and respect. He did not venture past the threshold into the bedroom to see the babies. No one asked him to, either.

"Wouldn't you like your supper, Señor?" Juana asked, gathering our patrón's tall laced black boots from the floor.

Señor Pico motioned her away with a wave of his happy hands.

"Should we draw you a bath?" she persisted.

"Leave the water on the coals for me," he said.

Luis ran off to warm Señor Pico's bathwater.

"It must have been painful. Was it painful?" Señor Pico asked his wife.

She smiled with a peaceful glow on her face. Juana placed Señor Pico's clothes in the armoire.

"Amabelle, Juana, you may both leave us now," Señor Pico said.

While the señor visited with his wife and children, I watched from a rocking chair outside the door to my room as Luis sat in the yard with a hurricane lamp, using his hat to fan the fire under Señor Pico's bathwater. As the flames grew, the night breeze teased them, forming dancing shadows on the sides of the tin bucket. Juana walked over to her man and handed him a bowl of stew. Luis placed the bowl of stew near the bucket to warm. He cleared a spot on the ground and spread a rag next to him for Juana to sit on. She told Luis of having had word (and dried coffee grains) sent from her sisters. Juana spoke excitedly about Señora Valencia's babies, how she could not believe that Señora Valencia—a child whose birth she had witnessed—was now a mother herself.

As she chattered, Luis looked at the dark around him, seeming afraid of being attacked by the trees. Yet he remained silent, waiting for his turn to speak. Finally, Juana fell silent, too.

"Señor Pico bought a goat that I must cut up and salt tonight" was what he said first.

"Where's the goat?" she asked.

Juana peered at the goat, hanging by its hind legs from one of the strongest branches of the flame tree. She then examined her man's face, perhaps sensing that something disagreeable had taken place, something he was not telling yet.

"How was the journey?" she asked.

"Too fast," reported Luis. "Don Ignacio went too fast going to the barracks. Señor Pico went too fast coming back. I thought you'd have to go and plant a white cross on the side of a mountain for me. They say those automobiles are made for automobile races. I felt like we were in one."

"Are you still shaking?" Juana asked, wrapping her large arms around his meager frame.

"I haven't told you even half the tale," Luis said. "Señor Pico was the one driving on the return. I have never seen a man so overjoyed. It wasn't his fault. Who can blame him?"

"Blame him for what?" Juana asked.

"Señor Pico was driving and talking. The closer we came to the house, the faster he went. He asked Don Ignacio all sorts of questions about the children. When Don Ignacio wouldn't tell him for the seventh and seventy-seventh time how big the children were, who they looked like and so much else, Señor Pico went even faster. When we reached the road near the ravines, we saw three men walking ahead—"

"Blessed Mother who gives life, forgive us," Juana interrupted. She raised both her hands up in the air as though to complain to the stars.

"Señor Pico shouted at the men and blew the klaxon," Luis continued. "Two of the men ran off. The other one didn't seem to hear the horn. The automobile struck him, and he went flying into the ravine. He yelled when the automobile hit him, but when we came out to look, he was gone. It was a bracero, maybe one who works at Don Carlos' mill."

I knew most of the people who worked with Sebastien at Don Carlos' mill, lived in Don Carlos' compounds, and toiled in Don Carlos' cane fields. The valley was small enough that most of us were familiar with one another. I thought immediately of Sebastien. Surely another worker would have come for me already had Sebastien been struck by Señor Pico's automobile.

Something rustled under the flame tree. We all jumped to our feet. I expected to see Sebastien running towards me, his body drenched in blood. Instead, it was Doctor Javier and his younger sister, Beatriz. Beatriz spent her days pounding her fingers on a piano in her mother's parlor and speaking Latin to herself. She wanted to be a newspaper woman, it was said, travel the world, wear trousers, and ask questions of people suffering through calamities greater than hers. Señor Pico had been courting Beatriz—who had no interest in him—before he began pursuing the señora. One day, when Beatriz had abruptly asked him to leave her mother's parlor so she could play her piano alone, the señor had stumbled down the road in a haze of lovesick rejection and seen Señora Valencia, who was plucking red orchids from her father's garden to put in the small vase at her bedside. Señor Pico, known to her only as Beatriz's frequent escort at local society gatherings, suddenly joined in the orchid picking and after a month of visits to the señora's parlor asked Papi for her hand in marriage. Papi said yes after consulting with the señora, on the condition that his daughter would stay in her own comfortable house rather than having to live in one of those meager isolated bungalows near the barracks, where Señor Pico often needed to be located due to his special military duties.

Juana rose to greet the doctor and Beatriz. Beatriz had braided some bright ribbons into her caramel-colored, calf-length hair; the braid swayed back and forth like a giant fish skeleton across her back.

Nodding to Juana, Doctor Javier asked, "Has the father arrived?"

"Yes, he has come," Juana said. "Good evening, Señorita Beatriz."

"Salve!" replied Beatriz in Latin.

"¡Hola! to you too, Señorita Beatriz," Juana said, dusting off the back of her dress. "Will you please go into the house?"

I didn't stop worrying about Sebastien. As the laughter and Beatriz's effortless Latin phrases echoed from Señora Valencia's bedroom, I walked over to the flame tree and peeked at the dead goat Señor Pico had brought home. Near the bloody spot where the goat's nose almost touched the ground lay my sewing basket and Sebastien's still-unfinished shirt. I had dropped them there when I'd heard Señora

Valencia's first screams. I picked up the basket and Sebastien's shirt and took them back to the rocker with me. The joyful reunion continued upstairs while Luis kept fanning the flames to keep Señor Pico's bath warm.

Soon after, Doctor Javier watched me from afar as he left with Beatriz. Señor Pico was ready for his bath; Luis carried the water to him.

"My wife wishes to see you," Señor Pico shouted at me from across the yard.

I went to her room. She was lying in bed, alone for a brief moment, her children sleeping nearby.

"I am grateful to you, Amabelle, for what you did today." She reached over and squeezed my hands.

When her husband entered the room in his sleeping robe, she quickly dropped my fingers. "Juana will stay here tonight," she announced.

Why Juana? Why not me? I thought. But maybe Juana had asked to stay. Perhaps she needed to cradle a cloud-soft child and pretend that it was hers. Besides, I had to go to my room and wait for Sebastien. Surely he would know what had happened, who had been struck by the automobile.

Juana was in the old sewing room of Señora Valencia's mother, piling blankets on the floor to sleep on. Behind her stood a four poster canopy bed that Papi had built long ago for his wife's afternoon siestas.

Señor Pico pulled shut his wife's bedroom door to keep out the night air. I waved good-night to Juana, who was already dozing off. Juana blew out her lamp, leaving me in the dark.

In their room, Señor Pico tried to make his wife laugh by

telling her how much he had missed her all those nights when he'd been sleeping on stiff, narrow, insect-filled mattresses in the barracks.

"Is it so terrible?" she asked.

Yes, it was, he said. Even worse than that, if truth be told. Away from her, everything was like a seat on a metal bench in Hell.

The señora asked her husband if he had to return to the barracks soon. The soldiers in his charge could wait awhile, couldn't they?

He'd try to stay through her lying-in period, he said, but things could change quickly. Had he forgotten to inform her? Where had his memory gone? The Generalissimo was spending some time with friends, not far from here. The Generalissimo's good friend Doña Isabela Mayer was planning to throw a lavish ball for him near the border. He—her husband, could she fathom it?—had been given the task of heading a group that would ensure the Generalissimo's safety at the border. They would also be in charge of a new border operation.

Wouldn't this take him away for even longer periods of time? Señora Valencia wanted to know.

She was not to worry at all, he assured her. The operation would be quick and precise. To tell the truth, part of it had already started.

She didn't sound as happy as perhaps he had wanted her to be. "Let's not speak of you leaving again," she said. "At least you are with us now."

In the parlor, Papi sat alone, as he did every night, in a corner near the parlor's accordion-shaped radio, straining to make out an announcer's voice without disturbing the others. He was an exiled patriot, Papi, fighting a year-and-a-half old civil war in Spain by means of the radio. On his lap were maps showing different Spanish cities that he consulted with a hand magnifier as he listened. The maps were cracked along the creases and edges, becoming closer to dust with every passing day.

"How is the fighting today?" I asked. "Is your side winning?"

"The good side does not always win," he said.

"Do you wish you were there?"

"In the war, an old man like me?"

Above Papi's head loomed a large portrait of the Generalissimo, which Señora Valencia had painted at her husband's request. Her painting was a vast improvement on many of the Generalissimo's public photographs. She had made him a giant in full military regalia, with vast fringed epaulets and clusters of medals aligned in neat rows under the saffron braiding across his chest. Behind him was the country's red and blue flag with the white cross in the middle, along with the coat of arms and the shield: DIOS, PATRIA, LIBERTAD. GOD, COUNTRY, LIBERTY. But the centerpiece was the Generalissimo himself, the stately expression on his oval face, his head of thick black hair (the beginning of gray streaks carefully omitted), his full vibrant locks swept back in gentle waves to frame the wide forehead, his coy gentle smile, and his eyes, which seemed oddly tender. Bedroom eyes, many had called them.

Papi seemed unaware of the Generalissimo's enormous presence as he listened for word from much farther away.

"Would you like some hot guanabana tea?" I asked. "Good for sleep."

He shook his head no.

"Amabelle, I am not a lucky man," he declared.

"Why do you say that?" I asked.

"I think we killed a man tonight," he said.

Then it seemed to me that the dead man was even less lucky than he.

"On the day my grandchildren are born, I was in an automobile that may have taken a man's life," Papi said. "My son-in-law did not want to stay and search, and I did not force him to do it. It was already dark. I didn't make myself or Luis go down into the ravine to look for the man, to see if we could save his life. You will tell me, Amabelle, if you hear of this man, if you hear that he lived or died. You will ask your friends and then report to me."

"I will."

"Good-night, then."

"Good sleep, Papi."

Outside, Luis skinned and chopped up the dead goat. He piled the legs in a bucket and covered them with clumps of rock salt.

When I was a child, my father and I used to play a game called oslè using the small front-leg joint bones from a goat. These bones are like dominoes, except they have a curved back and three hollowed sides. I'd spent hours alone trying to get a handful of five to land on the same side. I never succeeded.

I asked Luis to cut off the two small bones for me.

Wiping off the blood, I took them to my room. There I undressed, taking off my sand-colored housedress and the matching faded square of cloth wrapped around my head. Nearly everything I had was something Señora Valencia had once owned and no longer wanted. Everything except Sebastien.

I spread an old sheet on the floor next to a castor oil lamp and a conch shell that Sebastien had given me, saying that in there flowed the sound fishes hear when they swim deep inside the ocean's caves. On the wall was pasted a seven-year-old calendar, from the year of the great hurricane that had plundered the whole island, a time when so many houses were flattened and so many people were killed that the Generalissimo himself had marched through the windswept streets of the Dominican capital and ordered that the corpses he encountered during his inspection be brought to the Plaza Colombina and torched in public bonfires that burned for days, filling the air with so much ash that everyone walked with their eyes streaming, their handkerchiefs pressed against their noses, and their parasols held close to their heads.

I lay on my mat on the floor, giving Sebastien time to arrive. If he didn't come soon then I would have to go and look for him in the compound at the mill.

In the meantime, I did something I always did at times when I couldn't bring myself to go out and discover an unpleasant truth. (When you have so few remembrances, you cling to them tightly and repeat them over and over in your mind so time will not erase them.) I closed my eyes and imagined the giant citadel that loomed over my parents' house in

Haiti, the fortress rising out of the miter-shaped mountain chain, like two joined fists battling the sky.

The citadel had been conceived by Henry I, a king who wanted to conquer a world that had once conquered him. My father loved to recount this tale of Henry I, a slave who, after the captives had rebelled against the French and formed their own nation, built forts like the great citadel to keep intruders away.

As a child, I played in the deserted war rooms of Henry I's citadel. I peered at the rest of the world from behind its columns and archways, and the towers that were meant to hold cannons for repelling the attack of ships at sea. From the safety of these rooms, I saw the entire northern cape: the yellow-green mountains, the rice valley, the king's palace of three hundred and sixty-five doors down in the hills above Milot and the Palais des Ramiers, the queen's court across the meadow. I smelled the musty cannonballs and felt Henry I's royal armor bleeding rust onto my hands, armor emblazoned with the image of a phoenix rising over a wall of flames and the words the king was said to have uttered often—Je renais de mes cendres—promising that one day he would rise again from the ashes of his death. I heard the wind tossing through the wild weeds and grass growing out of the cracks in the stone walls. And from the high vaulted ceilings, I could almost hear the king giving orders to tired ghosts who had to remind him that it was a different time— a different century—and that we had become a different people.

Imperceptibly Henry I's murmurs became Sebastien's. I rose and walked to the door. Sebastien was standing there. He handed me two yams with the roots and dirt still clinging to them. The yams were from the small garden behind his room at the compound. Sometimes I cooked for him. Whenever we could we ate together.

"I almost dreamt about you," I said. "I was home and I wanted you to be with me."

"I've been waiting outside, watching for the right moment," he said.

His shirt, one of the many I had made for him from indigo-dyed flour sacks, was covered with dried red mud and tufts of green grass. There were cactus needles still sticking to the cloth and some to the skin along his arm, but he did not seem to feel their sting. One of his eyes was swollen, the pouch underneath visibly filled with blackened blood. He tried to smile, holding the side of his face where the smile tore at him and hurt.

"Did you fall in the cane fields?" I asked, already sensing it was not so. I touched the scruffy beard that he had grown the last few days. Some clumps of the hair were stained green as though his face had been pressed down against crushed grass for a long time.

"I cannot stay," he said. At least he was speaking normally, I thought. His voice had not changed. "Old Kongo's waiting for me at the mill. His son Joël was killed. Joël is dead." His dirt-stained forehead was sweating. He brushed the sweat off with a single swipe of his hand.

"Joël dead? How?"

"Yves, Joël, and me, we were walking along when an automobile hit Joël and sent him into the ravine."

"And you? Did you break any bones?" I asked, as if this

were the only way in which a person could be wounded, only when his body was almost crushed, pulped like the cane in the presses at the mill.

"Yves and I were lucky," he said. And then I thought how truly fortunate he was. He was not crying or yelling or throwing rocks at the house, or pounding a tree stump against the side of the automobile that had killed his friend. Perhaps the truth had not yet touched him deeply enough. But, then, he had seen death closely before.

"What's Kongo doing?" I asked. Perhaps Sebastien was staying calm by thinking of the next step, the next action.

"The first thing is to put Joël's body in the ground," he said.

"Does Kongo know whose automobile hit Joël?"

"At this time, all he knows is that his son is dead. He needs to make a coffin. Don Carlos won't pay for a burial."

Luis and Papi had gone to bed. I led Sebastien behind the latrines. There Papi had a stack of cedar planks that he used for his leisure occupation, making tables and chairs and building miniature houses. Sebastien took four long boards, stained and polished, enough to build a coffin for a grown man.

I offered to help him carry them, but he refused.

"You stay," he said. "I will come back."

I looked down at the yams, leaning against the wall where I had laid them soon after he had given them to me.

"With all this, you had time to bring these yams?" I asked.

"You stay here until I come back," he said, "don't try to go anywhere."

I heard him breathing hard, struggling with the weight of

the wood as he hauled it away. I went back to my room, lay down, and waited for his return.

Poor Kongo. Condolences, Kongo. Two new children came into the world while you have to put your son in the ground.

9

It is a Friday, market day. My mother, my father, and me, we cross into Dajabón, the first Dominican town across the river. My mother wants to buy cooking pots made by a Haitian pot maker named Moy who lives there, the best pot maker in the area. There is a gleam to Moy's pots that makes you think you are getting a gem. They never darken even after they have been used on outdoor cooking fires for years.

In the afternoon, as we set out to wade across the river again with our two new shiny pots, it starts to rain in the mountains, far upstream. The air is heavy and moist; a wide rainbow arc creeps away from the sky, dark rain clouds moving in to take its place.

We are at a distance from the bridge. My father wants us to hurry home. There is still time to cross safely, he says, if we hasten. My mother tells him to wait and see, to watch the current for a while.

"We have no time to waste," my father insists.

"I'll carry you across, and then I'll come back for Amabelle and the pots," my father says.

We walk down from the levee. My father looks for the shallows, where the round-edged rust-colored boulders we'd used before as stepping stones have already disappeared beneath the current.

"Hold the pots," my mother tells me. "Papa will come back for you soon."

On the levee are a few river rats, young boys, both Haitian and Dominican, who for food or one or two coins, will carry people and their merchandise across the river on their backs. The current is swelling, the pools enlarging. Even the river rats are afraid to cross.

My father reaches into the current and sprinkles his face with the water, as if to salute the spirit of the river and request her permission to enter. My mother crosses herself three times and looks up at the sky before she climbs on my father's back. The water reaches up to Papa's waist as soon as he steps in. Once he is in the river, he flinches, realizing that he has made a grave mistake.

My mother turns back to look for me, throwing my father off balance. A flow of mud fills the shallows. My father thrusts his hands in front of him, trying to keep on course. My mother tightens her grip around his neck; her body covers him and weighs him down at the same time. When he tries to push her up by her legs, a cluster of vines whisks past them; my mother reaches for the vines as though they were planks of a raft.

As the rain falls, the river springs upwards like an ocean riptide. Moving as close as they can to the river's edge, the boys throw a thick sisal rope to my parents. The current swallows the rope. The boys reel it back in and wrap it around a boulder. The knot slides away from the boulder as soon as it leaves their hands.

The water rises above my father's head. My mother releases

his neck, the current carrying her beyond his reach. Separated, they are less of an obstacle for the cresting river.

I scream until I can taste blood in my throat, until I can no longer hear my own voice. Yet I still hold Moy's gleaming pots in my hands.

I walk down to the sands to throw the pots into the water and then myself. The current reaches up and licks my feet. I toss the pots in and watch them bob along the swell of the water, disappearing into the braided line that is the river at a distance.

Two of the river boys grab me and drag me by my armpits away from the river. Their faces seem blurred and faraway through the falling rain. They pin me down to the ground until I become still.

"Unless you want to die," one of them says, "you will never see those people again."

10

When Sebastien returned from the compound that night, he was wearing a clean shirt and had washed most of the grass from his beard and face. He sat and leaned back against the wall, watching a lizard dash across the ceiling. I made room for him to lie down on the mat next to me.

"Señor Pico's at home now," I said. "You have to be careful coming and going."

"At this moment, what I want more than anything is for Señor Pico to try and strike me," he said, in an angry tone that I was not used to. Perhaps it was all becoming more familiar to him now. His friend had died. He could have died. We were in the house of the man who had done it. Sebastien could go in and kill him if he really wanted to.

"Señor Pico has rifles," I reminded him, "and we are on his property."

"Is the air we breathe his property?" he asked.

"How was Kongo?"

"No one can find him," he said.

"Where did he go?"

"After we brought the body to him—"

"What condition was the body in?" I asked, regretting the words as soon as they left my mouth.

"He fell from a great height into the ravine," he said.

"What did Kongo do with the body?"

"He let a few people see," he said calmly. "Then Yves and I helped him take Joël down to the stream. We washed him and cleaned off all the blood and brought him back to Kongo's room. Kongo said he wanted to stay alone with the body, then while I was waiting here to enter your room, he took it away."

It was hard to imagine Kongo hauling Joël very far on his back. Joël was much taller and larger-boned, the kind of man who was called upon to pull an oxcart full of cane when the oxen were too fatigued to do the job.

"They say a son's never too big to be carried or beaten by his father," Sebastien said, rubbing a balled fist against his swollen eye. "If Kongo carried off Joël by himself then there's more truth to that than I thought."

"Maybe Kongo wished to say his farewell alone," I said, raising his fist from his eye.

"The others have been out looking for him," he said. "I think he took Joël's body away because he wants us to let him be. I'm going to respect his wishes. He'll come back when he wants."

He ran both his hands up and down my back. He had been this way the whole year we'd been together. His favorite way of forgetting something sad was to grab and hold on to somebody even sadder.

"You're sweating," he said, letting his fingers slide along my spine.

"I had my dream of my parents in the river," I said.

"I don't want you to have this dream again," he said.

"I always see it precisely the way it took place."

"We'll have to change this thing, starting now." He blew out the lamp. The room was pitch black. I squeezed my eyes shut and listened for his voice.

"I don't want you to dream of that river again," he said. "Give yourself a pleasant dream. Remember not only the end, but the middle, and the beginning, the things they did when they were breathing. Let us say that the river was still that day."

"And my parents?"

"They died natural deaths many years later."

"And why did I come here?"

"Even though you were a girl when you left and I was already a man when I arrived and our families did not know each other, you came here to meet me."

His back and shoulders became firm and rigid as he was concocting a new life for me.

"Yes," I said, going along. "I did wander here simply to meet you."

"I don't give you much," he said, "but I want you to know that tomorrow begins my last zafra. Next year, I work away from the cane fields, in coffee, rice, tobacco, corn, an onion farm, even yucca grating, anything but the cane. I have friends looking about for me. I swear it to you, Amabelle, this will be my last cane harvest, just as it was Joël's."

I knew he considered Joël lucky to no longer be part of the cane life, travay tè pou zo, the farming of bones.

"Tonight, when Yves and me, we carried Joël's corpse into

the compound," he said, "I thought about how both Yves' father and my father died, his father organizing brigades to fight the Yanki occupation in Haiti and my father in the hurricane."

I reached up and pressed my hands against his lips. We had made a pact to change our unhappy tales into happy ones, but he could not help himself.

"Sometimes the people in the fields, when they're tired and angry, they say we're an orphaned people," he said. "They say we are the burnt crud at the bottom of the pot. They say some people don't belong anywhere and that's us. I say we are a group of vwayajè, wayfarers. This is why you had to travel this far to meet me, because that is what we are."

11

I am sick in bed with a fever that makes my body feel heavier than a steel drum filled with boiling tar. I sense myself getting larger and larger and at the same time more liquid, like all the teas and syrups my mother pours into me. My father says that I am in fact becoming smaller, shrinking closer to my bones, and there is little that is liquid in me that the fever does not dry up.

"It is a sickness we brought home to her from someone else," my mother concludes while standing over me one day, her lips puckered, her mouth switching from side to side as it always did when she was in deep thought. "I suppose it might be the young girl we treated two weeks ago, you remember?"

My mother makes me a doll out of all my favorite things: strings of red satin ribbons sewn together into the skin, two pieces of corncob for the legs, a dried mango seed for the body frame, white chicken feathers for flesh, pieces of charcoal for the eyes, and cocoa brown embroidering thread for the hair.

There are times when I want to be a girl again, to touch this doll, because when I touch it, I feel nearer to my mother than when her flesh is stroking mine in the washbasin or in the stream, or even when she's reaching down to plop down a compress heavy with aloe on my forehead.

As I lie in bed with my doll and my fever, during the few moments when I'm alone, the doll rises on her corncob feet, yanks several strands of her thread hairs and uses them to jump rope. She sings my favorite rope jumping songs, plays with my oslès, and says, "You will be well again, ma belle Amabelle. I know this to be true." Her voice is gentle, musical, but it echoes, like she's speaking from inside a very tall bottle. "I am sure you will live to be a hundred years old, having come so close to death while young."

While I am watching her play, I want to give the doll a name, but I don't remember names other than my own, and that one only because I've just heard her say it while addressing me.

When I am well, like the doll said I would be, I ask my mother, "What name should I give to this doll who walked about the room and played for me, and looked after me when I was sick?"

"There is no such thing and no such doll," my mother says. "The fever made you an imbecile."

12

The sweet fleeting smell of lemongrass at dawn has always been my favorite scent. Standing at the top of the hill, I saw Luis in front of his house, using a flour-sack rag to wash Joël's blood off one of the two automobiles owned by Señor Pico, Packards they called them, the type of vehicle the Generalissimo himself loved to be driven in at that time.

I walked to the stream behind the neighboring sugar mill where the cane workers bathed at daybreak, before heading out to the fields. It was the first day of a new cane harvest. The stream was already crowded, overflowing with men and women, separated by a thin veil of trees.

Everyone was unusually quiet, even in their whisperings. Instead of the regular loud morning chatter, there was only the sound of hummingbirds chirping, the water gurgling, circling around all the bodies crammed into its path.

I waved to Mimi, Sebastien's younger sister. She slid her face in and out of the water, making bubbles with her mouth. Mimi had followed Sebastien to the valley when he'd moved here four years earlier. These days she worked as one of the maids of Doña Eva, the widowed mother of Doctor Javier and Beatriz.

"This afternoon Doña Eva is having a Mass and a sanco-cho for the anniversary of her birth," Mimi announced. My feet floated above the warm pebbles at the bottom of the stream. It was as if nothing else of much importance had taken place, and for want of other information she had announcements from her mistress' life to share. "The doña is fifty years old. Will your people be coming to her Mass?"

Mimi always called Señora Valencia and Señor Pico "moun ou yo," my people, as though they worked for me. While pedaling in the stream, she ceremoniously raised her arms above the surface of the water and picked a small leaf off my nose. On her right hand, she had a bracelet made of coffee beans, painted in yellow gold and threaded on a string, just like Sebastien's. It was something their mother had made them for safety and luck before they left her on the other side of the border after the hurricane had killed their father.

Thinking of the fiftieth anniversary of Doña Eva's birth being on the first day since Joël's death, and that perhaps I would never have a chance to utter a farewell to Joël's closed eyes, I murmured to Mimi, "Do you think you and I will live long enough to be as old as Doña Eva?"

"I don't want to live so long," she answered in her usual abrupt manner. "I'd rather die young like Joël did."

"Do you really want to end like that, in a ravine?" I whispered to her so the others would not hear.

"I'd rather have death surprise me," she said loudly. "I don't want to wait a long time for it to come find me."

Mimi was at least four years younger than me and, not counting this sudden death she was saying she wanted, had more time ahead of her than I did. There were women in the stream who were ancient enough to be our great-grand-mothers. Four of them were nearby, helping a few of the orphaned girls to wash themselves. Among the oldest women, one was missing an ear. Two had lost fingers. One had her right cheekbone cracked in half, the result of a runaway machete in the fields.

The oldest cane-cutting women were now too sick, too weak, or too crippled to either cook or clean in a big house, work the harvest in the cane fields, or return to their old homes in Haiti. So they started off every morning bathing in the stream, and then spent the rest of the day digging for wild roots or waiting on the kindness of their good neighbors.

Mimi's face grew sad and serious as she observed the other women, especially Félice, a young woman, the housemaid of Don Gilbert and Doña Sabine, a rich Haitian couple who lived among the valley's well-to-do families. Félice had a hairy beet-colored birthmark like a mustache over her lip. She was reasonably pretty, but the birthmark was all you saw when you looked at her face.

Félice had been Joël's woman for some time. Kongo, Joël's father, had disapproved of the whole affair because he knew firsthand some of Félice's family history. In a moment of desperate hunger during the first years of the Yanki occupation, Félice's grandfather had stolen an old hen from the yard of Kongo's mother in Haiti. He couldn't bear having his son take up with a woman whose family had a thief for an ancestor, Kongo had said. There was always a risk that this type of thing could run in the blood. He didn't want to take any chances with his only heir.

Now Kongo was bathing in the middle of the stream,

scrubbing his body with a handful of wet parsley, while the sun climbed up in the sky above his silver-tipped hair.

We used pèsi, perejil, parsley, the damp summer morning-ness of it, the mingled sprigs, bristly and coarse, gentle and docile all at once, tasteless and bitter when chewed, a sweet-ened wind inside the mouth, the leaves a different taste than the stalk, all this we savored for our food, our teas, our baths, to cleanse our insides as well as our outsides of old aches and griefs, to shed a passing year's dust as a new one dawned, to wash a new infant's hair for the first time and—along with boiled orange leaves—a corpse's remains one final time.

The other men stood apart, giving Kongo more space than usual. He moved slowly as he scrubbed his wide shoulders and contorted himself to allow the parsley to brush over the map of scars on his muscular back, all the while staring at the water's surface, as though he could see more than his reflec-tion there.

Sebastien and his friend Yves were standing closest to Kongo, nudging away those who wanted to pay their respects.

"I keep asking myself what Kongo's done with Joël's corpse," Mimi muttered in my ear, leaning forward.

No one would dare dispute Kongo, no matter what he had done with his son's body. He was the most respected elder among us. We all trusted him.

Kongo dropped the used parsley in the stream and raised his machete from the water. Holding his work tool up to the sun, he stroked the edge of the blade as though it were made of flesh. Kongo was still an active worker. He had toiled side by side with his son for more than a dozen cane harvests. Before the full harvest, during the dead season, Kongo, Joël, Sebastien, and his friend Yves had cleared tobacco fields together; on Sundays they cut down trees to make charcoal to sell.

"If one of our men had killed Kongo's son, they'd expect to die," Mimi said. "But since it's one of them, there's nothing we can do. Poor Kongo, this must be killing him inside. I say, An eye for an eye, a tooth for a tooth."

A few more people arrived. They shed their clothes and squeezed into the spaces left in the water. Void of ceremony, this was a silent farewell to Joël, a quiet wake at dawn.

"Your people killed Joël rushing home to their twin babies, didn't they?" Mimi asked. "I hear this is how it happened."

"Yes. That's how it was."

"Beatriz thinks she'll be the godmother of one of the twins."

"The señor and the señora will decide."

"What Beatriz wants, she is often given."

"Do you always call her Beatriz?" I asked.

"I don't have to christen her 'Señorita' in your presence, do I?"

I thought of Señora Valencia, whom I had known since she was eleven years old. I had called her Señorita as she grew from a child into a young woman. When she married the year before, I called her Señora. She on the other hand had always called me Amabelle.

"I don't call her 'Beatriz' in her presence," Mimi explained. "But what would be so terrible if we did say only their Christian names?"

"It would demonstrate a lack of respect," I said. "The way you'd never call one of these old women by their

names. You call them 'Man' even though they're not your
mother."

Mimi flinched and looked down at her coffee bean
bracelet. She seemed pained for a moment as she glanced at
the old women, perhaps searching for her mother's smile
beneath their scowls.

"What does it matter if Beatriz and your lady become
angry with us?" she said. "If they let us go, at least we'd have
a few days of freedom before dying from hunger."

"There is your brother who counts on you," I said, wanting to halt this needless quarrel in light of the heavier pains
in the air. "Even when he's buried in debt, he can always
secure a meal from you."

"Or from you," she insisted.

"But you are his blood," I said. "With myself, if we quarrel, he won't eat from me."

"I thank you for reminding me why I'm so bound to the
misery of that woman's house," she said. "When you and my
brother set up house together, then perhaps I will be free."

Everyone watched Kongo as he emerged from the stream.
He walked off, leaning on a broken broom handle that
served him as a cane. Sebastien and his friend Yves, who had
also been on the road when Joël was killed, followed behind
Kongo, ready to catch him if the broom handle failed. Yves
had a shaved head that shimmered as bright as Kongo's
machete under the morning sun. He and Sebastien followed
Kongo back to the compound.

"When will you and Sebastien start living in the same
house together?" Mimi asked. "If my brother is too timid to
ask, I can act as a go-between."

"Yesterday Juana called me a nonbeliever because I don't normally pray to the saints," I said. "She asked me if I believed in anything, and all I could think to say was Sebastien."

"I'll have to tell Sebastien." Mimi splashed the water with her palms. The others turned to stare, cutting their eyes at her for seeming too joyful on such a day. She paddled the water with more force, making it rise up and shield her like a curtain of glass. She was like a naked statue in one of those fountains at the town square with water sprouting out of her navel and mouth.

"No sad faces," she said. "Joël's well enough where he is. He'd want us to be glad for him. We should give him a joyous wake to send his spirit on its way. He would want us to laugh and be grateful he's not here now."

Félice walked out of the stream and went to dress in the bushes. Mimi was one of the last people still left in the water.

"Mimi's only a child," I said, following Félice. "She didn't know what she was saying."

"This must be what it means to get old," Félice said, in her usual urgent voice, which sometimes blurred the words when she was speaking. She covered the hairy birthmark with her hands as she chose her words and forced them out. "I could hate no one when I was young. Now I can and I do."

Dropping her head onto my shoulder, she pressed her forearms into my ribs as she leaned against me. Her body felt heavy and limp; I was afraid she was going to faint and fall right there at my feet.

"Courage, dear one," I said, trying to hold her up.

"He was too young," she said, "and Kongo will not even let the others act in response to this."

"What can be done?"

"An eye for an eye, as Mimi says."

"No eye for no eye," I said. "We cannot start a war here."

"It would not be a war," she said, "only something to teach them that our lives are precious too."

"What will this do for Joël now?"

"Everything's lost to Joël," she said. "It's too late for him. But we should do something to keep them from taking others."

She pulled herself away from me, to stand on her own feet.

"We must leave it to Kongo," I said. "It is his son who died. He will know best what to do."

13

Every night Sebastien talks in his sleep.

"Do you know what I would like to do?" he asks one night.

"Tell me what you would like to do." You feel masterful making a sleeping person respond while you, awake, question the person. In some ways it is a miracle, like being loved, or watching a parrot—such a small animal—repeat words that have just crossed human lips.

"I'd like to fly a kite," Sebastien answers in his sleep when I ask what he would like to do.

"What manner of kite?"

"A piece of clear paper over a bamboo spine, a girl's red satin ribbon for the tail."

"If I offer you my red satin ribbon?"

He turns over and buries his head in the pillow.

If I offer him my red satin ribbon?

No retort.

14

Between the stream and Don Carlos' mill were the houses of those Sebastien called the non-vwayajè Haitians, the ones who were better off than the cane cutters but not as wealthy as Don Gilbert and Doña Sabine and their friends, the rich Haitians.

The stable non-vwayajè Haitians lived in houses made of wood or cement. They had colorful galleries, zinc roofs, spacious gardens, cactus fences with green vines crawling between the cactus stems. Their yards were full of fruit trees—mangos and avocados especially—for shade, nourishment, and decoration. They were people whose families had been in Alegría for generations: landowners, farmers, metalworkers, stonemasons, dressmakers, shoemakers, a married schoolteaching couple and one Haitian priest, Father Romain. Some of them had Dominican spouses. Many had been born in Alegría. We regarded them all as people who had their destinies in hand.

That morning I thought of Sebastien's decision to leave the cane fields after the harvest as I greeted those of them who were already outside, some sitting in cane back chairs while they had their morning meal of bread and coffee, corn mush, and mangú, others marching around their property like sentinels before rushing out to their day's work. I saw Unèl, a dwarfish stonemason, and called out to him. He waved back with a wide toothy smile. Unèl had once rebuilt the workers' latrines in Señora Valencia's yard along with a group of friends he called his brigade.

Parents were walking their children to the one-room school started by Father Romain and a Dominican priest, Father Vargas. The flat cinder-block building was already too crowded, and the parents who were taking their young ones there complained as they did every morning about the limitations on their children's education.

"I pushed my son out of my body here, in this country," one woman said in a mix of Alegrían Kreyòl and Spanish, the tangled language of those who always stuttered as they spoke, caught as they were on the narrow ridge between two nearly native tongues. "My mother too pushed me out of her body here. Not me, not my son, not one of us has ever seen the other side of the border. Still they won't put our birth papers in our palms so my son can have knowledge placed into his head by a proper educator in a proper school."

"To them we are always foreigners, even if our granmèmès' granmèmès were born in this country," a man responded in Kreyòl, which we most often spoke—instead of Spanish—among ourselves. "This makes it easier for them to push us out when they want to."

"You heard the rumors?" another woman asked, her perfect Kreyòl embellished by elaborate gestures of her long fingers. "They say anyone not in one of those Yanki cane mills will be sent back to Haiti."

"How can the Yanki cane mills save anyone?" the Dominican-born woman with the Dominican-born son replied. "Me, I have no paper in my palms to say where I belong. My son, this one who was born here in this land, has no papers in his palms to say where he belongs. Those who work in the cane mills, the mill owners keep their papers, so they have this as a rope around their necks. Papers are everything. You have no papers in your hands, they do with you what they want."

I thought of my own situation. I had no papers to show that I belonged either here or in Haiti where I was born. The children who were being taken to school looked troubled as they glanced up at their parents' faces, which must have seemed—if I remembered the way a parent's face looked to a child—only a few inches away from the bright indigo sky. I found it sad to hear the non-vwayajè Haitians who appeared as settled in the area as the tamarind trees, the birds of paradise, and the sugarcane—it worried me that they too were unsure of their place in the valley.

After joining the group, the stonemason, Unèl, began to talk about Joël.

"Did you hear that they attacked an innocent man with an automobile and threw his corpse into a ravine?" Unèl asked.

This is not the way it was, I wanted to say. But who was I to defend Señor Pico?

Many of them had heard about Joël, but this was not anything new to them. They were always hearing about rifles being purposely or accidentally fired by angry field guards at braceros or about machetes being slung at cane workers' necks in a fight over pesos at the cane press. Things like this happened all the time to the cane workers; they were the most unprotected of our kind.

"First it is someone like Joël, and then it will be someone like us," Unèl said, showing a braver sentiment than the others, "unless we gather together to protect ourselves."

Don Gilbert and Doña Sabine had erected a circular wall along the road enclosing them inside their expansive villa. As we moved towards their gate, I saw Félice standing on one of the raised verandahs between the two arched stone staircases at the front of Doña Sabine's house. Doña Sabine stood in front of her, gesturing in our direction.

The people ahead of me all spun around to look at Doña Sabine. Each adult in turn pointed at his or her chest, asking with hand signals whom she wanted. Doña Sabine kept pointing until Unèl realized that she was calling to him.

Unèl broke away from the group and moved towards the tall wrought-iron gate to Doña Sabine's house. Her ten Dominican guards stood in a crowd at the gate, ready to defend her in case Unèl proved dangerous. She waved them off and motioned for Unèl to follow her and Félice past the foliage in her garden, the flowering bushes lined up in cropped rows, like schoolboys' new haircuts.

Félice looked up and gave me a quick shy smile as I walked past the gate, then returned her gaze to the amber-tinted mosaic designs on the path as she walked at Doña Sabine's side.

Doña Sabine had once been a famous dancer who had traveled everywhere in the world. Her husband owned a rum enterprise, which had been in his family for five generations, first on Haitian soil and then on what became Dominican soil during the two governments' land exchanges some years before. Doña Sabine herself was a short woman, thinner than was perhaps beneficial to her health. From behind she looked more girlish than most girls, but each of her steps was like a long practiced dance. Now her elegant feet were engulfed in large cowhide slippers that probably belonged to her husband. Her hands were weighted down by a ring on every finger, except the thumbs. It was as though she were wearing all the jewels she owned, guarding them on her person rather than sheltering them in a cache.

Unèl followed her and Félice up the covered passageway to the main house. She likely had some work for him to do. Doña Sabine's husband, Don Gilbert, was standing out in the sun in a beige nightshirt, shouting orders to a large group of people who were scattered about the garden. When he looked up to see Unèl, his wife blew him a silent kiss, which he returned with a wave of his hand.

In spite of their smiles and kisses, there was a feeling of distress about the place; it was as though another Yanki invasion was coming. I had never seen so many people working for Don Gilbert and Doña Sabine: clusters of anxious faces peering out from everywhere in the garden, people who looked tired and ill, some with bandages on their shoulders and pieces of clothing acting as slings to hold up their arms.

On the way back to Señora Valencia's house, I stopped at the parish school to visit with Father Romain. Father Romain was younger than most of the priests I had seen. He was dressed in his cassock, running through the yard with a large ring-shaped kite giving his pupils a lesson on the principles of light and colors, terrain and landscape, earth and sky, and the precise direction of the wind at the exact place in which they were standing.

"It is Amabelle," he said, handing the kite to one of the older boys to fly, "she who is from the same village of the world as me, Cap Haitien, the city of Henry I's great citadel."

Father Romain always made much of our being from the same place, just as Sebastien did. Most people here did. It was a way of being joined to your old life through the presence of another person. At times you could sit for a whole evening with such individuals, just listening to their existence unfold, from the house where they were born to the hill where they wanted to be buried. It was their way of returning home, with you as a witness or as someone to bring them back to the present, either with a yawn, a plea to be excused, or the skillful intrusion of your own tale. This was how people left imprints of themselves in each other's memory so that if you left first and went back to the common village, you could carry, if not a letter, a piece of treasured clothing, some message to their loved ones that their place was still among the living.

Priests were not excluded from this, and Father Romain, though he was devoted to his students, missed his younger sister and his other relations on the other side of the border. In his sermons to the Haitian congregants of the valley he often reminded everyone of common ties: language, foods, history, carnival, songs, tales, and prayers. His creed was one of memory, how remembering—though sometimes painful—can make you strong.

The children crowded around him, yanking at his fingers, begging him to continue with the kite-flying class. He calmed them by taking turns touching each of their heads. When he had tapped all the children, he reached over and stroked my hand, and removing his instructor's spectacles to look straight into my eyes, he told me, "I am needed, Amabelle."

"Certainly I see that, Father," I said.

"I have already told this to Kongo," he said. "Please tell Sebastien for me, too. I am sad for Joël's death. These things happen too often. People die unfairly, innocently. His father will need kind words from all of us."

"Thank you, Father," I said, feeling that he had given me what I had come for, a fresh measure of hope.

"Thank you for your visit, Amabelle."

His students dragged him away, fighting for control of the kite string.

Walking up the hill to Señora Valencia's house, I saw Doctor Javier's sister, Beatriz. She was wearing an old green sundress and twirling a matching parasol above her head. The morning breeze went through her skirt, raising it above her knees, but she did not seem to notice.

Beatriz walked into the parlor where Papi was sitting near the radio, listening for word from Spain. He had his note-book on his lap, in which he scribbled a few words, looked up, then scribbled again, between loud fits of coughing.

Beatriz kissed Papi on the cheek, showing him a kindness she reserved only for old men who had no interest in marrying her. Papi kept his eyes on his notebook and continued to write. Beatriz picked a wicker sofa across from him and sat down. She swung her long braid from her back to her shoulder. The end of the braid landed on the closed parasol on her lap. "Papi, you haven't strolled past our house in some time." She played with the braid while talking.

"I was staying here in case Valencia's labor pains began," Papi said.

"Now that the babies are here—"

"I will be walking your way again," he said.

Juana rushed out from the pantry to meet Beatriz.

"How kind of you to visit us so early, Señorita Beatriz," Juana said as a greeting.

"Thank you," answered Beatriz, looking annoyed that Juana had disturbed her conversation with Papi.

"The señora did not have a restful night, with both the children waking at different hours," Juana announced. "It seems they already have dissimilar temperaments, those children."

"Do you have my tea?" Papi coughed as though he were drowning.

"The tea is boiling," Juana said. "It must stew; you need it for that cough." Juana turned back to Beatriz. "Would you like a taste of my good strong coffee, Señorita Beatriz, some that my sisters sent for me from my birthplace only yesterday?"

"Whatever pleases you, Juana," Beatriz said.

"Come, Amabelle." Juana grabbed my hand and dragged me back to the pantry where she busied herself making everyone's morning meal. Luis stood in a corner eating quickly before starting his day's work.

"Take this." Juana handed me two boiled yuccas in a large bowl. "Build up your strength. This day will be full of comings and goings for us."

I ate while she lined up the cups and saucers on a tray for Papi and Beatriz.

"Take your time with your food, Amabelle," she commanded.

Luis wiped his hands on his pants when he was done eating. He squeezed Juana's behind as he headed out.

"Don't forget the goat meat you must take as a gift to Doña Eva from Señor Pico," Juana reminded him.

When I came back into the parlor, Beatriz was bending over the radio with Papi as he turned the large dials to get a sound. The radio remained voiceless. He conceded defeat and turned it off.

"What are you writing there?" Beatriz asked, peeking into Papi's notebook.

"I'm trying to write what I recall of my life," Papi said, closing the notebook. He cleared a space for me to put the tray in front of him, tore a piece from the bread on my tray, and crammed it into his mouth.

"Papi, can I see what you have written?" Beatriz asked.

"I'm writing only for my grandchildren," Papi replied. "I feel like a bird who's flown over two mountains without looking at the valley in the center. I don't know what I will or won't retain in a few more years. Even now there are many things that took place yesterday I don't remember."

"Your grandchildren were born yesterday. I know you have not forgotten this, have you?" Beatriz teased, sliding her cup and saucer off the tray. The smell of Juana's coffee scented the entire parlor, like smoke from a green-wood fire.

I put the tray down on a side table near the radio and started walking back to the pantry.

"Stay, Amabelle," Papi said. "I may need you to warm my tea again."

"You've had a colorful life," Beatriz said to Papi.

"What do you know of my life?" Papi sipped his tea as he waited for her reply.

"I know what Valencia has told me," she said.

"Valencia knows only what I tell her, and for an adoring child a foothill can seem like a mountain if her father's painting the picture."

"So you didn't like being an officer in the Spanish army, is that so?" Beatriz asked.

"This was almost forty years ago," Papi said. "Spain was at war then too, a splendid little war, fighting for colonies with Los Estados Unidos. I fled from bloody battles to come here, the great battles of El Caney and San Juan Hill. But even if things were peaceful, I still would have left my country."

"Do you like it here?" Beatriz asked.

"I married here. I've raised my daughter here and now my grandchildren—"

"But does it please you, honestly?"

"Why do you ask so many questions?"

"I read in *La Nación* that there are women fighting in the International Brigade in Spain," Beatriz said, twisting her long caramel-colored braid.

"Is that what you see in your dreams at night, visions of the International Brigade?" Papi puckered his lips and moved his head from side to side in apparent disapproval.

"Do you enjoy it here?' Beatriz asked like a paid inquisitor.

"Should I tell you the truth?" he asked.

"Certainly, the truth," replied Beatriz

"Do I like the way things are conducted here now, everything run by military men? Do I like the worship of uniforms, the medals like stars on people's chests? Do I like this?" He looked up at Señora Valencia's spectacularly large portrait of the Generalissimo.

"Do you like it?" Beatriz persisted.

"No," Papi said. "I don't like any part of it."

"When you were in the army, did you kill anyone?" Beatriz asked.

"This is between me and my conscience," he said.

"You did, then?"

"What good can it do you to know what evil things I have or have not been part of?"

Beatriz threw back her long braid, almost hitting Papi's face with it. Papi was seized by another fit of coughing. Beatriz hurried to pat his back.

"You want to know what I'm writing to my grandchildren," Papi said after catching his breath. "I've begun with my birth in the seaport of Valencia. My father was a baker there. There are times when he gave bread to everyone in our quarter for nothing. I was his only son but he would never let me eat until everyone else had eaten. He lived to be ninety years old only to be killed in this evil war."

Like me, Papi had been displaced from his native land; he felt himself the orphaned child of a now orphaned people. Perhaps this was why he often seemed more kindly disposed to the strangers for whom this side of the island had not always been home.

Señora Valencia was nursing her son when I took her morning meal to her. Her husband motioned for me to enter as soon as he saw me in the doorway.

"Señorita Beatriz is here for a visit," I told him as I put the tray down.

I took the children's dirty linen from a corner and carried it down to the basin of rainwater that Juana kept out in the yard for the wash.

From the hill I could see some of the cane workers heading towards the fields. Kongo was at the head of the group, with Sebastien close behind. Mimi and Félice were walking with them on their way to buy provisions in the marketplace. I waved to them, but it was Doctor Javier who waved back instead as he climbed up the hill. He walked over to the washbasin before going inside the house.

"Have you given thought to what I asked?" He spoke Kreyòl like a Haitian, with only a slight Dominican cadence. "Soon, I'll be going back to the clinic for two days," he said. "If you want, you can come with me and some others. There'll be many children with us, perhaps ten orphans. The clinic itself is nothing more than a small house. At night some of the workers sleep there. You'll live there in the beginning. You'll be paid a wage, though not a big one. The mothers pay with food. Some make you the godparent. I'm godfather to twenty-six children."

With Joël's death, I hadn't given myself much time to think about this, to consider returning to a place I had not seen since I was a child. The cane workers had all turned at the bend in the road. Sebastien would soon be in the fields for the first day of what he hoped would be his last harvest. He was going to work hard, too hard, to save a few pesos, hoping to change his life. Maybe I too had been waiting for an escape, looking out of the corner of my eyes for a sign telling me it was time to go on to another life, a life that would fully be mine. Maybe I had been hoping for a voice to call to me from across the river, someone to arrive saying, "I have come for you to bring you back." Maybe this was that voice, that someone disguised as the doctor. Perhaps I should seize this chance. But not unless Sebastien was prepared to leave also.

"Javier, is this you I hear?" Señor Pico called to Doctor Javier from the parlor.

"It's me," Doctor Javier replied.

"Come, then."

"Amabelle, I need you," Juana signaled from the pantry doorway. I scrubbed my hands in fresh water and rushed to her.

"I must go and buy some things for the midday meal," she said. "Señor Pico wants rum and cigars brought to him in the parlor. I already have them prepared."

Señor Pico and Doctor Javier were sitting out on the lower verandah overlooking Papi's vast orchid garden when I brought them the rum and cigars. The garden had always been a great source of pride for Papi, who had forty-eight different species of orchids growing there, including a special hybrid with wide feathery petals that glowed like Christmas lanterns, the kind Señora Valencia had been plucking for the vase at her bedside the day she and the señor, as it was often repeated, had their hearts joined together.

"You have had your first night as a father," Doctor Javier said to Señor Pico. "I see you survived."

"No one slept." Señor Pico laughed as he drew on a long cigar. He handed another one, unlit, to the doctor. "Is that how it will always be, no one sleeping?"

"They grow and become calmer," the doctor said, biting off the end of his cigar.

15

My mother's cooking takes all day. She goes to the stream to wash our clothes and visits with our neighbors while the pot lies on the rocks, the contents bubbling up as if to make the pot talk.

I am always curious as to what is boiling inside and whether it is yet mashed into something thick and edible. Dry red beans take the longest, but I like to see them each float up to the surface and shed their skin to the water's heat.

It takes me half a morning to make my way to the boiling pot. I start at the kowosòl tree across the yard and slowly progress towards the fire. I stop on the way to jump rope, to smash marbles against each other, to watch some of the vendor women mutter to themselves as they pee under their long skirts, standing up in the middle of the road, when they think no one is looking.

Finally I am at the pot. The steam is rising, the lid clanking against the water's force. I reach over and raise the lid from the side and immediately my forearm is scalding and I am blinded by the fog of red kidney beans.

I feel a hand descend on my burning forearm and I release the pot lid in the dust.

It is my father and he is laughing.

"Soon you will have to be near a pot every day," he says, turning my face to show me that I am blind only when I am looking straight into the steaming pot. "For now you don't have to be and you should not be."

16

Sometime after Joël's death and Kongo's disappearance with the body, I walked into the orchid garden that on his very first day in the Dominican Republic Papi had bought, along with the house, with a gentleman's handshake from Don Francisco, Doña Eva's husband, and Doctor Javier and Beatriz' father, may he in eternal peace rest. Papi was tending to the orchids in this same garden, stroking petals and yanking weeds and rocks from the earth beneath them. He was wearing his well-worn, mud-stained shirt and gardening pants, the pockets bulging with seeds. Juana had given me a large cup of water to bring to him.

"I brought you some water, " I said, "so that you'll suffer less with this heat."

"How kind you are," he said, removing the old straw hat from his head and fanning his face with it. He took the water and drank.

"I have finally heard of a man dying," he said, when he was done with the water. "Don Carlos himself told me that one of his men died some days ago. But there are so many who work for Don Carlos, he did not know the name of the man who died."

"I have given four planks of your wood to a cane cutter who wanted to make a coffin," I said.

He put the water cup down on a piece of open ground. Staring ahead, he moved his lips in a hurried conversation with himself.

"Even though we did not go down into the ravine," he said, "we left the automobile and looked for his body along the incline. There were two other men with him who ran, so when we didn't see the one we hit, we thought—I hoped—that he'd run, too." He pressed a closed fist down on his hat, now on the ground. "The wood you took, who was it for?"

"It was for a man who was struck by Señor Pico's automobile," I said.

"Do you know this man's family?"

"He had only his father."

"No brothers or sisters?"

"Only the father and a woman who had promised herself to him."

"And is the father here?"

"He works in Don Carlos' fields."

Papi sank heavily onto the dirt and pushed his face down between his knees.

"You are aware, Amabelle, that I have no son," he said, without raising his head. "I would like you to bring me to visit the dead man's father. Will you take me?"

"To be prudent, I should ask first to see if he would like to receive you."

"I would like to speak with him."

"I should first request his permission to bring you there."

"It was a frightful accident," he said. "Please don't tell

Valencia, she need not concern herself with such things now, at her time of greatest risk."

"I will tell Kongo you want to visit him," I said.

"Is this the father's name? Kongo?"

"I know he has another name, but Kongo is what everyone calls him here. I think only his son knew his true name."

Just then the cane harvest began: the first moment saw the fires set to clear the fields, singeing the leaves off the cane stalks before they could be chopped down. Clouds of thick white smoke blanketed the sky. The smell of burning soil and molasses invaded the air, dry grass and weeds crackling and shooting sparks, vultures circling low, looking for rats and lizards escaping the blaze.

Señor Pico rushed out to watch the fires. Juana was at the open markets buying provisions and there were no visiting relations in the house, so I went inside to see if the señora needed help moving the babies, to get away from the drifting smoke.

Señora Valencia was sitting in the middle of her bed with the children sleeping next to her, their tiny rumps raised in the air.

"It's another harvest already. They've set the fires." She sniffed the air to enjoy the scent of the burning cane fronds, which smelled like roasting corn.

"Amabelle," she said, as if her thoughts were faraway, elsewhere. "He believes, my Pico, that during one of his long evening promenades, the Generalissimo will march into our house, admire my portrait of him, and make a gift of the whole nation to him and our children."

Rosalinda woke from her sleep with a wail. Señora

Valencia rubbed her fingertips against the crocheted bootie on her right heel to try to calm her. At the same time, she leaned over to have a closer look at her son's sleeping face.

"His sister's cries will wake him," she said.

His sister's cries did not wake Rafi. There was no movement in him, no signs of life.

Señora Valencia picked up her son and held his face against her breast. The little boy was still, his tiny arms hanging limply, not feeling his mother's embrace.

I picked Rosalinda up so Señora Valencia would not crush her as the mother thrashed around the bed trying to revive her son. Rafi's cheeks were drawn, his jaws had collapsed, his face bore an even more pallid shade in death.

"Mijo, my son, do not leave me!" Señora Valencia shouted into the child's face. "It's too soon for you to go. Mami is talking to you. It's too soon for you to leave."

"We should send for Javier," Señor Pico said when he ran in, peeling the señora's fingers off her son, who, if he were alive, would have been wailing from the way her fingernails were dug into his plump flesh, trying to bring him back to life with pain. Señor Pico planted his lips on his son's tiny mouth and attempted to breathe life back into him, succeeding in expanding the tiny chest, only to have it flatten and cave in once again.

Juana took Rosalinda to her grandfather's room. Soon the doctor arrived and offered some of his own breath to Rafi.

"We must send for Father Vargas," the doctor finally said.

Señora Valencia sat in the middle of the bed where her son and daughter had been sleeping not long before, and wrapped her arms around her own shaking body. Her husband pressed his head against the side of her face, and though he could not stop her from shaking, his hair did catch and soak up some of her tears. Señor Pico also appeared to want to cry, but instead kept looking at the señora's empty hands while she opened and closed them as though something had been yanked out of them.

Señora Valencia leaped up from the bed and ransacked one of her armoires for something proper to put on the little boy's body. She found an old lace and satin gown and matching bonnet in which she had been baptized as a child. Señor Pico took charge of changing his son into it without saying a word. The lace was browned and the satin shriveled with age, the gown too large for young Rafi.

Papi went for Father Vargas, the Dominican priest who said Masses at the chapel near the school, at the end of the almond path, a macadam road lined with almond trees. Rosalinda was awake in her mother's arms as the priest mumbled the final words to the little boy. "Rafael, from the sadness of death rises the joy of immortality. We release you into the arms of God. May you rest in eternity with your Maker."

"Padre." Señora Valencia put her trembling hands on the priest's shoulder. "Please say a blessing for my daughter, something that will protect her life."

Father Vargas traced a cross with his thumb on Rosalinda's forehead. The girl stirred, opening her mouth in a spacious yawn to receive the priest's blessing as Juana threaded her rosary through her fingers calling on Santa Agnès under her breath.

"Father, can you be at the family grave site at dawn tomorrow?" Señora Valencia asked. "My son will be buried next to my mother and my brother who died while he was being born."

The priest rested his own hand lightly on the señora's shoulder as if to calm her maternal distress with the power of Heaven flowing from the tips of his fingers.

"Please have him ready for tomorrow then," he said.

With the cane fire smoke still floating in the sky above their heads, the men went out to the garden to make Rafi a casket from the cedar that Papi kept piled behind the house. Señora Valencia watched from the patio as the jagged teeth of a saw drilled in and out of the wood, shaping her son's final bed.

Once the coffin was built, Señora Valencia was determined to do something herself for her lost child. She wanted to decorate the lid with red orchids before her son could be placed inside. The men carried the coffin to the old sewing room of Rafi's grandmother, where the body lay in repose behind the dreamy gauze of the lowered mosquito net framing the four-poster canopy bed, his hands crossed over his heart and a crystal rosary laced between his tiny fingers, the glassy beads spilling over onto the bedsheet like frozen tears.

Señora Valencia took her pencils, her paints, and her brushes out of their case and said, "Amabelle and Javier, stay. Pico, please go and see about Rosalinda."

Señor Pico did not want to go. He looked around the room, from the plain coffin to the ceiling, to the four-poster bed where Rafi was resting. He then used the back of his hands to wipe shadows of the coffin dust and a few bubbling tears from his eyes. Before the tears fell, however, he hurried out of the room, pulling the door shut behind him.

As soon as her husband was gone, Señora Valencia asked, "Why did my son die?" She looked up at Doctor Javier, her eyes reddened, somber. "You have examined the body, Javier. I want you to tell me why he died."

"It seems he simply lost his breath." Doctor Javier covered his face with his hands, aware as he must have been of the weak nature of his own explanation. "He stopped breathing. I thought Rosalinda was the one in danger, but he was the one whose strength failed."

"And Rosalinda?" She closed her eyes for a moment and rubbed her temples with her fingertips. "I know you cannot tell me if she will live or die," she said. "You could not do this with my son. But tell me, please, is she sad? Can they be sad so young?"

"If she is sad, it will not last for long," he said.

"You told me the children could not see me the first week, Javier. You said they could see only light and dark. Then, he never saw my face? I know he saw my face. Many times, he looked up at me, even smiled. Is this too much to hope, that he beheld my face and smiled at me too?"

I could tell he regretted having told her that. "What I told you is not true for all children," he said.

"I will go to his burial," she declared while sketching a large orchid in red pencil on the lid of the coffin. The wood was still damp from the varnish; her pencils slid off the surface.

"You should stay inside and observe your period of confinement," Doctor Javier said. "Do you want to risk your health and your daughter's, too?"

She sketched another large orchid. The paleness of the cedar showed through in the lines where the varnish had still not dried. "Javier, go to my husband and tell him my daughter will not die. He needs your assurance."

I stayed with Señora Valencia while she painted her father's orchid garden upon her son's coffin. On the sides, near the handles, she painted four small hummingbirds. Every once in a while she looked up at the mosquito net behind which her son lay, then continued with renewed devotion.

"Amabelle, today reminds me of the day Papi and I found you at the river." She wiped her paint-stained hands leaving red finger marks on the front of her housedress. "Do you remember that day?"

I did.

"After my mother's death, the house was so filled with her presence: her voice, her clothes," she said. "Papi and I went to visit some of his friends near Dajabón. Papi was more adventuresome then. He took me hunting for birds and taught me to shoot a rifle, as if I were the son who took Mami's life in childbirth. I told Papi I wanted to see the Massacre River where the French buccaneers were killed by the Spaniards in my history lesson.

"We went to the river and there you were, a bony little girl with bleeding knees. You were sitting on a big rock, watching the water as if you were waiting for an apparition. Papi paid one of the boys by the riverside to interpret for him while he asked you who you belonged to. And you pointed to your chest and said, yourself. Do you remember?"

I remembered.

Magenta-colored paint dripped on the floor as she added more to the coffin. We heard voices coming from the parlor, people arriving in small groups.

Señor Pico walked into the room and moved towards the carved posts on the old bed.

"Where's Rosalinda?" she asked him.

"Javier is examining her again," he said, moving closer to inspect the rainbow orchid paintings on the coffin.

"We cannot put him in the ground in this coffin," he said. "We have to make another."

"No, this is the one he'll have," she said. "He's a child. The coffin should be playful. I will drape something over it for the burial, one of Mami's lace tablecloths, one she never used. A beautiful one made from a fine French lace, Valenciennes lace."

"Many of our neighbors are here," he said, averting his eyes from the bed.

"I don't want them to see him," she said. "I don't want a wake for him. No wake, Pico. It would be too sad for such a short life."

"No wake." He bent down and kissed his wife on the side of her face.

"You go to them now," she said.

He shut the door and walked out to greet his neighbors.

"Do you believe in paradise, Amabelle?" she asked me.

I shrugged. I wasn't sure.

The coffin was now covered with a whirl of colors, one seeping into the other, like a sky full of twisted rainbows.

"Amabelle, I was so joyful when Papi said I could bring you to live with us," she said. "After my mother died, I was desperate for someone my age to come live with us in this house."

The mixed smell of wood varnish and different-colored paint made my head throb, and I imagined it did hers too. I removed the brushes from her fingers and pulled her hands away from the coffin. Somehow I envied her. At least she could place her hands on it, her son's final bed. My parents had no coffins.

17

I am in my room listening for music in the trees, the flame tree pods flapping against each other as the hummingbirds squawk back in fear. They know the sound of flame tree pods in motion, the hummingbirds do, but it is a sound that shifts all the time, becoming muted or sharp with the strength of the wind.

I close the door and lock out the tame night breeze that barely reaches my bare body, naked because Sebastien has made me believe that it is like a prayer to lie unclothed alone the way one came out of the womb, but mostly because I am hoping to feel the sweat gather between the cement floor and the hollow in my back, so that when I rise up, there will be a flood of perspiration to roll down over my buttocks, down the front and back and between my thighs, down to my knees, shins, ankles, and toes, so that there will not be a drop of liquid left in me with which to cry.

18

Doña Eva's birthday celebration became Rafi's unofficial wake. All of Doña Eva's guests from the Mass came to offer their felicitacións for the child they could see and their silent condolences for the lost one. In spite of her earlier insistence that there would be no viewing of her son's body, Señora Valencia allowed anyone who asked to file past the bed where he lay, looking as proud of him in death as she would have been in life. During those moments when the friends and distant relations peeked through the mosquito gauze, sniffing with sadness and crossing themselves as they caught a glimpse of the pale round face of the boy child, Señora Valencia, sat alone in her room with her daughter in her arms, as if guarding her from bad thoughts and omens. And there I saw a stillness in her eyes similar to the dead boy's face, something like the shadow of a lost dream entering and leaving through her vacant stare.

In the parlor, Juana wore her rosary around her neck as she and I served cafecitos to the visitors. Many of the neighbors had not seen Rafi in life and were lamenting to one another the loss now marked on Señor Pico's face.

It was easy to tell how much Señor Pico wanted to be

with his son, in the last hours that he could look at his face, hold him in his arms before he had to lay him in his coffin.

With a shiny black feather decorating her cloche hat, Doña Sabine's gaze stayed on Señor Pico as he looked towards the room where his son lay. Every now and again the señor's eyes would circle the room he was in, with no interest in what was being said. His eyes grew wider when someone smiled at him or addressed him by name, and occasionally he closed them and covered them with his fingers.

"You're so brave, both of you." Doña Eva's voice rose above the others. Doña Eva bore a great resemblance to both her daughter Beatriz, and her son, Doctor Javier—or rather they did to her—except Doña Eva's hair was crinkled like sawdust and mostly gray. Doña Eva strove against the natural curl of her hair by parting it in the middle and then coiling her tresses into two knots, one above each of her ears.

Señor Pico accepted Doña Eva's compliment about their bravery with a gracious but tired smile. Don Carlos, the mill owner, who was quite thin, was sitting on a wicker banquette between his wife and Doña Eva. Don Carlos had an abundance of veins showing under the surface of his sheer white skin. Sebastien had joked that if Don Carlos had as much money as he had veins bulging from his right hand alone, then he would own the whole island.

I tried not to look at his hands as I served Don Carlos his cafecito. Papi strolled to the radio and turned it on. A merengue by La Orquesta Presidente Trujillo came on and silenced the voices in the room. After three long patriotic songs, an announcer introduced fragments from a series of old speeches given on different occasions by the Generalissimo.

Señor Pico motioned for everyone to be quiet. He walked over to the radio and increased the volume, as though seeking comfort for his personal loss from the most powerful voice in the land, a voice that for all its authority was still as shrill as a birdcall.

"You are independent, and yours is the responsibility for carrying out justice," the Generalissimo shrieked. A buzzing hum intruded at many points, and some words, sometimes even whole phrases, were lost to the distance the transmission had to travel to Papi's radio.

"Tradition shows as a fatal fact," the Generalissimo continued, "that under the protection of rivers, the enemies of peace, who are also the enemies of work and prosperity, found an ambush in which they might do their work, keeping the nation in fear and menacing stability."

The neighbors listened, nodding their heads in agreement as the Generalissimo's voice rose, charged with certainty and fervor.

"The liberators of the nation did their part," the Generalissimo went on, "and we could not ask more of them. The leaders of today must play their parts also."

Doctor Javier got up to leave, excusing himself to his mother by whispering in her ear. Beatriz's eyes narrowed as she mouthed many of the Generalissimo's words, which it seemed she had heard recited before.

Papi slumped down in his chair and nodded off to sleep. Señor Pico stood staunch and erect as though about to charge across a field of battle. Juana threaded her rosary through her fingers while Luis, outside, listened through the shutters.

"My best friends are workers!" the Generalissimo shouted. "I came into office to work, and you will find me battling at every moment for the earnest desires of my people."

Kindly, the neighbors did not stay for long after the Generalissimo's radio broadcast ended. They filed out in small groups until only Señora Valencia and her husband were left.

Juana was entrusted with the care of Rosalinda, and the señor and señora sat in their room most of the evening. As he held her, she groaned now and then, trying not to cry too loudly. He did not know how to ease her pain, not very well in any case; he kept shifting as she tried to find a comfortable nook to claim for herself, her own place to sink into, within his arms. He was silent while she sobbed, not offering a word. Perhaps he was suppressing his own tears, but his silence seemed to me a sign of failure for this marriage, the abrupt union of two strangers, who even with time and two children—one in this world and one in the other—had still not grown much closer. The short courtship and the even shorter visits after marriage had not made them really familiar with each other. The señora did not know him well enough, nor he her. He was still learning his role now, and she hers, and perhaps neither of them imagined that this test would arrive to transform them from a newly joined pair to the parents of a dead child.

Finally she said, "You should bury his clothes before we bury him. This is something I would like you to do for me."

If he thought this strange, he raised no question at all. He got up abruptly and stretched.

"I will have to leave for the border soon," he said, "for that operation I spoke of earlier."

If she thought this a strange development, she too said nothing at all.

19

You walk half a morning to get there, a narrow cave behind the waterfall at the source of the stream where the cane workers bathe. The cave is a grotto of wet moss, coral, and chalk that looks like marble. At first you are afraid to step behind the waterfall as the water in all its strength pounds down on your shoulders. Still you tiptoe into the cave until all you see is luminous green fresco—the dark green of wet papaya leaves. You hear no crickets, no hummingbirds, no pigeons. All you hear is water sliding off the ledge and crashing in a foamy white spray into the plunge pool below.

When the night comes, you don't know it inside the cramped slippery cave because the waterfall, Sebastien says, holds on to some memory of the sun that it will not surrender. On the inside of the cave, there is always light, day and night. You who know the cave's secret, for a time, you are also held captive in this prism, this curiosity of nature that makes you want to celebrate yourself in ways that you hope the cave will show you, that the emptiness in your bones will show you, or that the breath in your blood will show you, in ways that you hope your body knows better than yourself.

This is where Sebastien and I first made love, standing in this cave, in a crook where you feel half buried, although the light can't help but follow you and stay.

I have always wished for this same kind of light on the grave of my parents, but now I wish it also for both Joël and Rafael.

20

Señora Valencia's face became as pale as a bleached moon after her husband left her and went to bury their son's clothes. After much cajoling from Juana, she left her daughter in her cradle where she was sleeping and slipped into the bed where both her children had been conceived and born. Juana sat on the edge of this bed, stroking the señora's hands to soothe her to sleep. I stood near the patio doors and watched through a tiny opening in the louvers as Señor Pico dug a hole under the flame tree to bury Rafi's layette.

Doctor Javier held the kerosene lamp while the señor shoveled up another pile of dirt and threw it over his shoulders. A flow of muddy perspiration rolled from Señor Pico's forehead down to his chest. Some of the area boys gathered around to watch and offer help, thinking perhaps there might be a vigil, if not an all-night wake. Señor Pico declined their offer. He wanted to carry out the task himself, not allowing even Luis to dig, as would have been expected. He stopped to take a breath, then, glancing up at the stars, which seemed to be blinking and falling a lot more frequently that night, he removed his shirt and undershirt, and laid them on one of the lowest branches of the flame tree before proceeding with the digging.

"I would like to go to my son's burial," the señora told Juana.

"Do not concern yourself with this now," Juana said. "Put your mind on the girl child. The other one is already lost."

"Juana, please talk to me of Mami," Señora Valencia said.

Juana looked around the room, at the old Spanish clock that no longer chimed the hour but still showed the time correctly after so many years. She stared at the armoire with the orchids and the hummingbirds carved on the front, at the crucifix hung above the bed to protect the house from evil.

"There is too much to tell," Juana said, stroking the señora's hair.

"Tell me," the señora pleaded.

"She was so shy when she became a wife, your mami. She was almost frightened of your father, who was some years older. But this changed very quickly after she became friends with the other young wives like Doña Eva and Doña Sabine. And of course when you were born, your mother and father were completely happy. Your father was so very unhappy when your mother died. It had been a joyful time with the hope of a new brother for you, but your mother's labor was difficult. It was a breech birth and both your mami and the child lost their strength."

"More of Mami," she said. "Tell me more."

"Your mami was kind," Juana continued. "She was always patient with me, with Luis too. She treated us not like servants but the same way she did her friends. She was a good-hearted lady, your mami, and she cherished you very much."

Outside, the evening breeze blew out the kerosene lamp held by Doctor Javier. Luis cupped his hand around a long wooden match and lit the lamp again.

Señor Pico dropped Rafi's layette in the hole, a bedsheet and three frocks, each of which I had sewn and which young Rafi had worn only once.

"I have had dreams of what my son's face would look like," Señora Valencia said, "first at one, then at five, then at ten, fifteen, and twenty years old."

"I always had similar thoughts about you, Señora," Juana said. "I am so pleased to have seen you at all those ages."

"I feel sometimes," said Señora Valencia, "that I will never be a whole woman, for the absence of Mami's face."

Señora Valencia was asleep by the time her husband came into the room. I did not want to leave that night, but I knew that Sebastien would not come to visit me if the dead child was in the house. I had to go to him. Besides, Juana had chosen to spend the night at the foot of the four-poster canopy bed, to keep company with Rafi.

Luis walked back to his and Juana's house alone, though on this night more than any other he seemed to want his woman to himself. Papi remained in the parlor near the radio, listening for news of the war in Spain. Another Spanish city had fallen while young Rafi's coffin was being made.

I walked out into the night, past the ravine into which Joël had been thrown. Lemongrass and bamboo shoots lined the road. A breeze raced down the incline, the rustle growing louder as the grass blades bent towards the gorge at the bottom of the ravine.

In Don Carlos' compound, children roamed, circling a wooden food stand run by a Dominican woman named Mercedes and her two sons: Reinaldo and Pedro. Mercedes was said to be a distant relative of Don Carlos, a peasant woman with city ways.

A group of cane cutters stood in front of Mercedes' stand, buying liquor and joking with her and her sons. The older son, Reinaldo, worked as a guard in the cane fields during the day while his brother Pedro operated the cane press inside. Mercedes—and consequently Don Carlos, at least by rumor—had some relations from the interior campos who lived in the compound and worked as cutters in the fields, but Mercedes never openly claimed these people. "They are peasants who fell blind into this life of the cane," she said to anyone who asked. "They have no reason to live like pigs. This is their country."

The compound children hopped around Mercedes' stand near the chatting men who shoved them away from adult conversations with slaps on their bottoms and orders for them to go find their mothers, whether they had mothers or not. The children then ran off to play, dashing back and forth behind the flowered curtains that served as doors for some of the rooms. Women were cooking on blackened boulders and sticks behind the cabins, pouring cups of water over naked infants to wash them before the evening meal. They were singing work songs, but their voices were so tired, I could hardly make out the words or the melody. Some men were dozing off in their doorways. They startled themselves awake when anyone walked by. I squeezed myself between two young lovers seeking a comfortable dark corner, their usual sapodilla tree taken over by a small group of men arguing over a domino game. The game was stopped now and again so a player could defend a bad choice or a loss. Sebastien's friend Yves, who was with Sebastien and Joël when Joël was killed, was one of the domino players. Yves shaved his head to keep cane ticks out of his scalp. His Adam's apple was as large as a real apple, his legs too short for his lanky body.

I motioned to a boy who was playing with pebbles on the ground at their feet. He was a beautiful child with a long manly face. He skipped from foot to foot, fidgeting while standing in front of me. I handed him the goat bones Luis had cut for me the night Señor Pico had come home. He smiled as he thanked me, pulled on the unraveling hem of his short pants, then ran off to show the other children his prize.

Félice was sitting on the doorstep in front of Kongo's room, her fingers trembling as she picked at the birthmark beneath her nostrils.

"Kongo here?" I asked.

She nodded.

"Why don't you go inside and sit with him?"

"He won't receive me," she said.

I peeked through the bit of palm frond that served as Kongo's door. The room was dim, except for an oil lamp at his feet. There were two old mats facing each other on the dirt floor and a pile of half gourds and earthen jars in the middle. Kongo sat on his own mat, squeezing a rare, precious, ball of flour dough in and out of the spaces between his fingers. He cursed the flour, murmuring that nothing ever took shape the way one wanted it to.

Félice motioned for me to go to Kongo. "I know he will receive you," she said.

"Old Kongo?" I called from the doorway. "It's Amabelle, come to see you."

Kongo moved aside the scrap of palm frond and let me in. I walked over to the mat where his son Joël had once slept. A pair of clean dark pants and a bright yellow shirt were laid out as though Joël had set them down to be grabbed in a hurry. I leaned towards the old man to better see his face.

"Too dark?" he asked.

"A little," I said.

"M'renmen darkness," he said. "In sugar land, a shack's for sleeping, not for living. Living is only work, the fields. Darkness means rest."

"Darkness is good," I said, simply to agree.

"Is she still there?" he asked of Félice. "I told her to leave, I did, but she won't go. She can't stay all night. I don't want her to stay."

Félice stirred and cleared her throat as though to remind Kongo that she was listening.

"You the woman who's with Sebastien?" he asked. "You Amabelle?"

"Yes."

"When he was killed, my son, Sebastien found the clothes you see next to you, to bury him in. Brought me a pile of wood, Sebastien did, to make a coffin for my son. Sebastien, he is like my own blood."

"Condolences," I said. "I am sad for the death of Joël."

He plopped the dough on the ground and pounded it with his knuckles.

"I was asked to make a request of you," I said. "Don Ignacio, the elder at the house where I am, would like to come see you."

He removed his hand from the dough and concentrated on digging the flour out from underneath his fingernails. Then he reached into his pocket for snuff and took a pinch.

"That is a strange request, Amabelle," he said. "What do they want with me, these people?"

"Don Ignacio wishes to talk to you of Joël's accident."

"I don't know if it was an accident, Amabelle. He was not one to die so easy, my son." He raised his face towards the ceiling to keep the snuff from sliding from his nose down to his chin. Outside Félice cleared her throat again, this time it sounded like she was crying.

"The elder, Papi, he would like to pay for Joël's funeral," I said.

"No funeral for Joël," he said. "I wanted to bury him in our own land where he was born, I did, but he was too heavy to carry so far. I buried him where he died in the ravine. I buried him in a field of lemongrass, my son." He lowered his head, letting the tobacco mix drop to his chest. "He was one of those children who grew like the weeds in the fields, my son. Didn't need nobody or nothing, but he did love his father. It wasn't ceremonious the way I buried him, I know. No clothes, no coffin, nothing between him and the dry ground. I wanted to give him back to the soil the way his mother passed him to me on the first day of his life."

I could hear the children outside drawing sticks to decide who should have the first turn at playing with the goat bones. I no longer heard Félice.

"Of all the things he's done, my son," Kongo was saying, "of all the ways I've seen him be, I'll never forget how he looked when he was born. So small he was, so bare, so innocent."

He picked up the dough again and crushed it between his fingers.

"You shouldn't spend too much time with this old man," he said. "I don't want to push you out, but kite'm. Go see Sebastien now."

"What word should I bring to Don Ignacio?" I asked.

"Tell him I am a man," he said. "He was a man, too, my son."

Sebastien was sitting in a corner in his room, rubbing an aloe poultice over some blisters along his calves.

"The body forgets how chancy a cane fire can be," he said, handing me the ointment.

Sebastien had a bunch of carbuncles over his hips and belly. As I rubbed the poultice on them, I didn't feel as though I was touching him. It was more like touching the haze of anger rising off his skin, the tears of sadness he would not cry, the move san, the bad blood Joël's death had stirred in him.

"There are new ticks in the fields with this harvest." He groaned while turning over for me to rub the ointment onto his back.

Papi's cedar planks were lined up against the back wall. The planks were glowing, even in the faint light. Papi's madder glaze had filled the grain in a way that made the surface sensitive both to the shadows and to the light. From the floor you could see the imperfections in the finish, the shading differences, places where the tint didn't match because Papi had waited too long before adding another coat, or where he had by chance brushed backwards, against the grain.

"Señor Pico's son died today," I said.

"This is what I heard," Sebastien said, his voice rising with a smile as though it were not a sad thing at all.

"You should not rejoice for something like this," I warned. "He was only a child."

"I am not rejoicing," he said. "And even if I was—"

"It would not be right," I said. "We would not have wanted them to rejoice when Joël died."

Silence was his most piercing weapon when he was angry. He said nothing for some time.

"Who are these people to you?" he asked, pushing at a few of the boils until the blood and pus bubbled to the surface. "Do you think they're your family?"

"The señora and her family are the closest to kin I have," I said.

"And me?" he asked.

"You too," I said, wanting to announce that he came first.

"We'll see," he said.

I thought of what Mimi had suggested in the stream the day after Joël had died. An eye for an eye, she had said. Did one only have to wish for it to make it true?

"What are you going to do with Papi's wood?" I asked.

"What am I going to do with what wood?" he asked.

"This wood," I said, pointing behind him. "The wood I gave you for Joël's coffin."

"Kongo didn't make use of it," he said. " Maybe I'll keep it for the next time somebody dies."

He sat up and leaned against the gray cement wall, looked at the doorway through the scarred fingers laced over his face. Yves yawned loudly from outside, waiting for the right moment to come in and bed down for the night.

Sebastien rose, put on his clothes, and walked me back out into the night. We said nothing to each other as we walked to Señora Valencia's house. On the way, we walked past the ravine where Joël had been buried. A fast breeze darted through the bamboo and lemongrass on either side of the road, blowing through them like a chorus of flutes and whistles.

Félice was ahead of us on the road, pacing back and forth over the steep edge of the ravine. Her posture as she tipped towards the gorge reminded me of myself standing at the river's brim the day my parents had drowned.

Sebastien and I accompanied Félice back to the gates of Doña Sabine's house. She went along with us, glad, I thought, to have been found.

The next morning, before dawn, while everyone was still asleep, Juana and I watched from the doorway of the old sewing room as Señor Pico padded his son's coffin with a pile of clean sheets from his wife's armoire and placed him in the casket. The señor was wearing his ceremonial khakis with his cap set in perfect alignment with his seashell-shaped ears. When he looked up, he seemed surprised to see Juana and me standing there.

"You have not slept at all, Señor," Juana reminded him.

"You should wake the señora now," he said.

Señora Valencia got up to drape a web of fragile lace over her son's colorfully painted coffin. Papi and one of the señora's maternal relations held the other end of the heirloom lace-bordered sheets, helping her to fold the cloth small enough to cover the casket without trailing onto the ground.

Señora Valencia bent down to kiss the coffin through the sunflower design of the lace and then walked back to her room. Her daughter was sleeping in her cradle. She picked her up and took her to her bed.

Señor Pico and Papi together carried the coffin away.

Once the casket was in the first automobile, Señor Pico came back to the bed where his wife sat with her daughter cradled against her chest. He removed his cap and placed it between his right armpit and elbow. Brushing his lips against his wife's forehead, he avoided his daughter's tiny hand, which she intuitively held out towards her father as if in recognition of his face or to ward off the stinging expression of disfavor growing more and more pronounced on it each time he laid eyes on her. Her gesture was like her own way of making amends for having lived in her brother's place, as if to say that she, too, wanted to be present for the burial and watch her brother's descent into the nothingness they had once shared as two.

"Don't be anxious, everything will go perfectly well," Señor Pico assured his wife as though he was discussing yet another military operation.

Señora Valencia watched her husband march out of the room. As his Packard pulled away, she covered her ears with both hands to protect herself from the noise. She then raised her daughter's face to her chin, closing her eyes to feel the child's breath against her cheek.

Once Juana took over the care of Rosalinda, Señora Valencia defied Juana's commands to lie in and rest and went out to sit on the rocker on the verandah outside her room. The sun had just risen over the valley, the dew still lingering in the curved petals of Papi's prettiest red lantern orchids. On the balcony, Señora Valencia made an altar for her son with two handfuls of white island carnations—which she chose and I fetched for her from her father's garden—and an unlit candle, which she had been saving to light in church, after a Mass.

We watched as Father Romain hurried past the house, as though on his way to administer last rites somewhere. Soon after him, my friends came drifting by on their way to the fields. Kongo led the group as usual, with Sebastien and Yves close behind.

Señora Valencia leaned forward on the balustrade as if to better see the orchids down below.

"Amabelle, you know some of the cane people?"

"Yes, Señora."

"Go and ask them—the ones who just walked by—to come and have un cafecito with us."

"All of them?"

"As many as will come."

I was breathless when I reached the almond tree road. A few ripe almonds had fallen off the branches. The seeds were cracked open, half buried in the soil. The broken fruits oozed a ruddy juice, which made it seem as though the ground was bleeding.

"What's chasing you?" Sebastien asked.

"The mistress of the house wants all of you to come for un cafecito with her," I said.

"Your mistress?" Sebastien asked.

"Señora Valencia."

Kongo raised his hand over his eyes and looked up at the house.

"It is not a place where we want to go," Sebastien shouted into the hollow of Kongo's ear.

Word of Señora Valencia's invitation passed from mouth to mouth in the group. Shoulders were shrugged. Eyebrows were raised. Burlap sacks and straw hats were removed from heads for a better look at the house. Discussions began and ended in the same breath. What did she want with them anyway? Maybe they were all going to be poisoned. Many had heard rumors of groups of Haitians being killed in the night because they could not manage to trill their "r" and utter a throaty "j" to ask for parsley, to say perejil. Rumors don't start for nothing, someone insisted.

A woman began telling stories that she'd heard. A week before, a pantry maid who had worked in the house of a colonel for thirty years was stabbed by him at the dinner table. Two brothers were dragged from a cane field and macheted to death by field guards—someone there had supposedly witnessed the event with his own eyes. It was said that the Generalissimo, along with a border commission, had given orders to have all Haitians killed. Poor Dominican peasants had been asked to catch Haitians and bring them to the soldiers. Why not the rich ones too?

"Tell me again the name of your mistress," Kongo said.

"Señora Valencia," I said. "Her son is being buried this morning, so she may not be fully well." I tapped my temples to explain any rifts in the señora's reasoning.

Kongo dug his broom handle into the red dirt and started towards the house. Most of the cane workers continued on to the fields, but some—at least twenty or so—were curious enough to follow us up the hill.

They crowded onto the porch, into the garden, any place where there was room to either lean or sit down.

Señora Valencia kept Rosalinda inside while Juana and I followed her orders. We poured coffee into her best European red orchid-patterned tea set and passed the first cups to Kongo, who handed them to the youngest in the group. Among the children was the boy I had given the goat bones to the night before. I poured him a full cup and then moved on to the others. Juana had rationed carefully, controlling the supply so everyone who wanted to could have at least a sip.

"We'll have the day's wages taken away if we don't go soon," Sebastien said. He did not want to participate in the señora's feast.

As Juana was handing out the last cups of the coffee her sisters had sent her, Kongo moved away from the others and walked boldly into the parlor where the señora was sitting with her daughter. Kongo leaned over to peek at Rosalinda's bronze face; he held out his hand as if to touch it. Señora Valencia reached up and blocked Kongo's hardened old fingers. Kongo grabbed Señora Valencia's extended hand and kissed the tip of her fingernails; Señora Valencia's face reddened, as though this was the first time she'd ever been touched so intimately by a stranger.

"My heart is saddened for the death of your other child," Kongo said in his best Spanish. He released her hand so that she could better grasp her daughter. "When he died, my son, the ground sank a few folds beneath my feet. I asked myself, How can he die so young? Did the stars visit him upon me in caprice? To teach me that a lifetime can be vast as a hundred years or sudden as a few breaths? Enjoy this one you have left. It all passes so fast. In the time it takes to draw a breath."

Señora Valencia watched as Kongo walked out. I followed him with my eyes as he strolled down the hill. He laid his hand on Sebastien's shoulder as if to summon the strength for one more step.

After everyone was gone, Señora Valencia went back to her bed and lay silently awake, watching her daughter sleep at her side. It seemed that she might have regretted exposing herself to the damp morning air and her daughter to outside forces that Kongo and the others might have brought with them, but her son's death had made her heedless and rash.

When her husband returned, before he could tell her anything about the burial, she told him what she had done for the cane workers.

He did not scold her, but once he discovered that she had used their imported orchid-patterned tea set, he took the set out to the yard and, launching them against the cement walls of the house latrines, he shattered the cups and saucers, one by one.

21

At Christmas, the hills beneath the citadel are full of lanterns. Parents and children join hands to light each other's faces by the glow of fragile paper shaped to the desires of their hearts. A fanal, a lantern, is like a kite, my father says, a kite that glows but does not fly.

My father always made me lanterns shaped like monuments, a task that took longer than most, the lantern of La Place Toussaint Louverture with a candle glowing inside, the plumed feather-capped hat of General Toussaint, the Cathedral of Cap Haitien with one set of paper used to dye another to look like stained glass, and of course the citadel, which takes twelve months of secret work.

I say to my father, Make me a lantern of your face to carry with me the whole year long.

He laughs, a chortle of paternal pride. It would be too vain, he says, to spend more time than God reproducing one's self.

22

Rosalinda's baptism took place only after Señora Valencia's period of lying in had formally ended. On the baptism day, at the chapel, the pews were filled with a waiting brood of mothers, fathers, godmothers, aunts, and uncles. They had brought their children to Father Vargas for a group baptism. Many of the children were already six or seven years old and were being rebaptized so the Generalissimo could now become their official, albeit absent, godfather.

Señor Pico forced his way past the crowd spilling over outside as his wife carried their daughter to the front row, which was reserved for the more privileged families.

Señora Valencia wore a pale cream dress with a mantilla bordered with the same Valenciennes lace as the tablecloth that had been buried with her son. Papi followed behind her, then Doctor Javier, and Beatriz.

I watched from a distance as Father Vargas poured holy water on Rosalinda's head welcoming her into the Holy Catholic Church.

After the baptism, I gave my space to the family of a nearly grown boy whose name was about to be changed to Rafael in the Generalissimo's honor.

Outside the chapel, the valley peasants waited for their turn before the altar. A few playful toddlers chased a baby goat around the church. Their mothers shouted threats that went unheeded. No supper for the rest of their lives. No sweets. No love, never again. The children, with the dust like a flying rug at their heels, were willing to hazard anything that might only be taken away from them later.

When they came out of the chapel, Señora Valencia held Rosalinda out to me for a baptismal kiss.

"Amabelle, when you last saw her, she was a Moor," she said. "Now, I bring you a Christian."

I leaned forward and grazed Rosalinda's cheeks with my lips. Her forehead was still wet where the priest had doused it with the holy water. Señor Pico yanked his wife's arm and pulled her away, almost making the señora drop the child. Rosalinda was startled by the abrupt movement and began to cry as they piled into the automobile for the short journey to the house.

Juana cooked a giant baptism feast. We spent the afternoon serving the neighbors, those who came into the house and others, the valley peasants, who gathered outside in curiosity and hunger.

The celebration was stilled by the memory of Rafi, whose shadow would no doubt follow his sister all her life.

That night, after the baptism celebration, Kongo came to find me. He was wearing the yellow shirt and black pants that Sebastien had given him to dress his son for burial; the clothes fit him as though they had been cut and sewn for his body.

"I am looking for Amabelle," he said through the crack in the door. Running his fingers over the verandah rail, he stood outside in the night and listened to the tree frogs croaking.

"Please come," I said.

He eyed the pile of cedar that Papi kept stacked near the latrines. "Let me stand here a moment," he said. "There is so much wood here. I've been on sugar land all over this country, and there's never enough wood to spare for us. I've seen people take doors off hinges to make coffins for their dead."

He reached through the doorway and handed me a papier-mâché mold of a man's face.

"I bring this offering for your house," he said. "I hope you will accept."

I took the mask from him. The face hinted at his, but many decades earlier. The forehead was curved and wide, the raised cheekbones standing out above the hollowed space over the jaws. The lips were half open, between a grin and a scream; it was the death face of his son.

I showed him to the mat where I prepared to sleep. He sat down. Picking up my conch shell, he blew into it, forcing out a clipped lively melody, a carnival rhythm.

"You hungry?" I asked him.

He yawned to show he was hungry without having to speak the words. I had some rice from the baptism meal that I had been saving for Sebastien. I removed it from three layers of plantain leaves and served it to him with a wooden spoon.

"Back home I earned my living making masks for carnival," he said between bites. "I was the only mask maker in my town. All I ever needed was a bit of flour and paper and

I could make this type of mask. Had a woman, thirty years she was with me, the mother of my son. She loved masks, she did. The more of them I made, the more she seemed to love me."

I gave him a small calabash full of water. He pushed his head back and drank until it was empty.

"At my age, my memory won't always serve me well," he said. "Could be I knew you when you were young. Could be you're one of those children who ran and hid when my woman and I came down the street with our masks to open the carnival parade. Could be you climbed the greasy pole in my yard to get the money at the top. I always had a big celebration for the children at carnival. Naturally one never remembers all the children."

"What is your true name?" I asked. "The name you had before you came here?" This was something I suddenly wanted to know. I was hoping that in the remembering he would want to share this too.

"Some things are too wasteful to remember," he said, "like burning blood in an oil lamp." His breathing grew louder as though his stomach was getting used to being full.

"After my woman died, I stopped the mask-making to do carpentry. But I wasn't good at making anything but masks, I wasn't. Still, I couldn't bring myself to go back to the masks without my woman. I sold all my land. My money went on things I thought I could buy to forget: mostly liquor, firewater, and happy people's company. Couldn't ever be alone when I was sad. Before you could tap your foot one time, I had nothing. Joël and I were used to working together. Both he and me, we would have been beggars if we did not come here. But I'm not here only to eat your food and tell you tales. I came because Sebastien sent me."

"Has something happened to Sebastien?" I asked. Because of the baptism, I had not been able to go and see Sebastien all day.

"Sebastien's well, he is," he said. "He decided after what happened at the ravine that he didn't want to waste more time. He sent me to ask you if you would promise yourself to him and keep yourself just for him. When a young man's serious about a young woman, the old customs demand he bring his parents to express his intentions to her parents. Since both your parents and his parents are absent, I came to you on his word."

I looked down at the mask in my hand. I couldn't help but think of the night Joël had died, how for a moment I'd thought it was Sebastien who had been struck down by Señor Pico's automobile. The old man glanced at me and then at the mask.

"Always hoped my son would find a woman like you," he said, "a good woman."

"Joël had a good woman," I said.

"You think of that one with the big black mark under her nose. I did not want her for him."

"She wanted your son," I said. "She desired your blessings. She still does."

"Blessings? What for? My son's only a remembrance now, if even this. The one with the big mark under her nose, she is young, and the young do not stay young by keeping watch on the past. Soon she will find another man, and my son will slip from her mind."

"She's still very troubled," I said.

"I hope Sebastien will let you keep the mask," he said.

"Are you certain you don't want to keep this face for yourself?" I asked.

"I've made many," he said, "for all those who, even when I'm gone, will keep my son in mind. If I could, I would carry them all around my neck, I would, like some men wear their amulets. I give this one to you because you have a safe place to preserve it."

"I'm happy to have it," I said, "though 'happy' is not the proper word."

"I'm glad to give it to you," he said, "though 'glad' is also not the proper word."

"Thank you for trusting me with something so precious to you," I said.

"My son was precious to me," he said. "This is only a sad reminder of him."

As he got up to leave, I straightened his collar and removed a clump of rice that was clinging to the top button of his shirt.

"Now you look handsome." I said.

"Sebastien, he let me keep the clothes," he said. "I put in some pleats and made them smaller."

"I am happy you were the one to bring this word from Sebastien," I said.

"I don't often have a chance to do these things," he said. "I also had another thought when I came here tonight."

"Tell me, please."

"The elder of your house, Don Ignacio, he's not asked again to come and see me, no?"

With Rafi's death, Papi did seem to have forgotten about him and Joël.

"I'm not surprised," he said, "that my son has already vanished from his thoughts."

After Kongo left, I rushed out to see Sebastien. I didn't go the ravine route but down through the footpath around the stream, which was a much cooler trail at night.

It was a dark night, but I knew the trail well enough to follow it in my sleep. I dashed around the stream, listening to the tree frogs and the cicadas trilling from far away.

I had been walking for some time when I heard the parting of tree branches and the flopping of footsteps landing in the mud holes behind me. The steps were faint at first, but slowly grew in force and concentration. They were coming closer, marching in perfect unison.

Jumping off the path, I tried to slip into the stream but landed on my bottom with a splash.

The night appeared clearer from the water. I reached down to the bed of the stream, feeling for a rock, something to use in defending myself. Looking back towards the footpath, I saw nobody there. Perhaps my fear had created all the noises.

"You in the water." A man's voice called from behind a shadowed tree. He spoke to me in Kreyòl.

I anchored my feet at the bottom of the stream, reached under, and finally grabbed a rock. Three men were standing at the causeway, each holding a machete, the blades reflecting the water's clarity.

"This is a time to sleep, not to swim," the same man said.

I could see all their faces now. They were stonemasons who lived in the neighboring houses, on the road leading to the stream. I walked out of the water, shivering as the night air dried my skin. Among the men was Unèl, who had once rebuilt the latrines in Señora Valencia's yard. Unèl handed me a blanket that he carried rolled up and tied with a rope on his back.

"Where are you going at this late hour, Amabelle?" he asked.

"To see Sebastien," I said.

"Haven't you heard all the talk?" he asked.

"What talk?"

"Talk of people being killed."

"That is just talk, started since Joël died," I said.

"You should tell Sebastien to come for you when he wishes to see you at night," he said.

I walked back to the trail that encircled the stream. Unèl rushed ahead as the others stayed behind me.

"It's not prudent to walk alone these days," Unèl scolded.

"Thank you for your counsel," I said.

"We want to protect our people," Unèl said. "After Joël was killed, we formed the night-watchman brigade. If they come, we'll be prepared for them."

"I am going back," another man spoke from behind me. "I won't wait for things to go from talk to bloodshed, I'm going back to Haiti. I won't take the automobile roads where all the soldiers are, I'll travel through the mountains. I'm going back this very Saturday. I'm prepared to leave all this behind. Thank you, Alegría. Our time here has been joyful, but now I must say good-bye to you."

"I will stay and fight," Unèl said. "I work hard; I have a right to be here. The brigade stays to fight. While we fight we can help others."

"All this because Joël's been killed?" I asked Unèl.

The coolness in my voice must have startled him, for he paused and looked at me before taking another step to follow his companions, who had left him behind. It wasn't that I had grown indifferent to Joël's death, but I couldn't understand why Unèl and the others would consider that death to be a herald of theirs and mine too. Had Señor Pico struck Joël with his automobile deliberately, to clear his side of the island of Haitians?

"Let me ask again. Haven't you heard the talk?" Unèl asked.

"I've heard too much talk," I said.

When we reached the compound, I returned the blanket to Unèl. He rolled it up, tied it with a short rope, and threw it back across his shoulder.

"Thanks to her, if I am cold tonight, I have a wet blanket to wrap myself in," Unèl told Sebastien as they shook hands. "I will take this opportunity to warn the others," Unèl said. "The times have changed. We all must look after ourselves."

Unèl and his men walked from shack to shack cautioning everyone to be watchful, not to walk alone at night. He enrolled a few more sentries among the cane workers, some who promised that they would walk the valley with him the following night. Others joked that only a woman could get them out of their beds to walk the valley all night after they had spent a whole day on their feet in the cane fields.

I hurried into Sebastien's room, my clothes dripping wet.

Both Yves and Sebastien looked as though they'd been about to put out their lamp and go to sleep.

"I thought Kongo was still with you," Sebastien said.

Yves got up, stroked his shaved head, and went outside. I stepped out of my clothes but remained in my slip. Sebastien went out to hang my day dress to dry. When he returned, we lay down on his mat. He raised an old rice sack sheet over our bodies. I could feel his boils and the sábila poultice sliding down his leg as he called Yves back into the room.

"Have you heard some talk?" I asked Sebastien.

"Unèl's talking of an order from the Generalissimo."

"Yes, that talk."

"I don't know what to make of it," Sebastien said. "I keep hearing it, but I don't know if all of it is true."

"Just before you came, we were speaking about you," Yves said, slipping back on his own mat across the room. "Did your ears burn?"

"What were you saying?" I asked.

"Yves was telling me I should sell the wood," Sebastien said.

"Papi's wood?"

"We can sell it," Yves said, twisting his neck and turning his large Adam's apple towards us. "I know someone who's looking for good well-cured wood to make tables and chairs."

"I don't want this wood near me," Sebastien said. Even though he was not speaking of the rumors, I could tell he was becoming as troubled as the others, distracted even. "Since we didn't use it for the reason we took it, I want to return the wood to its owner."

"There's no taking it back." Yves yanked a few sisal strands from the edge of his straw mat.

"Then, it is your wood now," Sebastien said. "I give it to you. It's yours to do with what you wish."

Yves coiled his body into a ball and turned his back to us. "There's no taking it back," he repeated, his voice already fading with sleep.

"You sent Kongo with word for me," I whispered to Sebastien.

"There are plenty of men who would have made a promise to you long ago," he said.

"Should we go to Father Romain for blessings?" I asked, becoming more and more impatient about being promised in a time-honored way to Sebastien. "I know you don't like priests and rituals, but Father Romain is our friend."

A piece of cooking wood held ajar the slat of lumber that served as Sebastien's window. The wood creaked as though about to fall. Sebastien got up and fixed it so the night air could freely enter and cool the room.

"We may not live together in the same house, you and me, until the end of this harvest," he said. "I don't want to bring you here, and I don't want to squeeze myself into your room on that hill and live with those people. Can you please wait for me?"

"I can wait," Yves shouted in his sleep.

"What can you wait for?" Sebastien asked him, laughing.

We walked over to Yves' mat. His eyes were wide open, staring at the wall with a glaze over his pupils, like the cloudy gloss of river blindness.

Sebastien waved his fingers in front of his face. Yves did not blink.

"Ask him how he is," Sebastien said.

"How are things with you, Yves?" I asked.

"Who is asking?" said Yves, still asleep.

"I have known him since we were both in short pants," Sebastien said as we walked back to his mat. "I've lived here in this room with him for many years. Never before has he talked in his sleep, plus with his eyes wide open. It started only after Joël's accident."

Yves and Sebastien both mumbled in their sleep all night, as though traveling through the same dream together.

"Papa, don't die on that plate of food," Yves said as dawn approached. He rolled onto his back, his eyes fixed on the dirty ceiling. His voice was clear yet distant, as though he were reciting a rote school lesson for the hundredth time. "Papa, don't die on that plate of food. Please let me take it away."

Sebastien turned over on his side and mumbled through his own nightmares.

"Is he still talking?" he asked as he woke up.

"About his father dying on a plate of food," I said.

"His mother liked to say that his father died over a plate of food," Sebastien replied in a wearied voice. "The father was put in a bread-and-water prison by the Yankis and let go after thirty days. First thing done by the mother is to cook him all the rich food he dreamt about in prison. The father eats until he falls over with his face in the plate and he's dead."

A cock's crow finally woke Yves. He jumped up and grabbed his work clothes, wanting to be among the first at the stream.

"Did you have bad dreams last night?" I asked Yves.

"Why do you want to know?" he asked, his Adam's apple bobbing up and down as though it were going to leap out of his mouth. "You want to use my dreams to play games of chance at Mercedes' stand?"

"We couldn't sleep," Sebastien said. "You were squawking like a crazy parrot all night long."

After most of the workers had left for the stream, Sebastien and I went to a mud-and-wattle cooking hut near a wooden fence where the compound met an open dirt road. He brushed two rocks against a dry pine twig and sparked a flame for our coffee.

We sat under the mesquite that leaned over the hut, and while he sipped the coffee out of one side of his mouth, I watched him and grinned against my will.

For some, passion is the gift of a ring in a church ceremony, the bearing of children as shared property. For me it was just a smile I couldn't help, tugging at the sides of my face. And slowly as he caught glimpses of me between sips of his coffee, he returned the smile, looking the same way I did: bashful, undeserving, and almost ashamed to be the one responsible for the look of desire always rising in a dark flush on the side of his face. His eyes searched everything around him, the live coals and ashes under the coffeepot, the pebbles opening the soil to fit themselves in, the patches of dirt-brown grass dying from being too often trampled underfoot.

When the morning breeze lifted his torn and leaf-stained collar, he pressed it back down with his cane-scarred hands. His eyes surveyed all the familiar details of his fingers, pausing only for an instant when our pupils met and trying to communicate with the simple flutter of a smile all those things we could not say because there was the cane to curse, the harvest to dread, the future to fear.

23

I dream of the sugar woman. Again.

As always, she is dressed in a long, three-tiered ruffled gown inflated like a balloon. Around her face, she wears a shiny silver muzzle, and on her neck there is a collar with a clasped lock dangling from it.

The sugar woman grabs her skirt and skips back and forth around my room. She seems to be dancing a kalanda in a very fast spin, locks arms with the air, pretends to kiss someone much taller than herself. As she swings and shuffles, the chains on her ankles cymbal a rattled melody. She hops to the sound of the jingle of the chains, which with her twists grows louder and louder.

"Is your face underneath this?" I ask. The voice that comes out of my mouth surprises me; it is the voice of the orphaned child at the stream, the child who from then on would talk only to strange faces.

"You see me?" she asks, laughing a metallic laugh that echoes inside the mask.

"Why is that on your face?" I ask.

"This?" She taps her fingers against the muzzle. "Given to me a long time ago, this was, so I'd not eat the sugarcane."

I begin to think inside the dream that it is Sebastien who always brings her here, that she is the hidden image of some jealous woman or the revenant of some dead love he carries with him into my arms.

"Why are you here?" I ask her.

"Told you before," she says. "I am the sugar woman. You, my eternity."

I wake up, pounding the arm Sebastien has draped over my breasts to awake him.

If I mumble in my sleep, it is either about my parents or the sugar woman.

"What dream this time?" he asks. Sometimes, he is impatient with my shadows.

24

The high cement walls around Doña Sabine's house were dotted with watchmen with deep brown peasant faces. Some looked too old, others too young to carry the ancient rusting rifles slumped over their shoulders, the holding straps digging flesh marks into their backs.

As I walked by, I looked up at the high patio doors, where a small cloister of men and women crouched behind fragile curtains while watching passersby on the roads.

Closer to Señora Valencia's house, Luis was standing in the road, his head swinging back and forth with every movement, every bull cart or peasant merchant on donkey back, every child on his way to the parish schools, every cane cutter heading to the fields.

"The patrón is leaving today," he said, smiling. "They come for him in a short time."

The patrón had already stayed much longer than his expected time. His pressing operation, he had told his wife, had been delayed until now. Because we were all so accustomed to having the señora alone to ourselves, we preferred having him gone. Now I suspected the señor was tired of watching his daughter grow plumper and happier every day while he was thinking of the male heir he had lost.

"How long will he be gone?" I asked.

He didn't know.

A burning piece of metal breezed past my face as I walked up the hill. I jumped aside, ducking my head. Señora Valencia and her husband were standing under the flame tree, each holding a short-barreled rifle aimed at the calabash trees in front of my room.

The air was filled with a gust of peppery smoke, some of which came to rest in the back of my throat. I closed my eyes to fight the feverish sting in my pupils.

"Amabelle!" Señora Valencia cried out, her voice hoarse with terror. She was in a loose housedress, leaning against the flame tree for support. Señor Pico had on all of his uniform except his cap, which was resting on the far corner of the bench where his wife sat between shots.

I waved my hand to show that I was still alive and then ran into the pantry where Juana was peering out, annoyed.

"I thought you'd caught the last one in your neck." She handed me a cup of water.

"Which saint must I thank for saving me?"

"All of them," she said.

Señora Valencia looked a bit depleted from the shooting but she pulled herself together in time to fire again. Looking towards the house, she appeared worried that the rifle blasts might wake her daughter.

"He should not make her do this," Juana said, "not so soon after she has given birth."

"The señora's strong. She's a good markswoman," I said, after the water had settled in my stomach.

I remembered how, for lack of a boy child, in spite of his saddening memories of the war, Papi used to take the señora hunting with real rifles when she was only a girl. With Papi the hunt was for birds. With her husband, what would the mark be?

Señor Pico guided his wife's hands along her rifle's trigger guard. "Remember, do not aim too high, or you will shoot over the head," he said.

He lined up her hands to fire once more. She shook her body free, leaned forward, lowered her eyes to the top of the gun barrel, then pulled the trigger. A calabash cracked from the tree across the yard and fell, toppling a few smaller ones on its way to the ground.

Señora Valencia lowered her rifle to her side and said, "No más."

With a towel draped over her shoulder, Juana brought out a large bowl of water. The señora washed her hands and wiped them dry with the part of the towel that fell down to Juana's stomach.

"You must know how to protect yourself," Señor Pico said as they walked back to the house. He held his wife by the arm as though they were reliving their wedding march.

"Papi and Luis will be here to look after Rosalinda and me," she said.

"They cannot be with you at every moment," he said.

"We have never had these fears before," she said.

"This is a different time," he told her.

Luis came into the parlor to announce that a truck full of Guardia had arrived.

Juana rushed off and came back with Rosalinda cradled in the arms of one of Señora Valencia's distant cousins, who had come from Higüey to visit the baby; her name was Lidia.

Lidia had a narrow face with slanted downcast eyes and shoulder-length black hair that swayed back and forth as she patted Rosalinda's behind.

Lidia stepped forward and held Rosalinda out to be embraced by her father. Señor Pico avoided the child and instead brushed his lips against the side of Lidia's face before springing out the door.

As he marched down the hill to one of the open-back trucks, the men of the Guardia saluted and cheered his approach. He waved to his wife one last time, then jumped into the passenger seat next to the driver.

"It almost seems like we are at war," Señora Valencia said, watching her husband's three-truck military caravan pull away. She chose to ignore his avoidance of their daughter and of herself, as she did all the other things he did that were not pleasing to her.

"With your man, everything is the great expedition." Papi walked back to the parlor with the señora. "Men like him have their names on plaques, on roads and bridges. Cities and villages are named for them. I came to live here in this valley because I wanted to escape such dealings, escape from armies and officers—"

"But your daughter loved the first soldier who strolled through your garden—"

"Love cannot always be explained," Papi said, his voice filled with a desire to understand. "I have seen this before. Your man, he believes that everything he is doing, he's doing for his country. At least this is what he must tell himself."

"He's a good man, Papi," the señora said.

"If you say it, I must believe you," Papi replied. "I'm going for a stroll now."

"Take Luis with you," Señora Valencia said.

"No, no," Papi said. "This I do alone."

25

The valley's dust storms bring me joy. The dust rises in funnels from the ground and sweeps down the road. Like a sheet come undone from the clothesline, it makes its own shadow, along with the birds that circle above, trying to spot the humans cowering with their heads mashed into their chests.

In dust storms, I always imagine there are people walking ahead of me, people I cannot see, but whose forms I hope will emerge again once the air is cleared.

I see my mother and father and myself. I am with them, a child who still must hold a hand to walk, a child who must look up to talk, to see all the faces. After the storm has cleared, I find myself with my hands raised up, in motionless prayer, as though some invisible giants were guiding me forward, my face tipped up towards the trees covered with a veil of white loam.

26

Doctor Javier came by later in the afternoon to examine Rosalinda. Juana was in the pantry while Luis swept the yard outside.

Doctor Javier seemed tired, his high shoulders drooping as he entered the house.

"Please listen to me," he whispered in Kreyòl. "You must leave this house immediately. I have just heard this from some friends at the border. On the Generalissimo's orders, soldiers and civilians are killing Haitians. It may be just a few hours before they reach the valley."

It couldn't be real. Rumors, I thought. There were always rumors, rumors of war, of land disputes, of one side of the island planning to invade the other. These were the grand fantasies of presidents wanting the whole island to themselves. This could not touch people like me, nor people like Yves, Sebastien, and Kongo who worked the cane fields. They were giving labor to the land. The Dominicans needed the sugar from the cane for their cafecitos and dulce de leche. They needed money from the cane.

"Is Pico here?" the doctor asked.

"He went to the border," I said.

"Oh the border," he said, as though this was the final sign he needed to confirm his tale. He was trying to make me see the truth in the pellets of sweat on his face, his knotted brows and hurried gestures urging me to trust him if I wished, believe him if I could. He had many more people to speak to besides myself.

"Will you go?' he asked.

I wanted to have had more warning. I needed to know precisely what was true and what was not. Everything was so strange. What if the doctor too was part of the death plot?

"I cannot leave my man and his sister," I said.

"A large group is crossing with me tonight," he said. "We have two trucks. I can make a place for them. We'll gather in front of the chapel. I've already spoken to Father Romain and Father Vargas. They are celebrating an evening Mass for Santa Teresa. It is almost her time. We will make it seem as if everyone is coming to Mass."

I knew nothing about this Santa Teresa. Perhaps it would help me to know more about these saints that Juana adored, that this whole valley seemed to adore. Señora Valencia appeared in the long corridor leading to her room.

"Why do you whisper, Javier?" the señora asked.

"I didn't know if your daughter was sleeping," the doctor said. "If she was, I did not want to wake her."

"My daughter is a deep sleeper," the señora said proudly. Then she turned to me, with her fingers buried in her hair, scratching her scalp. She asked, "Amabelle, has Papi returned?"

Help me, Señora, I wanted to say, but what could she do? How much did she know? Would she be brave enough to stand between me and her husband if she had to?

"I'm uneasy about Papi strolling for this long," she said before showing the doctor to the room where Rosalinda was sleeping.

I tried to think of a plan. Be calm, I told myself. I had to act calmly.

Just in case the doctor was right, I went to my room, sewed one of my skirts at the waist, made it into a sack, and threw a few things into it: Kongo's mask of Joël's face, Sebastien's unfinished shirt from the day the señora's children were born, and one change of clothing. If the doctor was wrong, I could always return. There was no harm in being prepared.

I walked down the hill and hid the bundle in a narrow gap between the banana trees in the lush grove behind Juana and Luis' house and then went back to the main house.

Señora Valencia was in the parlor with the doctor.

"Papi still hasn't returned?" she asked.

"No, Señora."

"Please tell Luis to go look for him."

First he would go the chapel, Luis said, where Papi sometimes prayed. Then he would go to the cemetery, where Papi might be visiting his wife, his son, and grandson's graves. There was no need to be anxious about Papi's wandering, but if the señora wanted him to go and search, this is what he would do.

I followed Luis out as if to help look for Papi, but I went to find Sebastien instead. He had just returned from the fields. His entire body was soaked with perspiration, as though he were sweating through a fever. He leaned back against the wall to feel some of the cool air from outside. Papi's cedar panels were still in the room.

I sat with Sebastien for a while without saying a word. I could tell that he was too tired to listen, and I did not want to speak until he was ready. Besides, I already didn't want to say to him what I had to say.

"I have found three places for you, Mimi, and me in a truck crossing the border tonight," I said finally.

"I've heard about the doctor's Mass," he said, "Santa Teresa, the little flower."

"The doctor offered me work in a clinic doing what my parents used to do," I said. "I think it's best we go with him. If he is wrong, we can come back."

"You never believed those people could injure you," he said with a scowl that seemed truly hateful, as though he were talking to someone other than me. "Even after they killed Joël, you thought they could never harm you." His hands were balled in fists the way they always were when he tried to hold in his anger. I reached for the fists and opened them to see the palms where the lifelines had been rubbed away by the cane cutting. Perhaps I had trusted too much. I had been living inside dreams that would not go away, the memories of an orphaned child. When the present itself was truly frightful, I had perhaps purposely chosen not to see it.

"Forgive me, please, Sebastien," I said, "for believing too much."

He released the tightness of his fists to my grasp. My chest was cramping with a kind of fear I had known only once before, when my parents were drowning: an unstrung feeling as when a gust of wind pushed a door shut behind you, as if to trap you inside.

"Let's talk to Kongo," Sebastien said. "He had a visitor in the fields this afternoon, the elder of your house."

"Papi?"

"He gave the field guards some money to let Kongo go away with him, and Kongo said yes."

We went to Kongo's room, where he was sitting with Yves. The two of them had a pile of almonds between them and were about to hammer them open. Kongo looked as rested as if he had not been to the fields at all that day. On his lap were wicker strands arranged in piles to make a basket.

Sebastien and I joined the circle around the wicker and almonds as though they were objects to be worshipped.

"Don Ignacio, Señora Valencia's father, came to see you?" I asked Kongo. "Do you know where he is now?"

"He said he was going to stroll awhile before going back to his house."

"What did he want with you?" Sebastien asked.

"He wanted to speak to me out in the woods, man to man, about my son," Kongo replied.

"He was not worth your breath," Yves said; his Adam's apple rose and fell several times faster when he was angry. "Only killing him would make things even."

"Things are never even," Kongo said. "If it was so, his life and my life would be the same."

"What did he say?" Yves asked.

"He asked me my son's name," Kongo said. "Wanted to make a cross and write my boy's name on it, he did. He wanted to put the cross on my son's grave. I told him no more crosses on my boy's back."

"You should have killed him and buried him in the woods," Yves said.

"He told me he killed people in a war when he was a young man," Kongo said. "He couldn't remember how many he'd killed but felt like each one was walking kòt a kòt with him, crushing his happiness. For his woman to die on the night his only son was to be born, for my son to be killed the day his grandchildren saw the first light, he felt this was the doing of the people he killed in the war, people still walking side by side with him. He thought his grandson's death showed this."

"He wants you to carry your own sadness and his too?" Yves asked, his Adam's apple bulging against the thin skin covering it.

Kongo reached over and tapped Yves' shoulder to calm him.

"I want nothing more from him." Kongo picked up a handful of almonds and pounded them with his fists to force them to surrender their kernels.

"Misery makes us appear small," he said, "but we are men. We spoke like men. I told him what troubled me, and he told me what troubled him. I feel perhaps I understood him a trace and he understood me."

"It's only a masquerade of kindness." Yves got up and paced back and forth in front of the mat where Joël had once slept. "Tonight I sell the wood in our room."

"Tonight a truck is leaving," Sebastien said. "Amabelle, Mimi, and me, we think of going."

"All the same, I'm staying," Yves said, running his fingers over his shaved head. "I'm selling the wood and I'm staying.

There are many who believe the rumors are simply meant to chase us away."

"Perhaps that is true," Sebastien said, "but I wouldn't like to sit like a dog in cage if they are true."

"What will you do?" Yves turned back to the old man.

"I've been here fifteen years now," Kongo said. "I'm too old for these types of journeys." He reached into one of his pots and fished out a fistful of maize flour. Sprinkling the flour, he sketched a large letter V on the floor, each side spread far apart, like arms stretched out towards an invisible sky.

"This is something my old grandfather used to do before I went on a journey," he explained. "'I make this mark for you,' he used to say, 'because we're one departing on two trails.' Your trail is the trail of rivers and mountains, and on your journey you will require protection."

Sebastien and Yves both seemed sadly content, as though their dead fathers had come back to offer them a benediction.

Kongo rubbed his hands together to brush off the maize flour once he was done. He looked up and winked at us. "Like a Saint Christophe," he said.

Yves got up and left Kongo's room. When I looked outside, a few moments later, I saw him heading towards the road in the dark with two of Papi's cedar planks on his back.

"Wait for tomorrow to sell!" Sebastien shouted as he rushed after him.

"Tomorrow you may not be here!" Yves yelled back. "When we're both home, we'll have a Sunday meal together, you and me, except we'll not eat too much, not enough to kill us."

I bent down and kissed Kongo's forehead good-bye. He kept his eyes on his maize-flour sketch on the floor.

Walking away, I couldn't help but think that once I was gone, I would never hear about it when Kongo died.

Outside, Sebastien took my face in his hand and kissed me on the mouth.

"I'm tired of the harvest and all the cane," he said. "Perhaps it's time to see my mother. My mother, she did not think I would be gone this long. I'll go find Mimi and we'll meet you at the chapel."

When I reached Señora Valencia's house, I found that Papi had not yet returned. Luis was still out looking for him. After she cooked supper, Juana joined him in his search. Lidia stayed inside with Rosalinda while Señora Valencia sat out on the front gallery watching the road.

To make her go inside, out of the evening damp, I wanted to tell her what Kongo had told me, that her father was well, at least he had been that afternoon—but I didn't want to reveal anything Papi might have wished to keep secret. Nor did I want to start talking and accidentally say more than I should about my own plans to leave her house, most likely for good. Where would such causerie begin and where would it end? At this point it was a matter between our two countries, of two different peoples trying to share one tiny piece of land. Maybe this is why I'd never let the rumors engage me. If they were true, it was something I could neither change nor control.

I had decided that when it came time to leave, I would not

say good-bye to the señora. But as soon as I was across the border, I would send word back to her with Doctor Javier.

While the señora was waiting for her father to return home, Beatriz came up the hill from her mother's house. She sat herself down next to Señora Valencia, in one of the rocking chairs on the front gallery. Señora Valencia got up and leaned against the corner post overlooking the main road.

"Where is your brother?" she asked Beatriz. "Maybe my father is with him."

"Javier is at the house preparing to leave for the border," Beatriz said. "Your father is not with him."

"I'd like to know what draws Javier to the border," Señora Valencia said. "Perhaps it's the same thing that keeps taking my husband there."

"Pico and my brother are not the only people going to the border. Mimi is leaving us," I heard Beatriz say. "Her brother took her away."

I came out and asked if they wanted a cooling drink. It would be my last gesture of kindness to Señora Valencia. She asked for a glass of cool water.

"Amabelle, do you know Mimi is leaving us?" Beatriz asked me.

I feigned shock as best I could. "¡Qué lástima!" A pity!

"My father has never disappeared for this long a time," Señora Valencia said as I served her the water.

"You're afraid for your father because you're thinking of only bad possibilities," Beatriz said in her usual nothing-is-ever-grave manner. "Perhaps he has a mistress."

"Why would he hide it if he was friendly with a woman?"

Señora Valencia slipped back into the rocker. "My mother has been dead for so long."

"Maybe there is something scandalous about his mistress. She could be too young or already married."

"This is not in Papi's nature," Señora Valencia said.

"Dies diem docet," answered Beatriz, showing off her Latin.

"What do you say?" asked Señora Valencia. "What does this mean?"

"A man's schooling is never complete," interpreted Beatriz.

Señora Valencia asked for another cup of water. When I brought it, she drank again without stopping.

"Perhaps my father's been arrested." She scanned the property for unknown faces as she handed the cup back to me. "He may have said something to the wrong persons."

"We will not think this now," Beatriz said, her voice composed enough to soothe the señora. "Let us think of happier things while we wait for your father to return. Tell me, what will you paint to follow this portrait of El Jefe inside?"

It took the señora some time to switch from thoughts of her father to thoughts of painting.

"Do you have another subject in mind?" Beatriz persisted.

"My son. I would like to paint my son," Señora Valencia said. "And you?" she asked, turning their chat to another course. "What of you? I'm told that these days you chase away young men like flies from your stew."

"You took Pico from me," Beatriz replied, laughing. "I have never found a man like him. Now I am waiting for the right one to arrive. Maybe he'll speak to me first in Latin, and the things he says I will not completely understand. This is a dream I had, that the man intended for me first spoke to me in Latin."

"Honestly, do you feel that I have taken Pico from you?" the señora asked.

"There is a side to Pico that I never liked," confessed Beatriz. "He's always dreamt that one day he would be president of this country, and it seems to me he would move more than mountains to make it so."

"He is a good man," Señora Valencia said, using her customary defense of her husband.

"Many good men commit terrible acts these days," Beatriz said.

"So you want to marry a priest who will first speak to you in Latin?" Señora Valencia asked, turning the conversation back to its original direction.

"A señorita who speaks Latin, my mother says, will never find a husband," added Beatriz. "My mother married when she was even younger than I am now. Look at her, she is alone all the same, a young widow in the end."

"So you are afraid of being more alone than you are now?" the señora asked.

"It is not that I am afraid," Beatriz said. "I would like to travel, escape, to go far away."

"Where would you go, to the capital?"

"I don't know. Maybe further. In Alegría, the girls dream only of going to schools of domestic science in Ciudad Trujillo. Elsewhere, in Spain for example, perhaps they have other aspirations."

"I don't think I will ever leave here," Señora Valencia said. "This is the place of my mother's grave, my son's grave. It is likely my father will be buried here. I will never leave here."

"Soon people will come to places like Alegría only for rest, for the tranquility of the land," Beatriz said.

"I think they will come for the wealth of the cane." Señora Valencia pushed her rocker forward and wrapped both her arms around the gallery corner post. "Since I was a child, the cane fields have grown. The mills have become larger and there are more cutters staying here after the harvests. This is our future."

There was still some time before the Mass would begin. I heard the rumble of automobiles and hurried out to the top of the hill. A truck was approaching. Señora Valencia and Beatriz got up and walked down the incline to the road. Beatriz was holding the house lamp, lighting their way.

By the time they reached the road, the truck had already sped by and disappeared. They both squeezed themselves into the narrow space between the drainage ditches and Juana and Luis' front door as another group of military trucks rushed by without stopping.

It took a while for the sun-baked dust to settle. The road was empty now, except for a few roaming goats regaining their footing.

The dust was too much for Señora Valencia, I thought. She was breathing hard and fast as though a pillow full of rocks was being pressed down on her face. Beatriz rushed into Juana's house and came out with an earthen jar of water. She spilled some of the water into her cupped palm and wet the señora's face.

Beatriz and I propped her up on each side and carried her back to the top of the hill as a few more army trucks raced

by, heading in the direction of the border. The trucks speeding by worried me, but more worrisome somehow were the
face-sized splotches of blood that I now saw on the back of
the señora's dress, stains that were growing wider even as we
carried her to her bedroom. In spite of this, I told myself I
would just see that the señora was put to bed and then I
would hurry to the church.

"Amabelle, please stay with me." Señora Valencia reached
up and grabbed my wrists as she was lowered into her bed.
She held me with almost the same force as when she was in
labor.

"Amabelle knows how to look after me," she told Beatriz.
"I did not give myself enough time to rest after the births,
isn't this so, Amabelle?"

"Por favor, Señora, release me so I can go and find you a
remedy," I said.

My wrists ached when she released them. Her eyes trailed
me out the door. Perhaps she knew that I wouldn't be coming back.

I went down to the pantry, intending to leave by way of the
grounds in the back. Lidia was pouring tea into a cup for her
cousin as Papi entered the house with Juana.

Papi dragged a cross made of freshly sawed cedar across
the red clay floor in the pantry. The cross had *Señor Joël
Raymond Lorier*, carved in small uneven letters.

"Amabelle, take this tea to the señora," Lidia said, "while
I make her a compress."

"Has something happened to Valencia?" Papi asked,
alarmed.

"She was overcome with dust from the road," I explained.

No need to tell him of the bleeding. She would if she wanted to.

"What was she doing on the road?" Papi asked.

"Looking for you," Lidia said.

I gave Papi the tea to take to his daughter, as he was going to her room anyway.

"Where did you find Papi?" I asked Juana.

"On the road with a cross on his back," Juana said.

The roaring of more engines could be heard from outside, mixed in with screams and loud voices. One of the voices was Señor Pico's.

We, all of us—Juana, me, Papi, then Beatriz, who came out of the señora's room—went outside to see what was happening. Two army trucks had stopped, crisscrossed in the middle of the road. Their front headlamps were ablaze, lighting a long trail from Juana and Luis' house down to Doña Sabine's gate.

The soldiers formed a wall, blocking a line of men from Unèl's brigade. Unèl and his friends had their machetes in their hands. Señor Pico stood on the front guard of the lead truck watching the confrontation.

Some cane workers had already been loaded into the back of the other truck, guarded by a small squad of young soldiers. The cane workers in the trucks huddled close, clinging to each other for balance. I recognized a few faces of those who worked in nearby towns, men and women I had seen once or twice when they traveled to visit friends to celebrate Christmas, Haitian Independence Day and the National Day of Independence Heroes, on the first and second days of the year.

Beatriz, Juana, and I moved towards the flame tree, where

we could see the road better. I felt Juana's nervous breath on the back of my neck. She muttered Hail Marys and supplications to saints whose names I had never heard her call on before.

"Kneel or sit!" Señor Pico shouted to Unèl's brigade. "Lower your machetes. We will put you on the trucks and take you to the border."

A few more soldiers jumped off Señor Pico's truck and joined the line in front of him. Luis wandered from the latrines and walked over to the flame tree.

We moved down closer to the road, standing on a sharp grade on the lowest part of the hill. We were now directly behind the truck where Señor Pico was standing. He had his back to us and could not see us.

"Kneel or sit," Señor Pico repeated. "Lower your machetes. We will put you on the trucks and take you to the border."

Unèl motioned for his people to stand still. No one kneeled or sat. Instead they took small steps towards the truck where Señor Pico stood giving orders.

"No kneeling!" Unèl cried out.

"What you do in the cane fields is worse than kneeling!" Señor Pico shouted back. "You work like beasts who don't even know what it is to stand. Put down your machetes. I have no cane for you to cut now."

The men called Señor Pico's mother the worst whore who was ever born to a family of whores; his grandmother and godmother were both cursed as disgraceful harlots. The day he was born was damned. Many of the men of Unèl's night-time sentinel brigade wished him a painful, tortured, macabre death, promising him that he would choke on his words one day, chew them up, vomit them, and chew them again.

The soldiers laughed at the cursing. I could tell by the points of light sprouting all over the hills that neighbors were coming out of their houses, trying to listen or watch.

Señor Pico looked down at Unèl's men as he considered his choices. Doctor Javier and Beatriz's mother, Doña Eva, ran through the crowd, brushing past the soldiers on her way to Señor Pico's truck.

"Could I speak to you, Señor?" she yelled out to Señor Pico.

He bent down towards her and said, "Doña Eva, have patience, please."

"I must speak to you now," she said. "It concerns my son. It concerns Javier."

"Doña Eva, wait in the house, please."

Beatriz stood and beckoned to her mother.

"Your brother has been arrested," Doña Eva said to Beatriz when she reached us. She was out of breath, and her whole body was trembling, including her face. "Javier was arrested at the chapel, along with Father Romain and Father Vargas. Someone ran to tell me, but by the time I got there the soldiers had already taken them away. I want to tell Pico. Perhaps he'll remember all his friend Javier has done for him, and help us."

If Doctor Javier was taken, what of Sebastien, Mimi, and all the others who were leaving with him?

"I don't understand it," Juana muttered. "In the sight of all our saints, we are losing our country to madmen."

Doña Eva gathered a thin flowered scarf around her back and pulled it closer to her chest. Beatriz walked her up the hill to the house. Señor Pico turned and watched them climb. He saw Juana, Luis, and me sitting at the foot of the hill.

"We are going to take you to the border now," he said, turning back to the men on the road.

The group chanted, "¡Nunca!" Never!

Unèl clapped his hands, encouraging the others.

Señor Pico motioned towards the soldiers blocking the road. The truck with the people from Don Carlos' mill slowly edged forward. One man ran toward it and fell in its path. The front wheel moved over his knees, his face twisting with each endless motion that took the truck through the rise and descent over his legs.

Two other members of Unèl's group rushed forward to help him, but scattered as the truck came at them. The wounded man fell on his back, then rolled onto his side, his face frozen in shock. He tried to lift his legs before the rear tire could pass over them.

I ran towards him, colliding with a few of my countrymen, who were now trying to escape. The truck stopped before the rear wheels could reach the downed man. A group of soldiers moved in, seized him, and threw him into the back.

It was a short drop from the deck of the army truck to the ground. The man with the crushed leg attempted the leap. He fell on his outstretched hands and crawled towards the brush alongside the road until the high grass engulfed him.

The soldiers seemed to have orders not to use their rifles; otherwise, they could have fired at those who fled. Instead they grabbed those in front of them. Two or three circled one person, seized that unfortunate by the arms and legs, and threw him into the back of the truck.

I heard Señor Pico call my name. "Amabelle, out of the road!" he shouted, as if my being there was a sign of disrespect to him and his house.

I dodged and ducked, trying to bypass the khaki uniforms. The soldiers were using whips, tree branches, and sticks, flogging the fleeing people. One of their bullwhips landed across my back; I felt the heated sting on my waist as I hurtled forward into the dense banana grove behind Juana and Luis' house.

Seizing my hidden bundle, I peered through the banana leaves. Juana and Luis were no longer where I had left them.

I moved to the edge of the grove, as close to the road as I could come without being seen. Unèl was one of three men still fighting. The others either were in the trucks with the soldiers' rifles aimed at them, or had fled.

Unèl hurled his machete at one of the young soldiers and cut him on the side of his face. As a small squad tried to grab him, Unèl twisted and dived between them, all the while screaming that he had never lived on his knees. All of the soldiers were racing after him now, except for Señor Pico who was standing on top of the truck, watching.

Unèl was trapped inside a circle. Three of the soldiers grabbed his right arm. Others grabbed the left, joining his arms behind him on his buttocks. One of the more anxious soldiers pierced one of Unèl's arms with the point of his bayonet, cutting a gash from wrist to elbow. Señor Pico jumped down from the truck and watched as Unèl was tied with a cattle rope and raised to the back of the truck. Unèl made jerky movements, trying to free himself from the soldiers' grasp. He was thrown into the back of the vehicle with the two remaining men. The gate was raised, shutting them in with all the others.

Señor Pico gathered a few of his men, and, after a brief survey of the road, he and half a dozen recruits marched up the hill to his house, while the others drove away with their prisoners. For him it seemed to have been regular work. He had seen to it and now was off to something else.

Once he'd disappeared, I turned and followed the stream up to Don Carlos' mill. Perhaps Sebastien had not yet left for the church. Maybe he was still at the mill with Mimi, waiting.

Two soldiers were drinking at Mercedes' stand when I got to the compound. I stayed out of view while they bragged to Mercedes and her sons about what had taken place at the church, telling them that their friends had arrested two recreants—Father Romain and Father Vargas—and many peasants, and of how the priests had pleaded to be brought to the same fortaleza as the peasants who had been arrested outside their church.

"You know how much I admire the Generalissimo," Mercedes said, her voice quivering beneath the weight of too much of her own firewater. "Even so, I say we are asking for punishment when we arrest the priests in their own churches."

"You should have been there to see it," one of the soldiers argued. "They cried like new widows, those priests."

The church was empty, with only a wooden Christ looking down at the silent pews from his uncomfortable place on the cross. I walked past every neat, untouched bench, hoping to find someone who might be crouching in the dark, another voice to tell me more about what had taken place there. So far as I could see, everything was as usual, nothing had been moved or pushed aside. It was as if no one had ever entered the church at all; the Mass had never started, the people had never gathered.

In the churchyard I heard only echoes that come with the night—the cicadas, tree frogs, and squawking bats. The gate around the school was chained. There was no light in the house behind the gate where Father Romain and Father Vargas and some of the orphaned school children lived.

Leaving the church, I stayed off the main road and followed a tangle of sword ferns, sapodilla, and papaya trees to a trench bordering a plot of Don Carlos' virgin cane.

I waited there awhile, hoping the soldiers would be gone by the time I reached the mill. When I finally entered the cane field, it was pitch black inside, as dark as it might be in a coffin under the ground with six feet of dirt piled over your face.

It was a darkness where the recollection of light did not exist at all, as if the bright moon overhead would never dare approach the compressed layers of cane leaves, spread over each other like house shingles.

The sound of crickets and grasshoppers echoed in the cane tent; I took tiny steps, holding my bundle close to my chest. As I moved forward, I didn't want to stir the cane too much in case the soldiers were waiting on the other side. Nor did I want my steps to arouse any animals that might be nesting in the sodden loam, gnawing at the cane roots: rabbits, rats, or garden snakes, which Sebastien and the others had often faced while working.

A scorching foul-smelling heat rose from the ground; the marsh underneath the cane sank with each of my steps. I felt the short cane spears cutting my legs and covered my face with my hand to keep the tall ones out of my eyes. An ant colony marched up my thighs. The more I smacked them away, the more they crept up my back.

I saw faint breaches of light as I moved closer to the shacks at the compound. Mercedes' stand was closed now, and the soldiers were gone. Lamps were lit inside the cane cutters' rooms, but no one was outside. I brushed the ants off my back as I approached Kongo's door.

"Kongo, it's Amabelle, come to see you," I whispered.

A few peered out with lamps from the shacks as I entered Kongo's room. My legs were bleeding, and a line of rust-colored ants were clinging to my arm. Kongo raised his lamp, brought the flame close to my skin, and brushed the ants aside. I felt a line of blood trickle from between my eyebrows.

"Did they take you too?" he asked, using his pocket handkerchief to mop the blood from my face.

"I walked through the cane," I said.

He pointed to Joël's mat and asked me to sit down.

"Sebastien went with Mimi to the chapel," he said. "They went there to meet you. Others tell me that army trucks came and took them away."

"Is it true?" I was not so ready to believe.

He lifted one of the pots in the middle of the room and took out a lemon. He cut the lemon and pressed both halves to the bridge of my nose.

"It will keep you from shedding more blood." He gave me the rest of the lemon to rub over the cuts on my legs. Gritting my teeth, I rubbed.

"And where is it thought they'll be taken?" I asked.

"If they don't kill them at once, they'll bring them to the border prison near Dajabón." He spoke in a distant voice, as if death no longer meant anything to him. "They used to take us to prison near Dajabón, then bring us to the bridge at the border and let us go. I don't know if they'll let them go this time. Sebastien's friend Yves is at that Doña Sabine's house. They did not take him. He's the one who came to tell me about Sebastien and his sister. He wanted me to go with him to Doña Sabine's house. I told him I'm staying here, and if need be, I'll die here."

A few ants were still crawling over my scalp, hiding in the short tresses of my hair. I scratched furiously, trying to frighten them out. There was blood under my fingernails when I pulled them out of my hair.

"I am going to Dajabón, then," I said.

"You certain you don't want to stay here?" he asked. "We are more protected here in the mill compound."

"I want to go to the border," I said.

"Do you know how to reach it?"

"I hear there are roads through the mountains."

"You follow the stream up the mountains. There are grottos and caves to sleep in at night. This is how I came here again and again many times, in the beginning. When you come down from the mountain, you know where to cross the river? Very shallow in some places, that river. This time of year, it's most shallow near the bridge."

"I will remember this," I said.

"There might be soldiers in the mountains," he added. "I heard from a man here in the compound that they're burning Haitian houses in the mountain villages."

"Before I go, I need to speak to Yves," I said.

He looked down at my bundle and saw the silhouette of his son's death mask in it. "Don't go through the cane again. I'll show you another way."

We tiptoed out and turned the corner through Sebastien's yam garden. I paused there for just a moment, thinking how much pleasure it gave Sebastien to plant and grow things for himself after he had been working the cane all day for someone else. I crawled under a wooden fence that opened to a narrow footpath leading to a side gate at Doña Sabine's house. Kongo took the hidden trail back to the mill without saying anything more.

I waited until I thought he was back at the mill, then walked to the front gate of Doña Sabine's house. I had to pound on it with a rock before my knock was heard. I was afraid the noise would be detected by soldiers somewhere farther up the road, but I had no choice.

Félice peered through the grille at the entrance, then pushed the metal door open and dragged me in. There were no watchmen at the gate.

"Your face?" she asked, the birthmark rising and falling with every movement of her lips.

"A scratch." I reached up to touch the bridge of my nose. "Where are the watchmen who were here before?" I asked.

"Don Gilbert and Doña Sabine sent them away," she said. "They were afraid the watchmen would change their allegiance and turn on them. Doña Sabine sent the people they were guarding and her young relations off to Haiti yesterday."

Félice pointed to the steps in front of the main house, where clusters of men and women were craning their necks trying to make out what was happening at the gate. A couple—an older woman and a young man who looked like they might be related—moved towards the entrance.

"I hear it was terrible on the road. We could hear all the noise coming from there," Félice said. "Is that where you were hurt?"

"They took Unèl and many of his men," I said.

"Anybody die?"

"Unèl looked bad."

"Some of the people on the steps just came from the road," she said. "Maybe I should stand here and wait in case more arrive. We don't want them to make so much noise knocking that the soldiers hear them."

The old woman and the young man peered into the darkness over Félice's shoulder. The woman was covered with leaf and mud stains. Her dress was torn on the side and in the back. The young man's clothes smelled of onion and garlic; his hands were callused, his fingers bent and curved the way some old men's were.

"The soldiers could be close," Félice concluded, "but Don Gilbert and Doña Sabine are here. Their money and position may protect us."

"We had planned to sleep in the cane fields," the old woman said. "Many people will sleep in the ravines tonight."

"I hear Sebastien was arrested at the church," Félice said. "Mimi too."

"They carried the doctor off with all those people who were to cross the border with him," the old woman said. "The priests they took alone in a separate automobile. The priests begged the soldiers to let them stay with the people. The soldiers wouldn't let them. One of the priests was crying."

We searched the grounds for Yves. He was sleeping in front of a row of servants' rooms. The last two planks of Papi's wood were leaning against the wall next to him.

Yves jumped to his feet as soon as I laid my hand on his shoulders. He rubbed the back of his hands against his eyes, looking around as though he didn't know where he was.

"I sold half the wood," he said.

"Yves, did you *see* them take Mimi and Sebastien?" I asked.

"I saw many taken," he said, dropping his face.

Doña Sabine called for Félice. She and Don Gilbert were sitting on one of the terraces, perched in two reclining chairs with only a hurricane lamp between them. Félice stepped across the yard and climbed a stone staircase to reach them.

"Who came?" Doña Sabine's voice carried across the grounds.

"A friend," Félice said.

"Who is this friend?" demanded Doña Sabine. "We must be cautious."

"Be careful who you let in." Don Gilbert echoed his wife's warning. "We are going to sleep."

On her way to her bed, Doña Sabine leaned over the verandah and examined their property. There was surrender in her voice when she said, "We will not be able to save everybody."

It was not even certain that they could save themselves.

After the doña and her husband had gone inside, I told Yves, "I must go to Dajabón. There is a chance of finding Mimi and Sebastien there. I should go at once."

I could tell Yves did not have much hope, but he agreed to come with me. When Félice returned, we told her we were leaving.

"Gather a few things," Yves told her. "Come with us."

"I cannot leave," Félice said. "I am afraid. This must be what it means to get old. I never was afraid when I was young. Now I am afraid all the time."

"Yves and I will be with you," I said.

"I don't want to die walking," she said.

"Gather your things and come," Yves insisted. "No one dies walking."

"I already have decided," she said. "I will stay here. This way I can look after Joël's father too."

I untied my packet and handed Félice Kongo's mask of Joël's face. She raised the mask up to her neck and stroked the paper lip with her fingers.

"It's a good likeness of him," she said.

Yves took the mask from Félice, glanced at it, and hastily handed it back to her.

"This wood was to be a man's coffin," he said, pointing at the planks of Papi's cedar leaning against the wall. "Since you're staying here, I'll trade this wood to you for a good machete."

Félice went into one of the workers' rooms and came out with a machete for Yves and a long meat chopping knife for me. The machete had a light brown cowhide sheath and a sling for carrying it across one's back. I wrapped the sharp knife in my spare dress and put it in my bundle.

Félice took us to the gate and let us out.

"Perhaps I will see you both again one day," she said through the grid.

We followed a trail up the stream. Yves grabbed a tree branch and tapped it against the side of his leg as he walked.

We journeyed side by side along most of the path. He let me go ahead when the trail became too narrow.

As the night wore on, we each drifted into our separate thoughts, our own visions of what might lie ahead.

27

The night thinned into a dawn of charcoal gray. We ran across a stream, where Yves bent down, took a handful of water, and whisked it around in his mouth. Dipping my head in the current, I jolted myself awake with the brisk coolness of the flow.

"When do you think we'll arrive at the border?" I asked.

"Tonight," he said, reaching across his back to make certain the machete was still there.

He got up and started walking again. The water trickling from my hair soaked my blouse, gluing the thin cotton cloth of the gray house uniform to my skin.

A crossroads split our trail into two paths: one led back to the valley, and the other up to the mountains. We heard the rattle of an oxcart struggling down the incline behind us and crouched beneath a croton hedge to wait for it to pass.

The cart was covered with a blanket made of brown sugar sacks sewn together. Two fat oxen puffed as they yanked their cargo forward. The oxen had pockets of water splashing from the folds of doubled-over flesh along their large bellies. Their horns were joined by ropes and a piece of wood that partially blocked their roving eyes.

Walking beside them were two men, their shirts tucked neatly into their pants, which were rolled to their knees, revealing wet and muddied feet. They were carrying rifles as well as whips.

The cart suddenly stopped, the wheels wedged in a ditch where the slope of the hill met the valley road. One of the men took out a whip and slapped it against the ground, damning the oxen for being so big and so slow. The oxen struggled, raising their front legs, but could not draw the cart out of the trench.

From the back of the cart fell a girl, seventeen or eighteen years old. I raised my head to have a better look at her. Yves shoved my shoulder down, but I could still see her. She was wearing an orange-yellow dress with a cloth of purple madras wrapped around her head. A machete had struck her at the temple and on both her shoulders.

Her face flapped open when she hit the ground, her right cheekbone glistening as the flesh parted from it. She rolled onto her back and for a moment faced the sky. Her body spiraled past the croton hedge down the slope. The mountain dirt clung to her dress, her arms, her face, her whole body gathering a thick cover of dust.

The men did not notice that she had fallen from the cart. They raised the whips menacingly once more, but the oxen could not budge it. Finally they strolled to the back of the cart.

"The blanket was loose," one said, tucking the sugar sack sheets beneath the cargo.

The loose blanket stirred. A groan could be heard coming from the cart. One of the men picked up a fist-sized rock and pounded on the head—or it might have been an elbow—pushing up the sack. There was no more stirring. The man threw the rock away. They shoved and bumped the cart out of the ditch, then the oxen took over and continued down the meadow, towards the valley.

The crowing of roosters echoed from the mountains. The girl's corpse had rolled out of sight. Perhaps she'd fallen into one of the ravines and slid into the water.

With the numbness of shock in his voice, Yves said, "At least we survived the night."

The casitas in the first mountain village were built on stilts, one-room houses with palm frond and thatched roofs. A line of vendors sold food from unsteady wooden stands on the shoulder of the road. Behind them, you could see the valley, dwarfed in the smallness imposed on things by great height and distance.

Yves used one of his two pesos to buy a few hog bananas, cocoplums, and small mangos, which he stuffed in his pants pocket. He offered me some, but I had no appetite.

As he ate, a religious procession strolled by. In front were three women carrying a statue of La Virgen in an ornate carved box covered with a white lace cloth. The women chanted under their breaths, sifting rosaries through their fingers. As they mouthed their slate of wishes and supplications, some of them looked like they were in a trance.

There is such a cord between desperate women that when I looked at them I knew what each one was hoping for even before their whispers brushed past my ears. They made novenas for lovers who had strayed, for sons and daughters to marry, for children who were sick, for the safe return of those who had traveled to the capital, forsaking them.

One of the women—the last one on the line—dragged a pack mule with one hand and carried a portrait of the Generalissimo with the other. She was praying for his good health and safe journey through life. "Let him continue to lead us with a strong hand and an even stronger heart," she implored.

Leaving the village behind, we started down the curve of a pebbly mountain road. We walked silently for a long time. The sun was scorching hot, and we had no hats or parasols for protection.

I tied the hem of my dress into a knot and raised it up to my thighs. Yves looked out of the corner of his eyes, pretending not to see the cloth brushing against the shredded skin on the back of my legs.

When it seemed like it was midday, we stopped on the side of the mountain to rest. I yanked up handfuls of the wild grass and dandelions growing out from between the rocks, remembering that my father had called them "pisannwit," saying that as he blew the dandelions' fragile fuzz into the wind, children were being cured of pissing in their beds.

A flock of rain birds squawked loudly as they passed overhead. Among them were fork-tailed swallows and swifts, trailed by a pack of yellow warblers, barely twisting their wingtips as they rode through the wind columns above the mountains.

Yves leaned back against a boulder and closed his eyes. I sat a few feet away, looking down at the land beneath us, the mesh of water, tobacco and cane fields, and the tiny houses terraced in the foothills.

Three women and two men trudged up a narrow track towards us. They looked like the straggling members of a vast family, except for two of the women who had coils of pumpkin-colored hair. Those two seemed like they might be Dominicanas—or a mix of Haitian and Dominican—in some cases it was hard to tell.

The man at the head of the line noticed me. The group rushed up the hill with a new sense of expectation. Everyone was carrying a small bundle, except a short man in the rear who was limping. He had taken off his shirt and tied it around his head to keep himself cool. The young man had uneven arms, one bulky, bulging with muscles, the other thin and withered, the skin clinging to the bones.

"Now I am even closer to the sun," the man at the head of the group said when he reached us. He had a deeply melodious voice, like the sanbas who told stories in song.

"There's no shade," the woman next to him complained. She used the wide, butterfly-shaped collar on her dress to fan her face. She and the man had the same musical voice, which made me think they were brother and sister, but I was wrong. She was his woman and he, her man.

Their speaking startled Yves out of his sleep. I asked the sanba-voiced man, "Where is your group coming from?"

He and his woman, Odette, were coming from a big sugar mill on the other side of the island, a big mill owned by North Americans, Yankis.

"We hear it's safe in the big mills," I said. "Why didn't you stay there?"

"Let them say what they will," Odette answered, cutting her eyes at me as though to reproach my ignorance. She turned in a circle and breathed in a passing breeze. Only she and her sanba-voiced man, Wilner, were from the same mill. The others they had encountered on the road, just as they were finding us now, Odette explained.

The two pumpkin-haired women and the man with the uneven arms crouched down to rest. They shared portions of foods wrapped in banana leaves and drank from old jugs and a worn-out wineskin.

"Do you have good luck?" Wilner asked Yves.

Yves laughed out loud. "Why do you want to know?" he asked.

"I like to know what type of luck a man has before I start on a journey with him," Wilner replied.

I moved towards the man with the uneven arms. I was drawn to him in part by curiosity but also because I pitied his condition. I wanted him to explain it to me. Was it tuberculosis or a flesh disease? Did it come from cutting the cane with one arm while neglecting the other? Was he born this way?

The young man seemed to forget his malformation unless someone's eyes lingered on it too long. He straightened his posture and pushed his chest forward to make his arms seem of one proportion.

Yves and Wilner discussed what roads to take to reach the border more quickly. Wilner had traveled through the mountains at least once before but could not remember the way clearly now. Odette recalled that there were some settlements high in the hills, which we would do well to avoid. They disagreed, though, on how long the journey should take.

"We'll be at the border before sunset tonight," said Yves.

"You have misjudged, my friend," shouted the man with the uneven arms, "how long it takes for men to cross mountains! Two days," he insisted, "and besides, we don't want to arrive at the border at night."

The pumpkin-haired women listened, even as they distributed their tiny portions of food and drink between themselves.

"Let's not squander time, then." Yves started walking. "If we stop to rest only at night, the journey will be shorter."

"M'se Tibon," the man with the uneven arms said, holding out his emaciated hand towards me.

"How long have you been traveling, Tibon?" I asked him.

"Five days on foot," he said.

"Did you see others being taken?" I asked.

"I am coming back," he said, "from buying charcoal outside the mill where I work, when two soldiers take me and put me on a truck full of people. The people who fight before going on the truck, they whip them with bayonets until they consent. After we're all on the truck, some of us half dead, not knowing whose blood is whose, they take us out to a high cliff over the rough seas in La Romana. They make us stand in groups of six at the edge of the cliff, and then it's either jump or go against a wall of soldiers with bayonets pointed at you and some civilians waiting in a circle with machetes. They tell the civilians where best to strike with the machetes so our heads part more easily from our bodies." Tibon used his bony hand to make the motion of a machete striking his collarbone. "They make us stand in lines of six on the edge of the cliff," he said. "Then they come back to the truck to get more. They have six jump over the cliff, then another six, then another six, then another six."

I didn't know how many groups of six he named. I shut my ears to him for a moment and tried to imagine Sebastien's voice, telling me he was alive. I knew this would be his great worry, that I didn't know what had happened to him and that perhaps I would think it was my fault he had disappeared. But he hadn't disappeared; I wanted to be convinced of this, invoking his voice and face on many past occasions: the night he came to tell me that Joël had died, other nights when he had been so careworn and weary, yet so happy that I had gone to his room to see him, nights when he was bothered by the heavy smell of cane that was always with him, in his room, in his clothes, in the breeze, even in his hair, mornings when he woke up and begrudged the sound of the cane being cut because it reminded him of the breaking of dry chicken bones.

Tibon went on naming another group of six, then another.

"Last they come for me," he said.

The others angled their necks towards him. They were paying close attention, as if they couldn't help themselves. Yves was the only one who did not seem interested. He kept walking swiftly, fixing his eyes on the road ahead.

"When I jump off the cliff," Tibon continued, "I tell myself not to be afraid. I say to myself, Tibon, today you and the birds become one. They say for a bird to stand on its two feet and not fly is laziness. Tibon, I tell myself, today you are a bird."

He opened his arms and spread them, like the rare large butterfly that drifted past us now and then, testing new wings against the unfriendly currents of the mountain air.

"It's a long way from the cliff to the sea," he said. "I fall and fall, passing the rocks where many of the bodies land on the way down. And then me, I fall in the water. I know it too when I strike the water because it is so cold and sharp, the water, more like a big machete than water. I have many cuts on my body where the water sliced me, some tears on my ankles, which now cause me to limp."

He raised his pants to show me the cuts on his ankle, many of them scabbed and deep, covered with the brown-red dust of all the different roads he had traveled.

"Now I'm in the water," he said, "but when I look at the beach, there are peasants waiting with their machetes for us to come out of the water, some even wading in to look for the spots on the necks where it's best to strike with machetes to cut off heads. I swim out into a sea cave. I hold on to a rock and fight the water until nighttime, and this is when, with another comrade who also survived, we take to traveling. My companion finds walking harder than those rocks we almost fell on, so he goes back to the mill. But me, I say now and until my last breath, if I die, I die on my feet."

The pumpkin-haired woman next to me was crying. Her body was slumped, her face sunk into her chest; her cheeks swelled up as if she was trying not to vomit. Still her tears were silent, almost polite. She muffled them with a man's handkerchief, embroidered with the word *Ilè* on each corner.

The other pumpkin-haired woman moved closer and put her arms around her.

When the comforter noticed me staring, she pointed to Yves and asked in Spanish, "Is he your man?"

"No," I answered.

"I thought he was your man," Tibon said, "the way he looks at you, like his eyes can protect you."

"I am promised to someone else," I said.

"Where is the man you're promised to? Was he taken?" the woman consoling the crying one asked.

"So I was told," I said.

"I am Dolores. This is my little sister, Doloritas," she said after a pause. "Our mother suffered much when each one of us was being born so gave us these grave names we have."

Doloritas swallowed a lump in her throat, removed the handkerchief from her face, and asked, "What do they call you?"

"They call me Amabelle," I said.

"Ah, Amabelle, like a taste of cool water in a drought," said Tibon.

"How long has your journey been?" the older sister asked in Spanish. The two sisters didn't seem to speak any Kreyòl.

"Only one day," I said.

"The sisters have been with us three days," Tibon said.

Doloritas covered her eyes with the handkerchief once more.

"Don't cry so much, Doloritas," Tibon said. "Save some of your tears to shed for joy when we find your man."

Doloritas lowered the handkerchief from her face as she considered this. If Tibon, a cripple, had escaped, why not her man?

"We are Dominicanas," Dolores explained.

"They took him," Doloritas added. "They came in the night and took him from our bed."

"We have yet to learn your language," Dolores said.

"We are together six months, me and my man," Doloritas said. "I told him I would learn Kreyòl for when we visit his family in Haiti."

"I know nothing," Dolores said. "Doloritas was lost when they took him. She wanted to go to the border to look for him. I could not let her go alone in her state."

"What is his name?" I asked, looking directly into Doloritas' reddened eyes. "Your man, what is his name?"

"We called him Ilè," she said, pushing her wet handkerchief towards me to show the embroidering of his name. "Ilè is a nickname for Ilestbien. He told me that it means 'he is well.'"

We walked through the afternoon without resting. The sun teased us by occasionally seeking shelter behind a dense cloud, often for long periods of time.

The mountain air grew cooler as dusk approached. Our fatigue limited our desire for more talk. Besides, each person's story did nothing except bring you closer to your own pain.

Now and then, Tibon would pierce the silence with his voice.

"Everyone says the Generalissimo is at the border now. Maybe he's there, waiting to greet us." He spat out his words, pausing for a reply, an agreement, or an argument.

Yves looked back to where I was walking next to the two Dominican women, with Tibon hobbling behind us. He had a sneer of disappointment on his face, as though he could not believe that I had forsaken him so early in our journey for newer company.

"They have so many of us here because our own country— our government—has forsaken us," Tibon started again, but no one replied. "Poor people are sold to work in the cane fields so our own country can be free of them."

The sun was setting, the valleys far below us fading into a void. The night brought with it a ghostly echo so that each time Tibon spoke it seemed as though you were hearing many people say the same thing at once.

"The ruin of the poor is their poverty," Tibon went on. "The poor man, no matter who he is, is always despised by his neighbors. When you stay too long at a neighbor's house, it's only natural that he become weary of you and hate you."

28

We found a point where the road widened into a broad level patch, and each person claimed the spot where he was standing when it was announced that we were stopping for the night. A few sheets were thrown open from the bundles, and we all fared well enough with something between us and the cool dirt and something else to throw over our bodies.

Wilner ordered us not to light any fires, which might make us discernible from a distance. Even a pipe, which Tibon desperately wanted to smoke, was not permitted.

There was a full moon overhead, but it was the stars that caught my attention. I had never seen them so massive and so close before. Every once in a while, one would plunge from the sky and crash someplace behind the mountains, fading from an explosion of fireballs into a hush of darkness.

Yves made his way towards me and offered two of the bananas he had bought on the road early that morning. He also gave me a block of coconut chunks, which I hadn't seen him buy. I ate the coconut first and then one of the bananas. Putting the other one in my bundle, I saved it for later.

"If I doze, awaken me," Yves whispered. "Don't let me speak in my sleep."

"Not all of us should sleep at the same time," Wilner said as he crawled into the small space near Odette. "There should be watchers to wake the sleepers if need be."

The three men divided among themselves the task of being sentinels. Yves was to watch during the last part of the night, into the next morning.

We all took turns sleeping and waking. Each time they woke up, the Dominican sisters had to remind themselves where they were, in murmurs, secret grunts, and mute conversations with each other.

I drifted off to sleep a few times myself, but when I woke up, it was so dark that if not for the coldness of the ground and the pebbles digging into my side, I still would have thought I was asleep.

Once when I woke up, I thought I felt the ground shaking. Powdered dust and pebbles sifted down from above us. I clung to the soil with my fingers. Then, realizing that this would be a cowardly way to die, I shook a mound of dirt off me and stood up.

Everyone rose and roamed in circles, trying to establish what was taking place. Then just as abruptly as it had started, the mountain's shaking stopped.

The night was still after this. The fireflies disappeared from the air. Even the bats must have been stunned.

"It's only the mountain settling," Wilner said, breaking the silence with his voice.

"Let it not settle on top of my head," Tibon said. Odette laughed and I was calmed.

We stayed awake for some time, waiting for the mountain to stir again. The stars stopped falling and slowly disappeared from the sky. We returned to our places, and perhaps because our bodies demanded it, most of us fell asleep.

Yves was the only one who did not sleep. Towards dawn, I saw him sitting on the edge of the hill with his body facing the road ahead. He was playing a game in which he buried a stick in a pile of dirt and then scooped away the soil until the stick was standing straight up in the least amount of dirt. When the stick fell, he would lose to himself and start the game again.

Over his shoulder, a funnel of dark charcoal smoke was rising from one of the small villages we'd left behind. Yves had become accustomed enough to the sight that he kept playing the game, only occasionally glancing in the direction the smoke was drifting before it rose high enough to thin out and become part of the air.

I tried not to wake anyone as I stood, but my movements caused more activity. Wilner's woman, Odette, woke up, then Wilner, followed by the Dominican sisters, then Tibon. By the time I reached Yves, everyone was awake and watching the fire burning through a village a few tiers below.

There was no mistaking the stench rising towards us. It was the smell of blood sizzling, of flesh melting to the last bone, a bonfire of corpses, like the one the Generalissimo had ordered at the Plaza Colombina to avoid the spreading of disease among the living after the last great hurricane.

Yves placed the machete on his back. He tugged on the game stick, ignoring the splinters stabbing at his fingertips. Odette raised her hands over her nose. Circling her frame with his embrace, Wilner rocked Odette's body back and forth in his arms. I felt Tibon shiver and then realized I was holding his skeletal hand.

Tibon leaned towards my left ear and whispered, "I almost kill a Dominican boy when I'm ten. I see him coming along the road in front of the mill one day and I decide to beat him to make him say that even if he's living in a big house and I'm living in the mill, he's no better than me."

I pulled my hand from Tibon's long delicate fingers. His voice grew louder as he continued. "I grab the boy by the neck. I beat him until I'm tired and he's biting the back of my hand and he's running. I still have the scar where he bit me. Do you want to see?"

He tried to show the scar on his normal-sized forearm, but no one looked.

"He never tells his family it's me beating him every day. I warn him 'I beat you worse if you tell.' He won't say what I want him to say, that we're the same, me and him, flesh like flesh, blood like blood."

"The mountains are dangerous for us now," Wilner announced, interrupting Tibon. "I say we follow this trail down and, soon as we can, go through the forest to a place where we can cross the river to the other side."

"We can get lost in the forest," Yves said, "walk the same path a hundred times and not know it."

"*You* can get lost in there," Wilner said. "Not me. I have two good eyes."

Wilner turned to the Dominican sisters who were still watching the smoke and addressed them in Spanish. "You will travel with us no more," he said.

"We cannot leave them here alone," Tibon protested.

"They are not good for us," Wilner said, as if the sisters had already disappeared from our presence. "I will not be roasted like lechón for them. This is their country. Let them find the border themselves. They can go to any village in these mountains, and the people will welcome them."

"What if they betray us?" Odette asked. "What if they send their people after us?"

"They will not betray us," Tibon said. "I can sense this."

"We will let you choose your road, and we will choose ours," Doloritas spoke up. "And we'll go on to Dajabón and I'll find Ilestbien."

Dajabón was a place I remembered as a barely developed town, a place I had not seen since I was a child. Now I imagined it full of people like us, searching for loved ones, mistaking the living for the dead.

As we walked away from them, I wanted to argue for allowing the sisters to come with us, but the fires down below made too strong a demonstration of the danger. Besides, the sisters would not have as many obstacles as we would in Dajabón. If they were asked to say "perejil," they could say it with ease. In most of our mouths, their names would be tinged with or even translated into Kreyòl, the way the name of Doloritas' man slid towards the Spanish each time she evoked him. Perhaps if we addressed the sisters publicly in Dajabón, someone might hear and at that moment decide that we should die.

I lingered and offered the sisters my remaining banana. They refused it, pushing my hand away. When Yves beckoned for me to hurry, I was surprised that I could yield so fast and leave them behind. But the most important task, I told myself, was to find Mimi and Sebastien.

We followed the mountain trail down, away from the fires.

The sun was fully up now. And going down into the woods seemed like a prudent idea. There were many more trees to cover us there, more places to hide, probably a creek or two to drink from.

It was late morning, and something reminded me that it was Saturday. I thought of past Saturdays spent sitting in the house with Señora Valencia, sewing baby clothes, going through the market stands with Juana, helping Papi in his flower garden, visiting Sebastien at the mill—even after long days when he had to do extra work outside the cane to earn a few more pesos to pay his debts. For so long this had been my life, but it was all the past. Now we all had to try and find the future.

I knew precisely what I would do when I crossed the border. I'd exchange the pesos for gourdes and look for a little house to rent on the citadel road, where I had lived as a child. I wondered who had our house now and if I could still claim the land as my inheritance. I had no papers to show, but it was probably recorded some place that the land was once my father's and mother's and—even though I hadn't been there for a long time—was still my birthright.

Tibon became as quiet as everyone else after we left the sisters. We were going down a steep part of the mountain, which required a lot of concentration from all of us but most especially from him because of his limp and wounded ankle. The grade was steep and we could easily trip, stumbling down the incline into a rough-edged gorge crowded with kapok trees whose branches rose as high as the hills and whose roots stuck out of the ground like the entrails of crushed animals.

We reached the foot of the mountain by mid-afternoon. At the mouth of the forest was a small deserted settlement of thatched huts and wood cabins with long vines of tobacco leaves drying in roped layers around them.

Tibon limped to the first of five doorways lined up in a short row.

"No one here," he called as he moved on to the next. Wilner and Odette rushed ahead of him. There was no one in any of the four other houses either, they discovered.

"Maybe the owners are out planting more tobacco," Wilner called. "Or maybe they've gone selling."

Wilner dashed in and out of the cabins, separating from his woman and then joining up with her again. He found bundles of corn and a water well with a bucket suspended from a rope. Odette discovered a few wooden bowls and distributed some water among us.

"When you're thirsty," Odette said, "no matter how much water you drink afterwards, nothing ever tastes like the first drop."

"I wonder why more people didn't travel the same way we did across the mountains," Wilner commented before drinking his water.

"It's a big mountain," Tibon said.

"Perhaps it was the fire," offered Odette.

"Some could have crossed before the fire," Wilner argued.

"Maybe there are no people left," Odette said. She splashed the rest of the water on her face, washing her armpits and the space between her breasts. Wilner wandered in and out of the huts, to see what other treasures could be found.

He ran out with a pile of land papers in his hand. "Look, this was under one of the mattresses," he said. "They are traders, Haitian traders. A big family."

"They were not poor." Tibon untied his shirt from his head and put it on. He fished a wooden pipe out of his pants pocket and crammed it with a piece from a tobacco leaf that still looked too damp for smoking. Puffing at the unlit pipe, he moaned after each smokeless draw. For the first time since we'd left the sisters, it seemed as though his guilt was waning.

At this moment we were all certain that chance had blessed us, that if these people came back, they would invite us to stay for the night and their presence would protect us. Each of us must have thought this, all except Yves.

Yves stood alone, far away from the others. He was leaning against the largest tree in the yard, holding a dusty brown sandal he had picked up from the dirt. He kept looking up, as if to find a patch of the sky between the tiny spaces left open by the wide kapok branches.

I moved towards him, wanting to say something quick-witted, like what a marvel it was that we not so long ago were looking down at these same trees and now were standing beneath their branches.

He looked up again, in spite of himself, it seemed. I followed the rise of his face. At first I couldn't tell what they were, these giant presences, which cast no shadows on the ground. They were dangling at the end of bullwhip ropes: feet, legs, arms, twelve pairs of legs, as far as I could count. Their inflated faces kept the nooses from releasing them. Three men. Five women. And two young boys.

A brown leather sandal was suspended, close to falling, from one of the feet, a man's foot. Yves had the other sandal in his hand.

I slapped the back of my neck where an insect—or a whole group of them—stung me. I cringed from the bruise of my own blow. Yves dropped the sandal on the ground.

"We must go," he said, moving towards the cabins. "If we go now, we reach Dajabón by nightfall."

It took some time to gather everyone.

"Why not stay here for the night?" Tibon asked when we found him. Well-lit now, his pipe stuck out between his lips.

"What if these people were chased away?" Yves said. "Those who frightened them will surely return tonight for all this tobacco. And the people who set the fires in the mountain villages, they may come this way, too."

Everyone agreed then that we should leave.

"I have people in Dajabón who may receive us," Yves said, as we entered the woods.

"We do, also," Odette said.

29

By the time we reached Dajabón, it was almost dark; still the whole town was lit up like a carnival parade. As we walked towards the square, we passed galleries full of people, some dancing, others drinking as they played dominoes with acquaintances peering over their shoulders. Rows of fringed colored paper were strung in front of the houses, with murals of the Generalissimo's face painted on side walls.

A wide new macadam road was filled with crowds heading for the town square, across from the cathedral. Musical groups grew from children beating on enamel and tin cups, women scraping forks against coconut graters, and men pounding on drums.

Ahead of us was a pack of schoolgirls and boys wearing blue, red, and white uniforms and carrying banners with the Generalissimo's name.

"Viva Trujillo!" The children echoed the chants of the crowd.

I looked down at my clothes, which were soil-stained and wrinkled. Yves, Tibon, Wilner, Odette, and me, we all looked the same. Our bundles, as carefully as we tucked them in front of us, gave us away as people who had hastily prepared for flight. We tried to mix, wanting to appear like confused visitors from the interior campos rather than the frightened maroons that we were.

I followed Yves as he wound his way through the dense crowd, trying hard not to let him wander beyond my sight. Tibon was walking behind me, and occasionally he'd put his skeletal hand on my shoulder when we had to stop and let a group of people squeeze by.

During one of those stops, Tibon leaned forward and told me that Wilner and Odette had left us. They'd gone to look for someone they could pay to help them cross the river safely. They wanted us to wait for them at the big fountain in the middle of the square.

I pushed my way towards Yves to tell him.

"We'll try to wait," he said, keeping his eyes down as we snaked through the tiny spaces between the swell of bodies.

The cathedral was covered with lights from the steeple down to the front door. Ladies in dinner frocks with nipped-in waists and crisscross necklines merrily skipped from their automobiles to the front door of the church, leaving their escorts a few bow-trimmed-shoe paces behind. I couldn't help but ask myself if Señor Pico was there. There were army trucks lined up in front and others scattered all around the plaza. The soldiers were reviewing the crowd, searching for threats of disturbance.

I gathered from many scraps of conversation that the Generalissimo was inside the church. Earlier he had given a speech to the crowd, restating that the Dominican Republic's problems with Haitians would soon be solved.

There was glee in the voices that recounted this. Some

thought the Generalissimo was going to war with Haiti to force all of us to return there. I also heard some worried Kreyòl-whispering voices, people who might have wanted to walk with us, but perhaps feared that gathering in large numbers would be dangerous for all.

Some of the Dominicans who were closest to us gave us looks that showed they pitied us more than they despised us. Others pointed us out to their children and laughed. They told jokes about us eating babies, cats, and dogs.

The crowd spilled into the square across from the cathedral. People waited anxiously for the Generalissimo to come out of the church. It was as though his presence were a sacred incident, something that might transform the rest of their lives.

La Orquesta Presidente Trujillo was playing in front of the fountain where Wilner had asked us to wait for him and Odette.

Yves grabbed my hand and pulled me away from the edge of the crowd. I turned around to make certain Tibon was following.

We moved towards a dark corner behind an acacia grove wreathed by crimson birds of paradise. A group of five young men watched us from beneath a frangipani a few feet away; they had deeply reddened faces as though, like us, they had spent the entire day walking in the sun.

"Best if we go to the border now," Yves said, watching them watch him. "I don't know if we can count on my friends. I don't even know if they're still here."

Tibon agreed, but he wanted to give Wilner and Odette some time to find us.

"We should go immediately," Yves spoke from behind his teeth, without moving his lips. "We should go while there's a lot to occupy the soldiers and the crowd."

The young men moved away from the frangipani and started towards us. They raised handfuls of parsley sprigs over their heads and mouthed, "Perejil. Perejil."

A few of the people on the benches walked away in fear as the young men came towards us. The soldiers were too far away, and I didn't think they'd want to defend us in any case.

The young men surrounded us, isolating us from most of the crowd faithfully watching the church doors and waiting for the Generalissimo to come out. As they circled us, Yves pulled out his machete and held it like a metal sash across his chest. Two of the young men lunged at him and wrestled the machete out of his grasp. The other three ripped off Tibon's shirt and poked a broomstick at his skeletal arm. Tibon tried to step back, but the young men shoved him forward, towards the stick.

I moved to an empty space on my left and found myself stepping on one of the young men's feet. His cheeks ballooned. He spat. I reached up and touched the glob as it rolled down my face. It was green with chunks of parsley.

Tibon thrust his muscular shoulder at one of the youths who was poking the broomstick at his chest. He was a child really, perhaps fourteen years of age, jabbing at Tibon as though he were sitting by a pond and teasing the small fishes circling around his feet. This boy was caught off guard when Tibon charged towards him; the broom fell from his hand as he staggered and tried to remain on his feet. Tibon encircled the boy's neck with his more developed arm and tightened his grip. He dug his teeth into the curved bone behind the boy's left ear, keeping the boy's scream buried in his throat by pressing his bony forearm down on the boy's lips. Two of the boys' comrades began pounding their fists against Tibon's back, but Tibon only squeezed the boy's neck harder. The boy began choking, blood flowing from his nose, down Tibon's forearm. The rest of the boy's face paled while he gasped for breath.

Yves attempted to tug Tibon away. Tibon would not let go. The boy was struggling for every breath now, his neck limp, his body shaking.

One of the other boys grabbed Yves' machete—Félice's machete, Doña Sabine and Don Gilbert's machete—and plunged it into Tibon's back.

Tibon seemed startled by the intrusion of the cold metal into his back. It was as though he had been in the middle of a dream. Releasing the boy, he reached behind him to check his wound. The boy fell to the ground, coughing, rolling beyond our reach.

Tibon thrust his hands in front of him once more, clutching at the air. The others kneed Tibon in the ribs and watched him fall to the ground. Tibon turned on his side and closed his eyes. The boy whose neck he had been squeezing slowly rose to his feet. He regained his balance and kicked Tibon in the chest.

Now the others circled Yves and me. La Orquesta Presidente Trujillo started playing the popular hymn "Compadre Pedro Juan." The crowd cheered as they watched one of the youngest players squeeze his accordion while holding it over his head.

I fumbled with my parcel and tried to find my knife. The bundle slipped from my grasp and someone grabbed it. I saw hands clutch it and then watched it disappear above the heads into the crowd.

Yves and I were lifted by a mattress of hands and carried along next to Tibon's body. Two soldiers laughed, watching. The young toughs waved parsley sprigs in front of our faces. "Tell us what this is," one said. "Que diga perejil."

At that moment I did believe that had I wanted to, I could have said the word properly, calmly, slowly, the way I often asked "Perejil?" of the old Dominican women and their faithful attending granddaughters at the roadside gardens and markets, even though the trill of the *r* and the precision of the *j* was sometimes too burdensome a joining for my tongue. It was the kind of thing that if you were startled in the night, you might forget, but with all my senses calm, I could have said it. But I didn't get my chance. Yves and I were shoved down onto our knees. Our jaws were pried open and parsley stuffed into our mouths. My eyes watering, I chewed and swallowed as quickly as I could, but not nearly as fast as they were forcing the handfuls into my mouth.

Yves chewed with all the strength in his bulging jaws.

At least they were not beating us, I thought.

I tried to stop listening to the voices ordering the young men to feed us more. I told myself that eating the parsley would keep me alive.

Yves fell headfirst, coughing and choking. His face was buried in a puddle of green spew. He was not moving. Someone threw a bucketful of water at the back of his head.

A few more people were lined up next to us to have handfuls of parsley stuffed down their throats.

I coughed and sprayed the chewed parsley on the ground, feeling a foot pound on the middle of my back. Someone threw a fist-sized rock, which bruised my lip and left cheek. My face hit the ground. Another rock was thrown at Yves. He raised his hand and wiped his forehead to keep the parsley out of his eyes.

The faces in the crowd were streaming in and out of my vision. A sharp blow to my side nearly stopped my breath. The pain was like a stab from a knife or an ice pick, but when I reached down I felt no blood. Rolling myself into a ball, I tried to get away from the worst of the kicking horde. I screamed, thinking I was going to die. My screams slowed them a bit. But after a while I had less and less strength with which to make a sound. My ears were ringing; I tried to cover my head with my hands. My whole body was numbing; I sensed the vibration of the blows, but no longer the pain. My mouth filled with blood. I tried to swallow the sharp bitter parsley bubbling in my throat. Some of the parsley had been peppered before it was given to us. Maybe there was poison in it. What was the use of fighting?

I thought I heard a bugle, a cannon blast, then another bugle. La Orquesta Presidente Trujillo stopped playing.

The air vibrated with a twenty-one-gun salute. People applauded and stomped their feet and sang the Dominican national anthem. "Quisqueyanos valientes," they began. Perhaps Señor Pico was there, somewhere, watching, listening, advising, participating. I heard sirens and cheers and the stampede of feet over my head, occasionally landing on my hands and shoulders.

The Generalissimo was leaving the church. The sirens. The voices. The hum of army trucks, then another twenty-one-gun salvo for good measure. Cheers erupted as the Generalissimo's car sped away with a caravan of soldiers and La Orquesta trailing behind him.

I attempted to get up many times, but was shoved back down by people rushing to glimpse the back of his head or to catch a last mote of the dust raised by his automobile.

Finally most of the crowd departed, leaving only a few dawdlers who cursed themselves for missing a glimpse of the Generalissimo, or a glance from him at them, even if only out of the corner of his eyes.

"Get up now." A couple was standing over us. "Rise."

Yves was already on his knees, trying to stand. He staggered to his feet and grabbed the side of the fountain to support his weight. Tibon's face was pressed into the ground, his back covered with foot marks.

A hand lifted me, a soft shoulder was offered for me to lean on.

"The river is not so far away," a woman's voice whispered in my ears.

"The river is not so far away," a man repeated.

I recognized the voices and immediately tried to speak, to ask, "Odette, Wilner, is this truly you?"

My voice came out in one long grunt.

"Save your strength," Odette said.

"We waited for you and Wilner, Odette," I tried to say, but I uttered only another long groan.

"Calm yourself," Odette said. "While these people are running after their Generalissimo, we're going to a house

Wilner knows of. Tomorrow we will go to the river. It is not so far, the river."

"Will they beat us again, Odette?" I tried to ask.

She thought I wanted to know about Yves and Tibon.

"Only Yves will be coming with us," she said.

Tibon's body was left face up near the fountain at the square. Yves and I were dragged down a dark alley between two small houses. Odette's nervous movements made me feel as though I were being attacked all over again. When I moaned in pain, she thought I was asking about Tibon.

"We leave the dead behind," she said. "Tibon is dead."

"We should not leave him," I tried to say. "Who will bury him? Besides, he was the one who wanted to wait for you and Wilner, Odette."

She stopped and looked at my face. That time I thought she understood what I was saying.

"We cannot take him with us," she said. "He is dead. Let your lip rest a bit now. It's as big as a melon, your lip."

"But how can we be sure he is dead, Odette?" I asked.

"Oh wi, your lips are as big as melons," she replied, "and you'll only waste more blood if you keep knocking them together like this."

They dragged us into a tiny room behind a house across from the square. The room was almost empty, with only a few sacks of cement piled against the back wall.

Wilner moved around as if trying to find something in the dark. He gave up, went outside, and came back with a cup full of salt water, which Odette held up to my lips. The salt stung my mouth. I spat it out on the front of what was left of my dress.

"We will rest here tonight," Wilner said, sounding like the echo of his own voice. "Tomorrow, we go to the river."

Yves sat with his back pressed into one of the cement piles, his shirt soaked with blood. He watched as Odette spread a coarse, itchy blanket over me while I shivered from a fever slowly rising from the hollow of my bones. My chipped and cracked teeth kept snapping against the mush of open flesh inside my mouth. All the pain of first being struck came back to me. I reached up to touch my misshapen face. Odette moved my hands away from my jaws. Wilner was pacing back and forth speaking to himself under his breath. The hand he lay on my forehead when he stopped smelled of parsley. Odette's clothes smelled of parsley. I closed my eyes and entered a darkness of parsley.

"You should sit," Odette told Wilner when he began pacing again. "Alberto said they would not look for anyone here tonight."

"I will have to find a good crossing place tomorrow," Wilner said, "a place where we can avoid the soldiers at the bridge."

"Do you know that you can trust him who offered this place to you?" Yves asked Wilner and Odette. He was lisping heavily himself, his enlarged tongue pushed out between his bloated lips. "How do you know he will not bring the soldiers here?"

"I paid him for this," Wilner replied.

"Even then?" persisted Yves.

"We've never lived lives of certainty," Odette said.

"Tell me, why don't our people go to war because of this?" Yves seemed to be asking this as much of himself as of them. "Why won't our president fight?"

Wilner did not have the answer right then, but he grunted as though he would come up with it if he had the time.

Yves, Wilner, and Odette stopped talking and listened to the night. I could still hear people squealing and laughing, the Guardia sending the drunken home. Footsteps glided through the narrow spaces between the houses. We waited for the footsteps to get louder and then quickly fade away like so many others had before.

There was a knock at the door, the knock of a fist.

"It is Alberto," a voice whispered through the crack that introduced a tiny sliver of moonlight into the room. "The Guardia is coming this way."

Wilner stumbled across the room and opened the door. The man on the other side of the threshold was carrying a kerosene lamp, which he pushed inside. The room was suddenly full of light, like an abruptly sunny day. Wilner thanked the man with the lamp and bid him good-night. The light disappeared from the doorway as the man took off running.

I could hear the soldiers at a distance chatting among themselves, the shrieking laughter of women they were lingering to tease, the loud kisses the women were blowing back at them.

Wilner jumped outside and held the door ajar for Odette. Yves limped out after her, then offered his hand to guide me over the threshold. Once outside, I clung to her shoulder as though it were a walking stick.

The voices of the soldiers died down with the humming of trucks out in the square. Wilner led us in a circle down a narrow alley around a string of half-finished cement houses. I

heard the soldiers pounding on the doors of the houses farther out on the square. We hurried to a soccer field, bordered
with a cinder-block wall. Wilner kept turning around to
glimpse the open spaces behind us, to make certain that no
one was following.

In a clearing, cows crouched, asleep. A few of them hastily stumbled to their feet as we hobbled past them. The scattered trees and shrubs of the savanna led into a grove of tall
coconut palms, which whistled in a breeze I could not feel.
Perhaps my whole body was beyond feeling now, beyond
healing.

"I think we left them behind," Wilner announced.

I couldn't make myself look back. The palms offered
enough protection now. Even if they came, we could scatter
far enough to delay their search. They would not find all of
us.

"Where to find Sebastien and Mimi? Where is it?" I mumbled slowly so they all would understand.

"Does she know the other one is dead?" Wilner asked.

"She knows," Odette answered for me. "Don't you know,
cherished one? You know Tibon died, don't you? The dead
cannot always come with us on such long journeys."

I tried to explain. I wanted to go to the fortaleza where I
thought they might be holding Mimi and Sebastien. My
words ran together, blurred and incomprehensible. They
stopped listening, perhaps thinking that each attempt at a
phrase was a complaint about leaving Tibon behind.

As we walked out of the palm grove, we found a tree-
arched path leading down to the river. From a distance, the
water looked deep and black, the bank much steeper than I

remembered. Chin-high grass surrounded the spot Wilner chose for our crossing. The bridge lay far ahead, the curve of its iron girders dotted with night lights. The lamps moved from one end of the bridge to the next, making the distant sentinels seem like giant fireflies.

We waited for some time to see if some guards would be coming that way. There were none in sight except for the sentinels at the bridge.

"We can perhaps cross now," Wilner said.

There was a splash from upstream; something had dropped from the bridge.

"They are throwing corpses into the water," Odette whispered.

"Don't listen," responded Wilner. "We need only look for the guards on patrol. I will go in last."

The marshlands led abruptly to the water's edge. The river reached up to our chests when Odette and I slipped in together. Odette turned her face back to the bank where Yves was still feeling his way in and to Wilner who was still watching the bridge.

A strong scent of wet grass and manure wafted through the current as we forded farther in. I tried to find footholds in the sand, wedges to anchor my feet. The water was so deep that it was like trying to walk on air.

When we were nearly submerged in the current, I yanked my hand from Odette's. I heard her sniffle, perhaps fearful and shocked. But I was only thinking of one thing: If I drowned, I wanted to drown alone, with nobody else's life to be responsible for.

An empty black dress buoyed past us, inflated by air, floating upon the water. It was followed by a clump of tree branches and three empty sisal knapsacks. A man floated past us, face down. I swam towards him and moved his head to the side.

Sebastien?

No.

I turned the head down again, wishing I knew a ceremonial prayer to recite over the body.

The water guided Odette downstream. She was not paddling or swimming but simply letting herself be cradled by the current; her head dipped under now and then, and when it came up again, she opened her mouth wide to gulp in the air.

I swam after her, grabbed her waist with one hand, and fended my way across with the other. When she raised her face above the current, she looked frightened, but stifled her coughs as the water spilled out of her mouth.

Behind us on the shore, someone was calling to Wilner, "¡He! ¡He!"

We stopped our struggles immediately, letting the current carry us downstream.

I reached for Odette's mouth and sealed it with both my hands when the shot rang out. Wilner did not even have time to reply.

During the dull silence after the shot, the soldier called out to his friends not to fret, that it was him, Segundo, and he, Segundo, was fine. Odette bit deep into my palm, scraping the inside flesh with her top and bottom teeth.

It is the way you try to stun a half-dead bird still waving its wings, a headless chicken courageously racing down a dirt road. I kept one hand on her mouth and moved the other one to her nose and pressed down hard for her own good, for our own good. She did not struggle but abandoned her body to the water and the lack of air.

The soldier who had shot Wilner continued marching upstream. Perhaps if he had wanted to, he could have seen us, but maybe the river itself, though good for discarding the corpses, was considered not favorable for shootings.

I covered Odette's body with mine and framed her in my arms as Yves and I continued swimming towards the shore.

Yves was the first to land on a sandbar on the other side of the river. He crawled back on his belly and pulled Odette away from my chest. Taking hold of a boulder, I eased myself out of the current.

We lay Odette facedown. Even though she was still breathing, she would not gain consciousness. It was as though she had already made her choice. She was not going on the rest of the journey with us.

All I had wanted was for her to be still, to do her part in helping us live.

Yves was staring down at Odette as though our futures were written in those eyes that she refused to open. She had saved us at the square, so we wanted to save her too.

He picked her up and carried her onto the dusky plains in the dark. Following the track inland, we approached a cluster of parrot trees whose furry leaves looked like soft hands reaching down from some higher place, encouraging us to pause once again and rest.

As we sat there with Odette under a canopy of trees in the middle of a grassy field, she spat up the chest full of water she had collected in the river. With her parting breath, she mouthed in Kreyòl "pèsi," not calmly and slowly as if she were asking for it at a roadside garden or open market, not questioning as if demanding of the face of Heaven the greater meaning of senseless acts, no effort to say "perejil" as if pleading for her life. Que diga amor? Love? Hate? Speak to me of things the world has yet to truly understand, of the instant meaning of each bird's call, of a child's secret thoughts in her mother's womb, of the measured rhythmical time of every man and woman's breath, of the true colors of the inside of the moon, of the larger miracles in small things, the deeper mysteries. But parsley? Was it because it was so used, so commonplace, so abundantly at hand that everyone who desired a sprig could find one? We used parsley for our food, our teas, our baths, to cleanse our insides as well as our outsides. Perhaps the Generalissimo in some larger order was trying to do the same for his country.

The Generalissimo's mind was surely as dark as death, but if he had heard Odette's "pèsi," it might have startled him, not the tears and supplications he would have expected, no shriek from unbound fear, but a provocation, a challenge, a dare. To the devil with your world, your grass, your wind, your water, your air, your words. You ask for perejil, I give you more.

30

We were found the next morning, at dawn, by a priest and a young doctor who were walking the savannas, looking for survivors. Yves had carried Odette's body some distance from the riverbank in the dark, far enough that we could no longer see the river and the bridge.

The priest called for help, and suddenly we were surrounded by men and women in different stages of hurt and healing, asking where we were from, had we seen this and that person from this or that campo or this or that mill.

Someone took Odette from Yves without questioning us. She seemed small and pliable, weightless in the stranger's arms.

We followed the one carrying her to another field dotted with large tents. Yves limped onward, his eyes fixed on Odette.

"What was her name?" asked the tired-looking priest with an open notebook in his hand. He wiped his mouth with a white handkerchief, the whitest thing I had seen since the lace covering the statue of La Virgen on the road up the mountain.

Yves said, "Odette, but we do not know her surname."

"Her relations?" asked the priest.

"We do not know where they are from."

The man with Odette in his arms was walking on the side

of the road where the corpses had been hauled and laid out in rows. Priests and a bishop in full dress performed the last rites for each of the dead. We did not ask where Odette would be buried, for we knew she would likely have to share her grave with all the others there. Besides, the priest had already moved on to someone else.

I took one last look at Odette's face. There was a stillness to it I nearly envied. She did not look like someone death had taken by surprise; her body had very hastily eased into it: her open hands, her bent knees, the relaxed face.

I must have been standing over her body for several hours. Wherever I go, I will always be standing over her body.

No farewell could be enough.

All I had wanted was for her to be still.

Yves took my hand and pulled me away from the body into one of the large tent clinics where people were squeezed together on benches and clustered on blankets on the floor. Two nuns greeted us from behind a small table.

"You don't look as bad as some," a nun with a manly, square-jawed, chocolat-au-lait face said to me in Kreyòl.

Two doctors were working behind wooden dividers inside the tents. Yves and I were crowded on a long school bench with many others and told to wait our turn.

We tried not to look at the people around us, especially those whose bodies were bared, as if giving you permission to gape deep inside them.

As we waited, many of them called the nuns' attention to their wounds.

"Sister, some cool water, please."

"Sister, don't you forget me."

"Sister, I feel so dead."

"Sister, has he come, my son? Have they come, my daughter, my man, my woman, my mother, my father?"

Their cries rose above the groans of others who like me were unable to speak their desires.

It must have been some hours before the nun with the square jaws finally came to fetch me.

"You don't look bad as some. You look rather well," she repeated.

Leaving Yves behind, I was taken past a line of people with burns that had destroyed most of their skin, men and women charred into awkward poses, arms and legs frozen in mid-air, like tree trunks long separated from their branches.

Behind the wooden screen, one doctor was seeing to many people lying on a row of jointed tables. Next to me was a woman with her leg dangling by a fragile bend of her right knee. The woman bounced her head up and down as she mumbled something to herself, a plea to keep her whole leg, a supplication to the doctor not to make her incomplete, to allow her to go into the next world the same way she had come into this one.

Another doctor came in with a small saw. The woman kept her eyes on the poles and ropes that formed the tent's frame and the tiny canvas windows with mosquito webbing above her head.

I saw my doctor's eyes peeking over the top of his soiled white mask. There was an urgency to everything he did. He stole glances at the other woman as he tore open my tattered dress. One hand turned my face away from the woman's operation, and the other hand raised my legs as he inspected my stomach for cuts. His eyes stood frozen for a single moment as the woman had her leg disjoined, as she gyrated in shock, making the other doctor's tasks difficult, as the blood shot from what was left of her thigh, a drop landing on my eyelids, as the other doctor stopped to announce, "She's not going to live," and as I closed my eyes against her blood, thinking this would be the last time I would see someone dying, so sure was I that when the doctor said, "She's not going to live," he was also talking about me.

When I came to, I was in a large room with wooden walls and a tin roof like the face of a dirty mirror. The midday heat burned through the ceiling, as if trying to set us all on fire. People fanned themselves for relief and to frighten the flies and ants away from their wounds.

I was lying on a thin blanket, next to a splintered post that held up most of the ceiling. Above me were two shutters; between them a breeze streamed in from outside.

My knees were bandaged, and so was my head. The house uniform was gone. I was wearing a different dress from the one I'd arrived in, a frock in faded denim made for a woman with a much longer and wider body than mine.

To distract myself, I pushed my hands in and out of the empty pockets. A whiff of wet pine breezed past my nose. I heard the moan of a man trying not to scream, saw Odette's dying face, and drifted back to sleep.

In my sleep, I see my mother rising, like the mother spirit of the rivers, above the current that drowned her.

She is wearing a dress of glass, fashioned out of the hardened clarity of the river, and this dress flows like raised dust behind her as she runs towards me and enfolds me in her smoke-light arms. Her face is like mine is now, in fact it is the exact same long, three-different-shades-of-night face, and she is smiling a both-rows-of-teeth revealing smile.

"I was saving my smile for when you needed it," she says, in a cheerful voice I do not remember, for she had always spoken so briefly and so sternly. "I didn't want you to think that love was not scarce because it is, that it flowed freely from every-where, or that it was something you could expect without price from everyone."

"And what of that time when I was dying and the doll came?" I ask her. "Why did you not love me then?"

"You were never truly dying, my precious imbecile," she says. "You were unbalanced in the head, as you are now. Your heart was racing and your blood was on fire, as it is now. So you felt like you were dying but you were not. It was never as hot as you remember. It could not have been. I would not have let it be."

"I will never be a whole woman," I say, "for the absence of your face."

"Your mother was never as far from you as you supposed," she says. "You were like my shadow. Always fled when I came to you and only followed when I left you alone. You will be well again, ma belle, Amabelle. I know this to be true. And how can you have ever doubted my love? You, my eternity."

I couldn't remember how long I had been asleep. But when I woke up this time, the nuns came through the room and handed out plates of corn mush with black bean sauce and a slice of avocado. I refused by shaking my head, but they left the plate near me anyway.

As they ate, people gathered in a group to talk. Taking turns, they exchanged tales quickly, the haste in their voices sometimes blurring the words, for greater than their desire to be heard was the hunger to tell. One could hear it in the fervor of the declarations, the obscenities shouted when something could not be remembered fast enough, when a stutter allowed another speaker to race into his own account without the stutterer having completed his.

"It was Monday, the last two days in September," a man began, as though giving an account to a justice of the peace. "I went to the fields in the early morning. When I came home at noontime, the Guardia was in my house. I'd heard talk, rumors of all these happenings at night. I took precautions not to lag outside. But this was the daytime. The soldiers came, picked out some chickens in my yard, and told me I was a thief. I tell you many a man was taken falsely as a thief."

Another group of voices argued for the right to speak next, as if their owners had been biting their tongues while this last man was speaking.

"Only a few paces from me," shouted a woman, "they had them tied in ropes and Don José, who has known me my whole life, went at them with his machete, first my son, then my father, then my sister."

My skin felt prickly, as if my blood had been put in a pot to boil and then poured back into me. Or maybe the tin roof was melting and streaming down on me in a light silver rain.

A man who had taken a bullet in the stomach told how he

had run for half a day, not realizing he'd been shot. He thought a bullet, especially one from a rifle like the Krag, would hurt worse. He was lucky to have been shot from a distance, he said. At first it felt like an insect sting, a bee sting, not even a wasp bite, which can be deadly to some people.

Another man spoke of how he was hiding behind a tree when a group of soldiers stormed a horse farm. They were so angry not to have found any Haitians there that they shot all the horses.

"I was there in Santiago," a voice shouted from the other side of the room, "when they shut seven hundred souls into a courtyard behind two government houses. They made them lie facedown in the red dirt and shot them in the back of the head with rifles."

In the heat's haze, the ceiling seemed to split in two, the pieces rising on silver wings to the sky, except there was no sky above, just a daytime darkness where a sun should have been.

"I was there," echoed a young woman with three rings of rope burns carved into her neck, "when they forced more than two hundred off the pier in Monte Cristi."

I felt my breath racing as if everything inside me was boiling, even though my body was still. Perhaps I had a fever, like my childhood fevers, but if I did have a fever, would the back of my hot hand know to discern its own heat from that of my forehead?

The next man who spoke had been struck with a machete on the shoulder and left for dead. When he awoke the next morning, he found himself in a pit surrounded by corpses.

"I felt like my woman on our first night together," he said. "She woke up in the middle of the night and started screaming. I said to her, 'Am I so ugly that you should scream so loud the first night you are with me?' She looked at me hard and said this was her first night outside her mother's bed and she'd plain forgotten where she was."

The group grew impatient with that one. He took too long to arrive at the center of his tale.

"I thought of my woman when I woke up that morning in that pit with all the dead faces around me and all the vultures overhead," he said.

"Oh, the vultures," everyone chimed in. They could not get enough, those vultures, covering the daytime sky like a midnight cloud. If you were not walking fast enough, they would try for your eyes, those vultures. It was as if they could sniff the scent of death on you, those vultures.

"It wasn't always just the vultures," someone added, "the 'good birds' became man-eaters too: the swallows, the warblers, even the tiny hummingbirds, they all wanted the taste of flesh."

"Waking up among the dead, I started screaming," the man from the cadaver pit went on. "And then I thought of my woman and our first night together, and in spite of all the corpses, I smiled."

The people around him smiled, too, at the beauty of such an innocent moment, when a young woman wakes up in her new man's bed for the first time and forgets how she came to be there. Had there ever been a time when such a thing as being a stranger in someone's bed could startle a person?

"Where is your woman now?" someone asked.

The man clapped his hands together and shrugged, a gesture of not knowing.

"It would take too much to kill me," bragged the next speaker. "I'm one of those trees whose roots reach the bottom of the earth. They can cut down my branches, but they will never uproot the tree. The roots are too strong, and there are too many."

"Who said this?" someone asked. "Wasn't it General Toussaint Louverture?"

"A smart man," someone said. "In those times we had respect. When Dessalines, Toussaint, Henry, when those men walked the earth, we were a strong nation. Those men would go to war to defend our blood. In all this, our so-called president says nothing, our Papa Vincent—our poet—he says nothing at all to this affront to the children of Dessalines, the children of Toussaint, the children of Henry; he shouts nothing across this river of our blood."

A woman was singing, calling on the old dead fathers of our independence. Papa Dessalines, where have you left us? Papa Toussaint, what have you left us to? Papa Henry, have you forsaken us?

"Freedom is a passing thing," a man said. "Someone can always come and snatch it away."

They went on to debate the wisdom of having traveled the forested valleys rather than the mountain roads. They wondered what would happen to their relations who had disappeared. Some had traveled in large groups and the nearly dead had to be left behind. They looked back and reordered the moments—second vision, hindsight. What could have been done differently? Whatever became of our national creed, "L' union fait la force"? Where was our unity? Where was our strength? And how can we not hate ourselves for the people we left behind?

At the same time, they dreamed of the first meals their mothers and sisters, who they had not seen for many years, would cook for them. They dictated step by step what the first domino games and cockfights with their fathers and compadres would be like, the first embraces given to lovers and children.

"It all makes you understand that the flesh is like everything else," the man who had been in the pit with the cadavers said. "It is no different, the flesh, than fruit or anything that rots. It's not magic, not holy. It can shrink, burn, and like amber it can melt in fire. It is nothing. We are nothing."

The woman with the rope burns engraved on her neck asked if she could have my food. I nodded and went back to sleep.

When I woke up again, the nun with the square jaws was tapping her fingers against the itchy wound dressings on my head.

"Do you know how long it has been?" she asked.

I shook my head no.

"Three days," she said. "You have slept for three days and three nights. You did not look bad as some, but you had such a fever, I was afraid you would die."

I tried to part my lips and smile to show her that I was far from dead, that I didn't want to die; Odette and Wilner had already died for me.

"Do you have a place to go to now?" she asked.

I shook my head no.

"Can you speak?" she asked.

No.

She motioned for me to open my mouth. I felt my face splitting apart as I did.

"What of the man who came, washed, and dressed you as you suffered through the worst of your fever?"

"Who?" I raised my eyebrows to ask.

"It must be someone you know."

I felt the large veins in my neck rise, the air catching in large bubbles in my throat. *His name is Sebastien Onius.*

"He said his name was Yves," she remembered.

Yves came to see me what must have been a few days later. I wanted to thank him for caring for me during my fever. But how?

He looked better now except for shreds of gauze taped in odd shapes on different sections of his head. His hair had grown in tufts around the gauze. He saw me staring at the tufts and said, "I can't yet shave my head."

I wanted to tell him that he looked well. He didn't need to have his head shaved. He seemed to be healing.

"I sleep outside with the moon," he said. "It's good unless it rains."

Good. Good. I nodded.

"I've been looking every place I can for Sebastien and Mimi." I could tell from the suddenly much graver expression on his face that he thought I was looking too hopeful. "The priests and the bishop try to question people and take their names. I have asked them about Sebastien and Mimi."

And now? I raised my shoulders to ask. "Nothing," he said. "Nothing at all. Maybe they passed through another border post. Maybe they were well enough to go directly to their mother's house."

In spite of my own wishes, I felt myself sliding back towards sleep. It was either cry or sleep. That's all my body seemed to be able to do.

His visits were like one conversation carried out over many days. Some of them I remembered and others I didn't.

"I'm going back to my land tomorrow," he said when he came another time. A little more hair had grown around his bandages, which were smaller now. "Tell me with a nod if you would like to come with me."

I tried to say yes, I would go with him. I would go with him wherever his home was, try to forget everything that had taken place on the journey, and wait for Mimi and Sebastien to return.

"Good," he said. "We will let you sleep tonight, and I will come for you tomorrow."

It rained all that night, and most of the people who were sleeping outside came running inside. The shutters above me were opened, letting a steady drizzle into the room. Someone finally woke up to close them, but by then I was drenched.

Yves made his way towards me and sat in the dark, with his back against a wooden beam nearby.

"I will take you to Sebastien's house," he said, "where you

can sit with him and Mimi and his mother and talk about all this like a bad dream."

"How long now since we have been here?" My throat felt like it was tearing from the effort of trying to speak.

"Six days," he said.

"What did I do when I had the fever?" I asked.

"Sleep and wake, again and again," he said. "But mostly sleep."

"And you have been caring for me?"

He nodded.

"With the rain, the river will overflow," I said. "And if Mimi and Sebastien are crossing, it will not be good."

"They say the killing has stopped," he said.

"There is a dream I have often," I said, "of my parents in the river, in the rain."

"Sebastien told me more than once about it," he said.

Someone shouted from the other side of the room. It was the man who had woken up in the cadaver pit. He said he heard his woman calling him from the river, and he wanted to go save her.

While Yves and a few other men restrained him, the nuns awoke from their sleep and forced him to swallow a few spoonfuls of a syrup that along with his grief made him suckle his thumb and cradle his body like an infant for the rest of the night.

The next morning, Yves went along with the priests, the doctors, and the others whose work it was to collect corpses along the riverbank. The work took the whole morning, even though the nuns too told us that the killing had ceased and there were hardly any more corpses to bury.

The room was full beyond its measure now, with everyone seeking shelter from the mud outside.

I looked for my face in the tin ceiling above me as I waited for Yves to return. With everyone lying face up and with their bodies so close together, I couldn't tell which face was mine.

The man from the cadaver pit lay on his mat all morning, mumbling his woman's name. Nounoune, Nounoune. Next to him was a crippled Dominican who could console him only in Spanish.

"Calmate, hombre," mumbled the Dominican. He was black like the nun who came to re-dress his wounds. He'd been mistaken for one of us and had received a machete blow across the back of his neck for it.

There were many like him in the room, I was told.

31

The sky was smeared with gray—gray like the inside of a broiled fish—when Yves and I finally left the clinic in a camión one afternoon. In that part of the country, the indigo mountains, cactus trees, large egrets and flamingos were great spectacles for the eyes, visions that made the people feel obligated to twist and contort their hurt bodies to peer outside and shiver with gratitude for having survived to see their native land.

Yves and I were pressed into a corner near the back of a crammed row; I knew my knee was pressing into his side, but I could find no room to shift into. Yves had not found Mimi and Sebastien that morning, and for this he was regretful. For this he was silent, watching his own twirling fingers with downcast eyes and grimacing, but not complaining, each time my knee rammed into his side during a sudden stop. Perhaps he thought I hated him and was tormenting him for being here instead of Sebastien; maybe he even thought that he deserved some kind of punishment for not being his friend.

The Cap was still an old new city when we returned to it, a city burnt to the ground many times for its own salvation.

These were tales that all the local children knew, for proof was sometimes found buried in their land: a gold coin, a silver saucer, which the ground would vomit up when it rained, like the bones of those laid to rest without caskets in shallow ground. The dream was to find a *ja*, a chest full of gold that a French plantation owner had buried along with the slaves he had killed and interred next to it so the slaves' souls could be the guardians of the treasure.

To the French generals who returned in fleets to reclaim these treasures and the souls of their slaves, Henry I had said, "I will not surrender the Cap until it's in ashes. And even then I will continue to fight on these ashes." He had given the signal to start the fires by torching his own house first.

The houses that were now built along the Place Toussaint Louverture—under a statue of Toussaint, where the camión left us—the houses of the Cap were now less grand, two stories at best, with wooden railings, double doors, and galleries on top. Not like the old vast plantations that were meant to last for centuries.

As soon as we descended from the camión, Yves parted from all the others. I followed him, looking up and searching the sky.

The giant citadel, Henry I's treasure, was leaning down towards the city from inside a wreath of sun-filled clouds. I wondered if Yves thought about such things. Or if he even noticed what was inside the shops as we ventured along the cleanly paved streets among small groups of men and women ambling past the shoe and fabric shops on the Rue du Quai. I was trailing far behind him with my face to the skies, trying to ignore the throbbing in my knees. The small bones of my bare feet were grating each other raw. Every movement required a pause, a thought to what I was doing, where my legs were going as opposed to where they were supposed to be.

Some of the merchants and shopkeepers and their workers moaned as we moved among them. They recognized us without knowing us. We were *those* people, the nearly dead, the ones who had escaped from the other side of the river.

I dragged my feet along, feeling now and then like other people were standing on them, people whose eyes were only a flutter away from mine, whose hands and fingers wandered freely towards me, whose lips shouted, "Podyab, poor devil," in my ear.

"Come, come," Yves called as we walked past the trellised doors of the old Hotel New York, and then past a sidewalk where someone was demonstrating the use of a phonograph and a sewing machine from a shop on La Rue A. Yves seemed to be searching for some place to enter while walking in circles as if he was lost and didn't even know it.

On La Rue B, he stood in the middle of an open tourist market, scratching the scabs on his unshaven head as he waited for me to catch up. When I reached him, he asked me to stand there, holding on to the front post of a pharmacy as he ran inside and bought a pack of La Nationale cigarettes. He smoked nearly the whole pack by the time we reached the cathedral.

In front of the cathedral, a woman moved so close to me that I could smell the chewing tobacco on her breath, the sweat that dried and then poured out again from her forehead, and the bitter thick-skinned oranges piled in a basket standing by itself on her head. Without looking where her hand was going, she reached up and pulled an orange from the basket and gave it to me.

"You warm this orange on an open fire," she said, "Let it burn until the skin turns black."

"I thank you," I said.

"I am not finished," she said. "When the skin turns all black, you know it's ready. Then you cut it open while the juice is still hot, slap the insides against your flesh, then you take a warm bath and wash the orange flesh away. All your cuts will heal. Your bone aching will stop."

I grasped the orange tightly so it would not fall. She walked behind me, then gave another orange and the same commands to someone else.

Yves was now keeping pace beside me. A few people recognized him as we walked down a gravel road, away from the commercial area. A man with a pile of embroidered tourist shirts on his arm followed us and announced to the people living in the small crowded limestone houses along the gravel road, "It's Man Rapadou's boy, Yves. He's returned from over there."

The man poked his hand out from underneath the heap of shirts he was carrying and gave Yves a joyous handshake.

"They didn't take you, eh," he said. "They couldn't take you. No more than the Yankis could take me."

The man with the tourist shirts talked endlessly about events that had taken place since Yves had left, how the Yankis had gone back to their country three years before, how Yves' mother was well, though always heart-crushed, anxious for him.

The house was one of many constructed from mismatched pieces of timber and rusting tin. Yves leaped towards a low step that led to his mother's front door. A large woman was standing on the doorstep, struggling to push her arms through the short sleeves of her rainbow-striped blouse. Her fingers were snarled in the fabric and she tore at it fiercely to free herself. Her chest was bare, the skin of her breasts the color of molasses. She was about to step into the road without the blouse when Yves jumped in front of her. He guided her clenched fists through the sleeves and calmly buttoned the blouse for her. She watched as he did this and rocked herself all the while, saying his name. When he was done, she grabbed his head and pressed it against her neck, then wept into the scabs on his scalp.

The woman did not see me standing there on the edge of a growing crowd of curious onlookers. I spun the orange in my hand and tried not to squeeze it too hard from anxiety.

"Man Rapadou, you're so happy to see your son, no?" said the man with the pile of tourist shirts in his arms.

Yves walked over, took my hand, and brought me out of the crowd.

"You have a woman. This is your woman?" his mother asked.

"Don't be so rash, Man Rapadou," Yves said.

The mother opened her arms and nodded her head, beckoning to me. I wasn't certain how to respond, so I stood there next to Yves, pretending I didn't understand what she'd said. She yanked my hand and pulled me into her arms. The gathering of observers laughed. The mother waved them off with a turn of her face.

"Her name is Amabelle," Yves said. Hearing him say it, listening to the mother repeat it, made me feel welcomed.

"Inside now," the mother said, waving good-bye to the onlookers. She was wearing one shoe on her foot. The other she had left inside in her haste to run out and greet her son.

We were in the first room of the house. The back room led to a courtyard shared among many families. It reminded me of the compound at Don Carlos' mill.

Yves went out to greet his relations who lived around the courtyard. They brought a chair out for him to sit in beneath a tree in the middle of the yard, a tall, vibrantly green traveler's tree with the palmetto branches spread out like the fingers on a hand.

The mother served us a hot cup of salted coffee. The inside of my mouth was scalded as I sipped, but I struggled not to spit it out because the saline taste washed out the taint of parsley and blood that had been on my tongue since the beating at the square.

Yves' relations from the yard put together and cooked a large meal for him. They fried and stewed all his favorite foods: goat meat and eggplants, watercress in codfish sauce, corn mush, and black beans.

Yves ate everything placed in front of him. Now and again his mother would interrupt his eating to tell a story about how much he had eaten as a boy, not only food and sweets, but also moist dirt from bean plant roots, which he liked to rub against his gums until they bled.

Yves stopped to listen to his mother's stories as though he too was hearing them for the first time. The mother was telling her tales, I realized, to stop him from eating too quickly, to force him to rest his mouth and stomach.

"Remember a man who was put in prison." The mother stood in a corner rubbing her large belly. "After nothing but bread and water for thirty days, they let him out of prison and he brought himself home. First thing I do is cook him all the rich food he had dreams about in prison. He ate until he fell over on his plate in the middle of eating. He died eating," she told the relations with a deep long laugh. "Please, don't kill my son. A man can die of hunger, but a man can also die over a plate of food."

Yves put his spoon down and pushed his plate away. His mother chortled, even though no one was cackling along with her. She seemed to be the only one who could laugh out of sadness, a sadness that made the laughter deeper and louder still, like the echo of a scream from the bottom of a well.

The mother stroked her hairy chin with her long thick fingers, still laughing. She reminded me of the old women at the cane mill with their cheeks split in half, the flesh healed because it had to but never sealed in the same way again.

I remembered what my father used to say as he would hurry off with a knapsack of bottles filled with leaves and warm rum, as he raced to a birth or to a death, thinking of ways to encourage or halt the event. "Misery won't touch you gentle. It always leaves its thumbprints on you; sometimes it leaves them for others to see, sometimes for nobody but you to know of."

The mother looked liked she'd had her own share of misery. The only thing it hadn't touched was a mouth full of perfect white teeth, curved like the round edges of an enamel cup, none of them her own.

My own mouth was still too bruised for hard foods. A full plate of fried goat meat remained on my lap. Yves' mother walked over to me and asked, "Some soup for you? It won't be too hot or too thick."

She took the full plate from my lap and came back with a small bowl of pumpkin soup. While the others watched, she fed me the soup with a tiny spoon as though I were a sick, bedridden child.

32

That night, the mother moved six cousins out of the second room so Yves could share his old bed with me. The bed was made from four posts mortared to the ground and a wooden platform that held a small mattress filled with old rags.

The room where Yves' mother slept was separated from ours only by a rattling beaded curtain. When she went to bed, he followed her there. I sat alone on the new bed and played with my bitter orange while listening to the noises from outside. Everything the people who lived around the courtyard said or did could be heard, their caresses and arguments, their gossip, and the cries of their restless children.

"Who is this woman?" the mother asked Yves. "Where are her people? Are they here or did they all die in the killing over there?"

Yves said nothing. I went out to the yard, found the cooking fire and a basin of water, bathed myself with the bitter orange the way the woman in front of the cathedral had instructed. I could hear some of the courtyard children giggling as they peered at me through the holes in their doorways. In spite of their curiosity, I knew that my body could no longer be a tempting spectacle, nor would I ever be truly young or beautiful, if ever I had been. Now my flesh was simply a map of scars and bruises, a marred testament.

Yves was still with his mother when I came back to bed. They had moved on to talking about other things unfamiliar to me, about old friends who had died or moved to other parts of the country, about his father's land, which had not been cultivated since Yves left.

Each time I closed my eyes I saw the river and imagined Sebastien and Mimi drowning the way my mother and father and Odette had. To escape these thoughts, I envisioned Henry I's citadel as I had seen it again that afternoon, its closeness to the sky, its distance from the river. With my childhood visions of being inside of it, protected, I fell asleep.

The next morning, I stumbled out of bed, ashamed to have slept so soundly and so late. The mother was sitting under the traveler's tree outside, pouring steaming hot water over the powdered grains in her coffee pouch.

"Where's Yves?" I asked. I didn't even know if he had come and lain in the bed with me the night before.

"He's on his father's land," the mother said. "He comes out of bed this morning and says he wants to go and plant some beans in his father's fields."

I didn't know what Yves had told her about me. She got up, walked towards me, clasped my face between her wet hands, and planted a kiss on my forehead.

"You call me Man Rapadou," she said. "I know your story."

Which story of mine did she know? Which story was she told?

"Everything you knew before this slaughter is lost," she said. Perhaps she was encouraging me to embrace her son and forsake Sebastien, even my memories of him, those images of him that would float through my head repeatedly, like brief glimpses of the same dream.

Yves stayed in the fields until nightfall. When he came home his hands were coated with mud and he smelled like the earth had been turned inside out over him.

"I planted a field of green beans," he announced to his mother.

"I told you. It is not the season," she said.

"We'll see," he said.

"When will you pay a visit to Man Denise?" his mother asked.

He did not answer.

"It is only respectful that you go and visit with her, since you and her son left here together," she said.

Yves walked out to the courtyard to wash himself. I went back to our room and lay down on the bed, hoping to fall asleep before he returned.

When he came in and called my name, I did not answer. He lay down and curled himself up on his side of the mattress. He did not speak in his sleep that night. Or any other night after that.

While Yves was in the fields the next day and his mother was visiting a friend, I asked some of his relations and found out where Man Denise, Sebastien and Mimi's mother, lived.

I made the promise of a mint confection to a boy who took me there.

The house was not too far from Yves' but was in a less populated area, with bigger residences and more trees.

I walked back and forth around the property. There was no activity, except for a girl rushing in and out of the yard, carrying jugs of water on her head.

"The woman who lives there, she will not come outside," the boy with me said. "Do you want to go inside and speak with her?"

"No," I said. What would be the use? She hadn't known me when her children were still hers alone, safe in her house.

Soon after that, my body began to feel better, even though I had a constant ringing in my ears and one knee would not bend all the time. Still, I walked by Man Denise's house every day to see if anything would change. Whenever there was more noise than usual on the roads, whenever people gathered in a group, I rushed out to see if it was the homecoming that would bring Man Denise out of her house. There were new arrivals all the time, people returning from the other side, people who were settling again in our quarter and in hers.

Thinking of Sebastien's return made me wish for my hair to grow again—which it had not—for the inside of my ears to stop buzzing, for my knees to bend without pain, for my jaws to realign evenly and form a smile that did not make me look like a feeding mule.

At night, lying next to Yves, I grew more and more frightened that Sebastien would not recognize me if he ever saw me again.

33

Yves spent all his days planting in his father's fields, then lingered with his friends and neighbors for late-afternoon talk after his work.

I never saw him but only heard him undress and slip into bed at night when he finally came home.

A few weeks after his first planting, I waited for him to climb onto his side of the mattress and asked him, "Did anything come up from the ground for you?".

Since we'd come back, we hadn't spoken of our situation, never even talked of changing it in a way that would make us both more comfortable at night.

"Only grass might come up this quick," he said. "And not every type of grass even."

His scornful voice made me think that he was not a fortunate planter, or maybe he didn't think he was one.

"I would like to go to the fields with you one day," I said.

"Why so?" he asked.

"I want to see your father's land."

"It's no different than other land," he said.

I could hear him suddenly sitting up on the bed as if in defense of what had just been said. I reached for his arms in the dark and pressed them down to show him that I truly wanted to be quietly grateful, to cooperate, to make the best out of our burden.

"I hear there are officials of the state, justices of the peace, who listen to those who survived the slaughter and write their stories down," he said. "The Generalissimo has not said that he caused the killing, but he agreed to give money to affected persons."

"Why?" I didn't think he would have the answer, but I wished he did know.

"To erase bad feelings," he said, as if he were no longer linked to the slaughter.

"And the dead?"

"They pay their families," he said.

I knew what he was thinking, that perhaps Man Denise should go, in case Sebastien and Mimi were already dead.

I stepped off the bed and crouched down in a corner of the room, as far from him as I could. I felt grateful that it was dark, that neither one of us could see the other's face.

"I want to meet that justice of the peace myself," I said.

"I don't know if you'll be given the money," he said. "The authorities might try to keep it all for themselves. They ask you to bring papers. They ask you to bring proof." But he knew that it was not money, it was information I was hoping for.

The next morning we went to see the justice of the peace. He was posted in a yellow police building that seemed to have been shaped out of one massive mountain rock. Outside was a group of more than a thousand people waiting to be allowed entry. A line of armed soldiers from the Police Nationale stood between them and the narrow entrance to the building.

As the morning went on, the waiting group became larger, so much so that when I pulled myself up and looked behind me, I could not see where the road ended and the faces began.

Yves had not said a word the whole morning. He occasionally ventured off to get water, or to help carry home some elder who had fainted from the heat.

In the afternoon, food vendors arrived and people shared their tales, as if to practice for their real audience with the government official. The man next to me had walked seventy kilometers to avoid the crowds in his own town. Another woman had come from even farther away. Others were planning to go to Port-au-Prince, which fewer survivors had yet reached.

There was only some vague order to the way people were allowed inside. The most mangled victims, the ones whose wounds had still not healed, were let in as soon as they arrived. Pregnant women entered quickly as well as those who could find some money to bribe the soldiers.

To pass the time waiting, I thought of many ways to shorten my tale. Perhaps Yves and I would go in together and make both our stories one. That way we would give someone else a chance to be heard.

The justice of the peace came to the entrance at sundown. He was plainly dressed in a light green house shirt and pants with a small watch on a gold chain dangling from his pants' side pocket. In one hand was a large leather covered note-book and in the other a shiny black case. His presence caused a stir in the crowd. The soldiers raised their rifles for silence so he could speak.

"I can do no more today," he said.

"Non," moaned the crowd.

"And if I say one more, each of you will want to be that one," he said.

"Non," the crowd disagreed.

"I will come tomorrow," he said.

"Tomorrow, listen faster," someone recommended.

The soldiers surrounded the justice of the peace as he went back inside, then we saw his automobile speeding away from the protected yard behind the station.

People rushed after him, but quickly gave up the chase, for many of them could not run far because of some injury or exhaustion from being in the sun all day.

The last person who'd had an audience with him was a woman, thirty or thirty-five years old. She was dressed all in white—as though she were going off to a religious ceremo-ny—and had a sun-bleached straw hat tied with a green rib-bon under her chin.

"What did they do for you in there?" Yves yelled out to her. Others in the crowd joined in, "Did they give you money?"

She removed her hat and surveyed the faces staring up at her.

"No, he did not give me money," she said, watching the soldiers for approval. "You see the book he had with him?" She glanced at the guards once more, then turned her face back to the crowd. "He writes your name in the book and he says he will take your story to President Sténio Vincent so you can get your money." She kept her eyes on the crowd, no longer watching the soldiers for approval. "Then he lets you talk and lets you cry and he asks you if you have papers to show that all these people died."

The soldiers from the Police Nationale, wearing the same khaki uniforms as the Dominican soldiers—a common inheritance from their training during the Yanki invasion of the whole island—approached the woman from behind and asked her to move away from the entrance. The crowd protested with hisses. Two of the soldiers took her by the arms and carried her down the station steps. She tried to twist out of their hands. Finally someone in the crowd pulled her from them for her own safety.

"If you make trouble," the sergeant—the station head—announced to the crowd, "you will not be allowed to return tomorrow."

The crowd dispersed slowly, perhaps wondering if there was any use in coming back the following day.

Yves and I went back there for the next fifteen days. New faces came and went. Some stopped coming. Some never left their places in front of the station, even when it rained.

The justice of the peace came there every day, except Sundays.

On the sixteenth day, we were waiting without hope in the back of the crowd when we saw her coming.

I knew immediately who she was when Yves leaped from his place and headed for her.

"Man Denise, you came," he said.

"I did come, yes," she said in a voice sharp and abrupt like her daughter Mimi's. "I want to stand here with all of you."

She looked too young to be both Mimi and Sebastien's mother. She was long-legged and slender, her face the color of wet terra-cotta. She wore a long tan dress that swept the floor as she walked. Bowing her long neck, she greeted those people in the crowd she knew and merely nodded to the others. She glanced at me, but she did not see me. Instead, as she stood there, she watched the soldiers. Her eyes followed the movements of their rifles from shoulder to shoulder; their offhand leanings to talk to one another about offhand things. She kept stroking her side, reaching in and out of the deep recesses of her pockets for something too tiny to be held in her hand.

At dusk, the justice of the peace did not come out to speak to the crowd. The head sergeant came out instead and announced that there would be no more testimonials taken. All the money had already been distributed. The justice of the peace had already gone away when no one was looking, knowing we would be enraged if we saw him depart.

It took some time for people to take in what this meant. Their disappointment grew as the word spread from mouth to mouth and was reinterpreted by one person for the next. There were moans and screams of protests, convulsions and faintings as rocks began to fly.

The people at the front of the crowd charged at the entrance. Trained by Yanki troops who were used to rebellious uprisings, the soldiers shot several rounds of bullets in the air.

A few of the soldiers were caught and passed from hand to

hand as blows were struck, but the crowd was not really interested in them. The group charged the station looking for someone to write their names in a book, and take their story to President Vincent. They wanted a civilian face to concede that what they had witnessed and lived through did truly happen. When they did not find such a person inside, they freed the ten male prisoners who were being held in the inner rooms and walked away with a few items the soldiers had left behind: seven chairs, six canteens, two water jugs, three handkerchiefs, fourteen coiled cowhide whips, seventeen cat-o'-nine-tails, two sets of keys to the cells, and a giant official photograph of President Vincent.

He was a sophisticated-looking man, President Sténio Vincent, with small spectacles worn very close to his eyes. He had a pair of beautifully large ears framing his moon face, a tiny dot of a mustache over pinched pensive lips, a poet's lips, it was said. In the photograph, he wore a gentleman's collar with a bow tie, the end of which touched the shiny medal of the Grand Cross of the Juan Pablo Duarte Order of Merit, given to him by the Generalissimo as a symbol of eternal friendship between our two peoples. The image of the Grand Cross caught the flames first when kerosene was brought and the photo, then the police post, was set on fire, though only the wooden doors and the thin coat of paint on the building burned, for the concrete walls of the station did not even scorch.

We dodged the rocks and torches and forced our way out of the crowd. Yves took Man Denise back to her house. Her neighbors who had heard about the melee came to console her. Soon her house was filled with her friends, the girls who ran errands for her, and some traveling vendors who paid to use her empty rooms as a night stop on their long journeys.

The vendors set up mats and sheets in the two bare rooms, places Mimi and Sebastien must once have used. Man Denise had moved all their things into her own room to make it less empty, and also so that the vendors would not walk away with them, one of the errand girls explained.

In the back of the house was Man Denise's room, containing a ring of old sealed-off oil drums filled with her own things as well as Mimi and Sebastien's effects.

The vendors helped her climb on top of a pile of clothes on her bed. They wanted her to take off her tan dress and change into her nightdress, but she refused.

"Forgive me," she said, excusing herself for the pile of clothes and the disorderliness of the oil drums in her room. "What a difficult day this has been."

The neighbors offered her many cups of tea. She raised herself to take a sip from each, then buried her head in the pillow.

"Leave me," she said, "please."

They left her, but we could all see her from the crowded room opposite hers since her room did not have a door.

Yves returned to his mother's house that night and I stayed at Man Denise's. After she fell asleep, I crept back inside and lay down at the foot of her bed. I heard her breath whistling, like someone who tried even in her sleep not to disturb others.

When she woke up in the middle of the night to use her blue enameled chamber pot, she tripped and nearly fell on top of me. I moved the pot closer to her and she climbed on it without questioning what I was doing there.

The next morning before dawn, I went out and sat with the women vendors, who made themselves coffee before moving to the next station on their journey.

As they drank their coffee, the women wondered out loud whether Mimi and Sebastien had disappeared forever in the country of death—as they called it—or if maybe things had returned to normal. Maybe everyone had returned to their everyday work, they hoped.

While they were talking, I heard Man Denise call for water. I hurried inside, ahead of one of the girls who looked after her, picked up the earthen jar leaning against the wall, and handed her a cup of water. She was not fully awake when I held it to her lips. After taking a few sips, she pushed my hand away.

The room had brightened a bit with the morning light. She narrowed her eyes, as if trying to recognize me.

"Which one of them are you?" she asked.

"Amabelle," I said.

"If you've come to pay for the night, put the money on one of the drums," she said.

"I have not come to pay," I said.

"What, then?" she asked.

I put the earthen jar and the cup back against the wall.

"I knew Mimi and Sebastien over there," I said.

She sat up and reached for my ears, rolling my cheeks between her fingers as though my face belonged to her.

"You knew my Micheline and my Sebastien," she said. "My Mimi and Sebastien, you knew them?"

"Yes," I said.

Her face broadened with a pained smile. She let go of me

and clapped her hands together. "I didn't want my children to go and stay there forever," she said. "Their father was killed in the hurricane; Sebastien had a cage full of pigeons that also died in the hurricane, and he was so sad. After the hurricane, this house was taken from us by the Yankis; they wanted to make a road of this house. It was given back to us only after they left. Because we had no house, my son went there first, and me, because I was weak in the lungs, I was to go live with my brother in Port-au-Prince. I had no money so my daughter followed Sebastien and they both sent me some. I came back from Port-au-Prince when the land was given back to us, but my children, maybe they didn't know that the Yankis left, maybe they didn't know that the house was ours again."

She fished in the pocket of her dress and pulled out three painted yellow coffee beans, the kind that Mimi and Sebastien's bracelets had been made of.

I tapped them with the tip of my fingers and watched as they bounced against one another in her palm.

"These are mine," she said, closing her hand around them, "from my own bracelet, which broke long ago. I made one bracelet for each of my children and one for myself, but when I was anxious over the children, I tugged too hard at the bracelet and the thread broke. This is all I have left of the beads from my bracelet."

I wanted her to let me touch the beads again. She reached into the pocket of her dress and lay them there.

"Sit for a moment," she said.

I moved closer and sat on the edge of her bed.

"So you knew my Micheline?" she asked.

"I did."

"She was always untamed for a young girl," she smiled. "Her father gave her the name Micheline. Did she ever tell you this?"

"No," I said. "She never did."

"But Sebastien, you knew more about him? You knew him well."

"Very well," I said.

She smiled a knowing smile, Sebastien's smile, her cheeks ballooning, then caving down on the sides of her lips.

"I named him Sebastien myself," she said, "after the saint. You know of Saint Sebastien, who died not once, but twice."

"No, I didn't know."

"The first time, soldiers shot arrows at his body and left him for dead. A widow found him and saw he was alive. The widow carried him to her house and treated his wounds. When he was healed, Saint Sebastien went back to the soldiers to show them the miracle of love that was his life; this time the soldiers beat him with sticks until he was truly dead."

She held her head between her hands as though it were an unfamiliar thing, a load now too heavy for her. Reclining, she clutched the pillow under her head.

"I named him Sebastien," she said, "because I knew it would be wise if a man could have two deaths. The first one comes quick enough, so it's good to have another one in reserve."

I moved towards her and adjusted the pillow beneath her head. I pressed my palm down on her forehead as she looked up, staring directly into my eyes. I could tell that she trusted something about me, even though she herself might not have known what it was.

"A young man came here to see me some days past." She reached up and pressed down hard on my hand as it was resting on her forehead. "He came here to see me on his way to Port-au-Prince. He said he saw my children killed, in a courtyard, between two government edifices there, in a place he called Santiago. He said he saw them herd my children with a group, make them lie face down on the ground, and shoot them with rifles."

I felt my fingers stick to her forehead as she pressed down harder on my hand. Her body was shaking, but she was not crying.

"In my place, would you believe this?" she asked.

"No, I would not believe this," I said. But in my heart I kept thinking, how could I not? Wouldn't Sebastien have come home already if he was still alive?

"You knew my Micheline. You knew my Sebastien. Do you believe it for yourself?" she insisted.

"No, I do not believe it for myself," I said.

But I did. I believed it because of what I had seen, in Dajabón, because of what I had heard of La Romana, because of what the people said in the clinic that day about those who'd died in Santiago.

"Leave me, please," she said, releasing my hand.

"I wish to stay," I said.

"Leave me."

As I was going, she stopped me in the doorway and asked, "Did you ever see my children wearing these bracelets I made for them?"

"They were never without them," I said.

"This is what they say, the people who come here to bring the word to me. It is not just one traveler, but many. They say that my children died with my bracelets on their wrists."

Pushing her hand inside her pocket, she pressed the beads against the side of her thigh.

"Those who die young, they are cheated," she said. "Not cheated out of life, because life is a penance, but the young, they're cheated because they don't know it's coming. They don't have time to move closer, to return home. When you know you're going to die, you try to be near the bones of your own people. You don't even think you have bones when you're young, even when you break them, you don't believe you have them. But when you're old, they start reminding you they're there. They start turning to dust on you, even as you're walking here and there, going from place to place. And this is when you crave to be near the bones of your own people. My children never felt this. They had to look death in the face, even before they knew what it was. Just like you did, no?"

I nodded yes. Mostly because I knew she wanted me to.

"I wish people would stop coming to tell me they saw my children die," she said. "I wish I had my hopes that they were living someplace, even if they never did come back to see me again."

"Maybe those who came with the word, maybe they are mistaken."

"They are always strangers, the people who come," she said. "They do not know me. Before they died, either alone or together, my son and daughter told them to come here and tell me about their fates."

She pushed her hands into her pocket and pressed them down on the beads.

"Leave me now," she said. "I'm going to dream up my children."

I strolled like a ghost through the waking life of the Cap, wondering whenever I saw people with deformities—anything from a broken nose to crippled legs—had they been there?

I followed the road from Man Denise's house out to the quay, where ships entered the harbor with horns blaring while others were being unloaded as they wobbled against the piers. The sacks of rice, beans, and sugar were being distributed among the merchants as a line of bare-chested young men waited with wheelbarrows to carry the stacks off for them. These men, with more than the weight of their bodies in sugar on their heads, shouted in an uneven chorus of rage in order to be allowed to pass through the streets.

34

When I went back to Yves' house, he had already left for the fields. I sat in the yard with my arms around the traveler's tree, trying not to pound my head against it.

Man Rapadou came out to the courtyard in her nightdress, smiling. She carried a low chair from her room and sat down next to me.

"You don't need the justice of the peace," she said. "You don't need a confessor. I, Man Rapadou, I know your tale." She pressed her face close to mine and whispered so the others in the courtyard couldn't hear. "I asked my son why there is no love between you and him, and he told me about Sebastien."

As I watched her flawless smile grow wider on her face—which should have been a lot sadder than it was—I stroked the traveler's tree, not sure what else to do with my hands. I reached up and touched the frilled yellow-green palmetto branches; the narrow stems had woven themselves together like the inside of an enormous wicker basket. I wanted to cry, but I couldn't. I wanted to scream, but summoning the will to do it already made me feel weak.

"When my son left here, I planted this traveler's tree, and

now look how it's grown," Man Rapadou said. "Yves told me you can make dresses and help give birth to children. Since I'm not to have children anymore, maybe you can make me a dress."

Kindness prevailed on Man Rapadou to let me spend the rest of the day inside, in her son's bed, by myself. She did not call me to eat, even when the mid-afternoon meal was ready. Instead, she whispered from outside the door that she was saving a plate of food for me to have whenever my stomach felt at ample ease.

As I lay in bed with my arms and legs coiled around myself, I ached inside in places I could neither name nor touch. I could not accept that I'd never see Sebastien again, even though I knew it was possible, just as I would never see my mother and father again, no matter how many times I called them forth both with my own loud voice and the timid one inside my head. When it came to my parents, the older I became, the more they were fading from me, until all I could see were the last few moments spent with them by the river. The rest blended together like the ingredients in a too-long-simmered stew: reveries and dreams, wishes, fantasies. Is that what it would also come to with Sebastien?

I feigned sleep when Yves came to bed that night, but unlike the other times he was not convinced by my frozen pose.

"My beans have sprouted," he announced. "Looks like I'll see a harvest."

I did not want to move. Perhaps he didn't know about Mimi and Sebastien, and I wasn't certain how to tell him.

"I hear," he said, "that the priests at the cathedral listen and mark down testimonials of the slaughter." This was his gift to me, like the gift the earth had given him in pushing his beans back up in a different form.

"They don't promise you money." His voice staggered between high and low, as though he were beginning to think that I might really be asleep. "They're collecting tales for newspapers and radio men. The Generalissimo has found ways to buy and sell the ones here. Even this region has been corrupted with his money."

I turned on my back, opened my eyes, and tried to find the silvery lines of rusting tin on the ceiling.

"Will you go yourself to see these priests?" I asked.

"I know what will happen," he said. "You tell the story, and then it's retold as they wish, written in words you do not understand, in a language that is theirs, and not yours."

"Will you go?"

"I have already gone and they looked in their books. Their names are not there. There are good days now waiting for me in the fields. This means we will start to have money. You can buy cloth and thread, sew for people, and make money on your own."

At that moment the future seemed a lot more frightening than the past. Perhaps working the earth, making beans sprout out of dry hard seeds and dust, could make him believe that he had forgotten. But I couldn't trust time or money to make me forget.

Sometimes I conjured up the group from the border clinic, especially Nounoune's man, who had woken up in the cadaver pit, and the woman with the large appetite and the rope burns on her neck. I imagined them going forward in their lives, cultivating their gardens, taking their animals to the stream, skipping out of the road to avoid speeding trucks, calling their children in for an evening wash, making love to the people they'd been reunited with.

I wanted to bring them out of my visions into my life, to tell them how glad I was that they had been able to walk into the future, but most important to ask them how it was that they could be so strong, what their secret was, how they could wash their lives clean, if only for brief moments, from the past.

"How did you keep on with the planting, even when nothing was growing?" I asked Yves.

I could hear him breathing loudly, tapping his tongue against the roof of his mouth, trying to find the right phrasing for his answer. "Empty houses and empty fields make me sad," he said. "They are both too calm, like the dead season."

He pushed his body down, farther into the mattress, as though our speaking together had made him feel like he was more entitled to do so.

After a long silence, he added, "The night when Joël was hit by the automobile, it was almost me who died."

"I think Sebastien felt like this, too," I said.

"No, no," he said. "Joël, Sebastien, and me, we were walking on the road together. Joël was in the middle, and Sebastien and me, we were on either side of him. I was on the side closest to the road. We saw the light and heard the automobile in the same instant. By the time we turned around, it was almost on my neck. Joël pushed me aside, so he had no time to run himself. He was struck and thrown into the ravine."

I listened for signs that Man Rapadou was in a deep sleep in the next room, her loud snoring and occasional shifts on the bed.

"Then the automobile stopped and the people came out," he said. "I didn't see Sebastien. I didn't know where he was. I thought he was hit, too. I ran off to hide behind a tree in the dark. The old man wanted to stay and look for us, but the other one, the son-in-law, was in a great haste."

I wanted to tell him that he was right to run, brave even, that perhaps it was Joël's day to die, that there might have even been a worse death waiting for Joël in the slaughter. I wanted to say most of those things that never comfort the person hearing them, but only the one saying them.

"It could have been me too at the church with Mimi and Sebastien if I hadn't gone to sell the wood." He continued. "Yes, I saw them put Sebastien and Mimi and all the others on a truck. I saw it all from the road. They made them stand in groups of six and then forced them to climb. The priests asked to stay with the people, but they took the priests separately, and then they took the doctor and the people together. If he wanted to be a Haitian, they told Doctor Javier, they would treat him like a Haitian. I saw Mimi climb when her turn came. Sebastien was in line behind her. Her knees went weak when she was climbing, and she almost fell. The doctor offered his hand to her, and Sebastien supported her from the rear. I saw all this from the road where I was hiding. I wanted to do for them what Joël had done for me, but I didn't. I couldn't. Even in the river, with Wilner, I couldn't. The thought came to me that I should swim across the river again, collect his body to be buried on this side. All the soldiers. All the guns. I couldn't. I have not been able to do for anyone what Joël did for me. And I never will. No. Never. Because the more I see people die, the more I want to guard my own life."

I reached over and placed my hand on his sweaty trembling leg, to keep him quiet, to keep him still. My fingers crept up his thighs with his hands guiding mine. I felt for his face in the dark and touched his large Adam's apple, which bobbed up and down as though about to slide out of his mouth.

He turned over on his side and slipped my nightdress off my shoulders. For a while we both lay on our backs staring at the darkness above us. What now? What then? Who else did we know to turn to?

"It could have been me too at the church with Mimi and Sebastien," I said. "If I hadn't noticed two bloody spots on the back of the señora's dress and stayed a while longer with her. And maybe Odette died in the river because I pressed down on her nose too hard, though this was not my intention."

"Odette died when Wilner died," he said. "They killed her when they killed him."

And for this I was grateful. More grateful than he knew.

His body immediately leaped up to meet mine when I climbed on top of him. I was probably lighter than he expected, bonier and smaller framed than he'd thought. For a while I felt as though he was carrying me, the way Señora Valencia had carried her son and daughter in her womb, the way

Kongo might have carried his son Joël, after he'd died, the way first he and then the stranger had carried Odette. Then it was me carrying him. After a while it was as though we were both afloat at the same time, joined in a way that we could never be speaking together, or even crying together.

For several months, as I'd imagined Sebastien's return, I'd wondered whether my flesh could feel anything but pain. Perhaps Yves had wondered the same about his own.

His breathing was loud and fast like the vapor raising the lid off a steaming pot. Then his body froze abruptly and became heavier and I thought that his heart had stopped, that he had died right there on top of me. He ground his teeth and mumbled to himself, trying to push out everything that wanted to remain safely hidden in him. In the end, all he let out was a flash flood of tears, tears that rolled down my forehead, stung my eyes, made me sneeze when they slipped into my nostrils, and tasted like my own when they fell on my tongue.

As he rolled back on his side of the bed, I felt an even larger void in the aching pit of my stomach. I put on my nightdress and slipped under the sheets. He stepped off the bed, put on his pants, and went outside, leaving the door half open. Sitting under the traveler's tree, he examined the sky and opened a new pack of La Nationale cigarettes.

In the moonlight, I could almost see the silhouette of bones pushing themselves out in his back. After smoking a few of the cigarettes, he threw the rest of the pack against the side of the house and came back inside. When he climbed onto the bed, I pretended to be asleep—or even dead.

35

The next afternoon, when I went back to Man Denise's house, the doors were bolted shut and one of the girls who had been looking after her told me that Man Denise had buried some coffee beads in the yard and then returned to her people in Port-au-Prince.

"Do you know where in Port-au-Prince her people live?" I asked.

She shook her head no, turned her back to me, and looked towards the lime-colored hills on the other side of the house.

"Maybe she was tired of being told the same thing, in so many ways," the girl said. "Might be she went someplace where only her children would find her if they come back."

She was mending a blouse that didn't need mending at all, something she was making smaller to fit her own body. I offered to fix the blouse for her, but she would not let it out of her hands. So I watched as she stitched her uneven seams and sewed it too narrow for her shape.

"Better you go," she said. "She is never coming back to this house. Her people will travel from Port-au-Prince to sell the house, is what she said. But she herself will never set her foot here again." The girl tore out the new seams she had sewn for the blouse and started making darts in the lining. I wished I could have been with Man Denise much longer. I wish I could have done more for her. But some sorrows were simply too individual to share.

"Better you go now," the girl said.

So I went to the Cap's cathedral, where a late afternoon Mass was being held. A group of consecrants lined up to accept the Eucharist at the feet of a giant crucifix that was bleeding crimson paint for blood.

I stood in the back near a slanted wall of votive candles and watched the whole assembly march to the altar and then back up again, crossing themselves and bowing to the crucifix one last time before they turned their backs to it.

A woman slipped in next to me with her hands outstretched towards the candles and a transparent window of La Vierge, whose dress was made of sun sieved through blue glass.

"No communion for you?" she asked, looking away from the Virgin's downcast eyes.

"No communion," I said.

"No confession?"

"No confession."

"Even as you say one simple word," she said, with an open-mouthed smile, "I know the sound of your talk. Did you just return?"

"Some time ago," I said.

"Me too. Some time ago," she said. "I used to have a little trade of my own, selling things there, but now I work for the priests here, cleaning the church, and cooking for them."

I looked her over for a mark, a scar, some damage that I could see. She was looking at my legs, wondering perhaps if that was the only way in which I'd been hurt.

"Where did you live there?" she asked.

"Alegría," I said.

"Never went there," she said.

"Where did you live?" I asked her.

"Higüey," she said. "Was it cane country where you were?"

"Small cane, small mills."

"The place where you lived, is Alegría what it was called officially or did our people christen it this way?"

"I've always heard it called this," I said.

"People I was with, they'd christen places. And the name they gave these places nobody outside knew. Was there much joy where you were, that they'd call it Alegría?"

For as long as I could remember, people had always called the cluster of rich homes and mountains, streams, and cane fields that surrounded Señora Valencia's house, Alegría.

"Maybe the people who called it this were jesting," I said.

She let out a laugh too noisy for any sacred place.

"You here to talk to the priests about the slaughter?" she asked. "Father Emil, he's the one who listens to the stories."

She pointed out Father Emil. He was the shorter and fatter of the two priests standing at the altar. The other one was older, French, and white, with hair like a mare's forelock falling into his eyes.

"You will have to wait some," she said, "until after the Mass and all the alms are given for the day."

After the Mass, the priests went out on the steps in front of the cathedral and distributed bread to the poor waiting outside. The woman ran to a back room and came out with two rolls of bread. She placed them in my hand without a word so I would not be shamed by accepting them.

As the fathers walked past us on the way back inside, she grabbed Father Emil's cassock and said, "Father, this one here has been waiting a long time to see you."

Father Emil looked down at the bread in my hand and gave me a nod of pity. The woman pressed her hands against my back and shoved me towards him.

I followed him to a room behind the altar. The room had a wide desk, two cane-back chairs, a small cross on the wall, and a glass case full of books for the school the priests ran behind the church.

"You've come to talk about the slaughter?" he asked, offering me one of the fragile cane-back chairs. He slipped behind the desk and sat down. "To all those who tell us of lost relations, we can offer nothing, save for our prayers and perhaps a piece of bread. So we have stopped letting them tell us these terrible stories. It was taking all our time, and there is so much other work to be done."

"Father, I have not come to tell you a tale," I said. "And I've already received a piece of bread."

"Then how can I be of service to you, my child?"

"I want to know if you have heard of Father Romain or

Father Vargas, who lived and served on the other side of the river?"

He joined his hands together and pushed his body forward, towards my chair.

"In churches all over this land, we have prayed for them," he said, glancing up at the simple cross on the wall behind me. "Word of their struggle has reached us through our other brothers in the faith."

He seemed pleased that there was at least something he could do for me.

"So they are not dead?"

"They suffered much in prison, but they are still alive. Some members of the church approached the Generalissimo on their behalf and they were both liberated. After he was released, Father Romain was asked to leave the other side, even though he wanted to stay and help those of our people who have remained there."

I reached across the desk and squeezed his joined hands.

"Did you know them?" he asked.

"I did know them, yes."

"Father Romain is living near the border, in Ouanaminthe, in a tiny shack with his younger sister, not a nun, a blood sister." He smiled. "A singer. The house is near an old grange where a clinic was erected during the crisis. He wanted to be as close to his old parish as possible."

"You are a miracle, Father," I said, kissing the still warm rolls of bread rather than him.

36

That night, I wrote a simple note to give to Father Romain if I saw him. My words were written for Doctor Javier, who, if he was not still in prison, might visit Father Romain at the border.

Por favor—Doctor Javier,
I would be most grateful for your guidance
as to where to find Micheline Onius and
Sebastien Onius, who are said to have
perished in Santiago at the time of
the slaughter. Desiring to know if you
have seen and know this to be true.
Signed,
Amabelle Désir

I added the location of Man Rapadou's house, along with the street number of the merchant on the quay who sold us most of our sugar and flour. If Doctor Javier was ever handed my note, he would know where to find me.

When Yves came to bed that night, he kept himself on the far end of the mattress and took great pains for our skins not to touch. Before he fell asleep, I told him I would be going to the border the next day to visit Father Romain.

The following morning, he started early for the fields, but left ten gourdes with his mother, some of it for me to pay for the camión to take me there.

During the journey back to the border, I was struck by the size and beauty of the mountains, their hiplike shapes becoming clearer as we drove alongside them.

The camión stopped in front of a field of dust-feathered grass surrounding the grange where the old makeshift clinic had been. As I approached the grounds where the dead and wounded had lain, I thought of Odette and my stomach churned.

The ground was slipping beneath my feet; the sun seemed to be moving closer until I felt like it was stationed next to my face, melting my skin and blinding my eyes. The rocks on the ground become as large as pillows and finally I fell, making of the earth a warm bed.

I knew I should call for help, but there was no one coming and going, alive or dead. Besides, I felt so rested, I did not want to be disturbed. Above me spun a sky full of grass and the planks nailed in twos across the grange door.

I remembered once, when I was a girl, watching an infant boy my mother and father had midwifed into this world. A month later, the mother left the boy with us when she went to market. While he was sleeping, he rolled himself into a ball and spun around on the bed. I watched him do this for some time before I called for my father, who was cutting wood outside, and my mother, who was washing clothes behind the house.

"I think this baby has the evil in him," I told them.

My father laughed and slapped the little boy's bottom, which made him stop his spasms. Then he explained, my father, that sometimes in the first year, babies remembered their births with their bodies and had to repeat it many times before they could forget. When they did this, you were to help them recollect the whole thing, especially their coming out, by tapping them on their bottom as had been done to them after their birth.

Some time later, I woke up and stumbled to my feet. Miraculously, I had not hurt myself. I wiped my face with the back of both hands and walked to a limestone house in the distance, a solitary lodging in a large open field. An old woman sat crouched in the doorway, shelling peas on her lap. Her thumbs dashed in and out of the soft green pods, thrusting out perfectly round green peas into a half filled bowl.

"I've come to see Father Romain," I said.

She pointed down the field to a boxlike clapboard shack with a zinc roof.

The front door was open, but I knocked anyway. A young woman came to the door, wearing a flowered sundress, the top of which barely covered her small flat breasts. She was fanning her face with two long flame tree pods that made a haphazard melody as she waved them back and forth.

"Is Father Romain here?" I asked.

"Who wants him?" She continued to swing the pods, making it hard for me to hear her voice above the clatter.

"They call me Amabelle," I said. "I knew him in Alegría."

Swinging the pods even harder, she said, "I do this when I'm not in view of my brother so he knows where I am. It comforts him."

Stepping out of the doorway, she motioned for me to walk inside.

"Do not be saddened if he does not remember you," she said. "So many people have come to him asking about their relations, but when he was arrested, he was always kept with the other priest, Father Vargas. He was never with the Haitian prisoners."

She stopped the rattling and led me through a bare room, then out to the yard, where Father Romain was sitting on a rocker beneath a cluster of mango trees.

"Jacques!" she shouted. "You have a visitor, someone who knew you in Alegría."

Father Romain was wearing a straw hat that covered most of his face. A thicket of sable hair peeped through the open collar of his long roomy shirt. His hands trembled as he squinted, fumbling to tie a piece of thin orange paper around the skeleton of a small kite. When his jaws quivered, he reached up and stroked his cheek to control the twitching.

"Who has come?" he muttered. Spittle was glistening from either side of his mouth. Though still young, he had the look of those who no longer recognized anything, people for whom life was blending into one large shadow, their vision clouding over as they surrendered their sight to very old age.

The sister left the yard, went into the room, and brought out another set of chairs. Father Romain's eyes traveled up and down, from the trunk of the mango trees and then back to his sister, before he saw me.

"Speak loudly and tell him what you must tell him," she said. "His mind wanders."

"Father, my name is Amabelle Désir," I said.

"Yes, Amabelle Désir." His voice was a distant mumble as he held the kite up to his face.

"Father, do you recognize me?"

He shook his head from side to side.

"You don't remember me?"

"No," he said.

"Father, I need to know if perhaps you encountered Mimi and Sebastien Onius before or after you were in prison."

The priest shook his head from behind the kite. "Prison? Wi. Wi. I encountered many people in prison."

"See how they aged him in prison," his sister said.

"Our country is the proudest birthright I can leave them," babbled Father Romain. He was staring up blankly at his sister as if trying with all his powers of understanding to make out her words and mine too.

"They forced him to say these things that he says now whenever his mind wanders," she explained.

"On this island, walk too far in either direction and people speak a different language," continued Father Romain with aimless determination. "Our motherland is Spain; theirs is darkest Africa, you understand? They once came here only to cut sugarcane, but now there are more of them than there will ever be cane to cut, you understand? Our problem is one of dominion. Tell me, does anyone like to have their house flooded with visitors, to the point that the visitors replace their own children? How can a country be ours if we are in smaller numbers than the outsiders? Those of us who love our country are taking measures to keep it our own."

"I cannot stop him once he begins," the sister said, using

her bare fingers to wipe the growing puddle of drool on either side of her brother's chin.

"Sometimes I cannot believe that this one island produced two such different peoples," Father Romain continued like a badly wound machine. "We, as Dominicans, must have our separate traditions and our own ways of living. If not, in less then three generations, we will all be Haitians. In three generations, our children and grandchildren will have their blood completely tainted unless we defend ourselves now, you understand?"

Perhaps finally tired of talking, he stopped and lowered his face, his chin down to his chest.

"He was beaten badly every day," the sister said, stroking his shoulder. "When he first came, he told me they'd tied a rope around his head and twisted it so tight that sometimes he felt like he was going mad. They offered him nothing to drink but his own piss. Sometimes he remembers everything. Sometimes, he forgets all of it, everything, even me."

"Forget," mumbled Father Romain. He went back to concentrating on improving his kite. With more strength than I'd expect his trembling hands to have, he ripped a piece off the front end of his shirt to make a longer tail for the kite.

"Non, Jacques," his sister scolded, like a young mother correcting an errant child. "He's ruined many of his shirts this way," she said, turning back to me.

"Did you know Doctor Javier at all?" I asked the sister.

"Jacques, do you remember a Doctor Javier?" she asked.

Father Romain tied the strip of cloth from his shirt to the end of his kite and said nothing.

"I didn't know all of Jacques' friends," the sister said. "He is a priest. I am a singer and not a singer of religious songs."

"How long will you stay here?" I asked her.

"As long as he wants to be here," she said. "Where do you live?"

"In Cap Haitien," I said, "at the house of a woman they call Man Rapadou."

"Our family has a fine house in Cap Haitien, near the cathedral," she said. "I hope he will let me take him there soon. Even in this state, Jacques still wants to go back across the border to find the people he served in that little valley town, but he will be killed if he crosses again."

The sister shook the flame tree pods once more. Father Romain looked up, his eyes suddenly gleaming like a hungry dog being called to a long-awaited meal.

When I said good-bye to him, he greeted me again as though he were seeing me for the first time.

I pressed my missive into his sister's hands. "Please give this to him during one of those times when he remembers," I said.

As I left his house, I wanted, but could not bring myself, to visit the river. Instead I dreamt of walking out of the world, of spending all my time inside, with no one to talk to, and no one to talk to me. All I wanted was a routine, a series of sterile acts that I could perform without dedication or effort, a life where everything was constantly the same, where every day passed exactly like the one before.

That night in bed, I told Yves that I had seen Father Romain at the border.

"Don't you think I have gone there too?" he asked. "Don't you think I have seen him, the poor bèkèkè?"

"Please don't call him that," I said.

"Did you see what state he was in, talking, talking like that without stopping? His sister was the one who told me first that all the killings were meant to look as if they had been done by farmers with machetes; no rifles were ever intended to be fired as was done with Wilner."

"Why didn't you tell me you had gone to see him? Do you know that Man Denise is gone, that people have been coming to tell her that Mimi and Sebastien are dead?"

"I don't always tell you what I know or where I go," he said.

His silence before he fell asleep was weighted with rage and guilt. Like Sebastien, he had always lived for work. The two most important cycles of their lives were the cane harvest and the dead season. Now all he could do was plant and sow to avoid the dead season.

37

The dead season is, for me, one never ending night.

I dream all the time of returning to give my testimony to the river, the waterfall, the justice of the peace, even to the Generalissimo himself.

A border is a veil not many people can wear. The valley is a daydream, the village, the people, and Joël, with a grave that only a broken-hearted old man would ever know how to find.

I would go back with Odette to say her "pési" to the Generalissimo, for I would not know how to say it myself. My way of saying it would always be—however badly— "perejil." For somewhere in me, I still believe that perhaps one simple word could have saved all our lives.

I had never desired to run away. I knew what was happening but I did not want to flee. "Where to?", "Who to?", was always chiming in my head.

Of all the people killed, I will wager that there were many asking like me "Who to?" Even when they were dying and the priests were standing over them reciting ceremonial farewells, they must have been asking themselves, "Go in peace. But where?"

Heaven—my heaven—is the veil of water that stands

between my parents and me. To step across it and then come out is what makes me alive. Odette and Wilner not coming out is what makes them dead.

I was never naive, or blind. I knew. I knew that the death of many was coming. I knew that the streams and rivers would run with blood. I knew as well how to say "pési" as to say "perejil."

You may be surprised what we use our dreams to do, how we drape them over our sight and carry them like amulets to protect us from evil spells.

My dreams are now only visitations of my words for the absent justice of the peace, for the Generalissimo himself.

He asked for "perejil," but there is much more we all knew how to say. Perhaps one simple word would not have saved our lives. Many more would have to and many more will.

The more days go by, the more I think of Joël's grave. (Of Wilner's, Odette's, Mimi's, and Sebastien's too.) I could no more find these graves than the exact star that exploded and fell from the sky the night each of them perished.

The more I think about their graves, the more I see mine: a simple stone marker with written on it only my name and the day I die.

But it must be known that I understood. I saw things too. I just thought they would not see me. I just thought they would not find me. Only when Mimi and Sebastien were taken did I realize that the river of blood might come to my doorstep, that it had always been in our house, that it is in all our houses.

I once heard an elder say that the dead who have no use for their words leave them as part of their children's inheritance. Proverbs, teeth suckings, obscenities, even grunts and moans once inserted in special places during conversations, all are passed along to the next heir.

I hear the weight of the river all the time. It creaks beneath the voices, like a wooden platform under a ton of mountain rocks. The river, it opens up to swallow all who step in it, men, women, and children alike, as if they had bellies full of stones.

It is perhaps the great discomfort of those trying to silence the world to discover that we have voices sealed inside our heads, voices that with each passing day, grow even louder than the clamor of the world outside.

The slaughter is the only thing that is mine enough to pass on. All I want to do is find a place to lay it down now and again, a safe nest where it will neither be scattered by the winds, nor remain forever buried beneath the sod.

I just need to lay it down sometimes. Even in the rare silence of the night, with no faces around.

38

I waited for Doctor Javier's reply by watching Yves leave for the fields every morning to return home after dark. I waited for Doctor Javier's reply by feeling my wider, heavier body slowly fold towards my feet, as though my bones were being deliberately pulled from their height towards the ground. I waited for Doctor Javier's reply by sewing clothes for everyone who came with a piece of cloth and held it in front of me and for my effort offered a few gourdes, a plate of food, and sometimes nothing but a kind grin. Yes, I waited for Doctor Javier's reply by growing old.

His sister had moved Father Romain to a hospital in Port-au-Prince, so I didn't see him again until May 1961, after the Generalissimo was killed in a monsoon of bullets as he was being driven out of the capital city on a highway named after him.

Father Romain was in the Cap then for a family event and came to stand out in the sun on the cathedral steps and watch a parade of survivors singing on the street:

Yo tiye kabrit la! Adye!
They killed the goat! Adye!
It was the first time since the crowds waiting for the justice

of the peace that I had seen a group remembering, a strange celebration of the living and the dead, the children and grandchildren of the slaughter.

Father Romain had been forced to age faster than most of us, but I could tell under his hollowed cheekbones and high round bounty of salt-and-pepper hair that he was experiencing his own share of uncertain joy. He seemed like a different person, the older brother—no, the grandfather—of the man he once was, the man who had taught the children about the properties of the wind and the invisible substances in the air by flying kites.

I didn't know where the sister was that day but she was not with him or with us, those of us who took to the once fire-engulfed streets of the Cap to clank pots and cans and sing to celebrate the Generalissimo's passing.

Yves came home from the fields to wander in and out of the small crowd, nibbling at his lower lip as though he wanted to weep for every scream of our happiness.

Man Rapadou and I walked arm in arm, her body nimble and spry as she entered the last years of her eighth decade.

Man Rapadou had been essential to me in the simple routine of my life. We'd wake up together at the same time every morning after Yves had left for the fields and she would help me with my sewing. I treasured my sewing; I enjoyed feeling my index finger cramped inside the thimble, found many hours' pleasure in watching the needle rise and fall, guarding the fragile thread with caution as it snaked through the cloth. I never used machines because that would have taken away a great part of the physical enjoyment.

Every morning at dawn, Man Rapadou and some of the

women from the yard would go to market and bring back fresh ingredients for a meal that wasn't ready until late afternoon, closer to the time when Yves came home. Even though she knew he ate elsewhere, or maybe even had another woman looking after him, she still treated him like he was her helpless boy who had just enough strength to make his father's land come alive.

As his fortune had grown, Yves had added four more rooms to the courtyard, two of them mine and mine alone. (His mother did not want to move elsewhere and leave her old relations and happy-sad memories behind.) There were times when I shut myself in those two rooms that were mine and took to bed for months, times when I had too much lint in my throat, or an aching arm that prevented me from sewing, when the joint of my knee would throb, and the ringing in my ears would chime without stop. Other than those moments, the Generalissimo's death was the only reprieve from my routine of sewing and sleeping and having the same dreams every night.

"Oh, Man Amabelle, look at you doing the kalanda," someone called out from the crowd in front of the cathedral.

I didn't even realize I'd been dancing. Didn't even know I could dance. Still, it wasn't the compliment I heard but the title belonging to an elder—a "Man" like Man Irelle, Man Denise, or Man Rapadou—before my name.

I saw young men and women leaping with maracas and tambourines that day who were not yet born when I'd returned, and I felt time slither around me in a way it didn't when I was alone with Man Rapadou and her people in the courtyard.

Yves walked ahead of all of us, staying out of the crowd

spilling over into the shops. He seemed younger than he was; with a sunken chest and narrow waist, he looked like he had lived through one or two famines. He had gone back to shaving his head bowl-bald even though he no longer had any reason to fear collecting cane ticks in his hair.

He was not pleased with us for taking part in the instant parade; I could tell. He spoke so little now that I could read whole phrases on his sweaty knotted brows. The questions posed on his face that day were ones I was also asking myself.

How dare you dance on a day like this?

What could we do but dance?

It's like dancing on all the graves.

There were no graves, no markers. If we tried to dance on graves, we would be dancing on air. Besides, this was a harmless, effortless dance, one our people knew well, the dance of farewell to a departed tyrant.

For twenty-four years all of my conversations with Yves had been restricted to necessary prattle. Good-morning. Good-night. What goes? Good-bye. The careful words exchanged between people whose mere presence reminds each other of a great betrayal.

I had often hoped that he would find a woman to love him and take him away from the courtyard. I couldn't escape myself because I had nowhere else to go. I didn't have the strength to travel in search of distant relations whose lives had gone well enough without me; I didn't even know if they would recognize me if they saw me. Some of them might have come looking for me after my parents drowned, but maybe they thought I had drowned, too.

So in spite of the solemn expressions on many of the faces

in the crowd, in spite of those who wept even as they were dancing, in spite of the dead whose absence trailed us as did the dust of their bones in the wind, even as our chances vanished of ever glaring and spitting into his eyes, we were still having a celebration, if only because the Generalissimo was dead and we had survived.

After the crowd had thinned out, I walked up the steps in front of the cathedral, leaving Man Rapadou and Yves to wait for me on the sidewalk. Father Romain was standing with a group of parishioners walking out of the cathedral.

"Mon pè, you are better?" I asked from the outer row of the group.

"By His grace, yes." His voice was as tranquil as his eyes were suddenly attentive, the two most visible signs of the young man he had once been.

"I am Amabelle Désir, Father," I said. "I came to see you when you were in Ouanaminthe. I lived in Alegría. How is your sister?"

"You knew my sister?" he asked.

"Yes. I saw her in your house in Ouanaminthe."

"She still sings in nightclubs in Port-au-Prince." He extended his right hand to me, watching it rise from his side as though his own flesh was a marvel to him still.

"Father, will you return to Alegría now?" someone asked.

He seemed surprised that so many others knew about Alegría. "Alegría, a name to evoke joy," he said, his voice rising as if for a group before a pulpit. "Perhaps this is what its founders—those who named it—had in mind. Perhaps there had been joy for them in finding that sugar could be made from blood."

Yves and Man Rapadou climbed the steps and went to sit inside the cool cathedral. Yves did not even look at Father Romain as he walked by, supporting his mother's steps by holding on to her elbow.

"Father, will you return to Alegría?" Another person asked the question again.

Father Romain looked down at our group as though we had just planted the seed of this idea in his head.

"Yes, I will return," he said, "to help those of our people who are still there if I can."

"When will you return, Father?" I asked.

"I am no longer a father," he said, then corrected himself. "I am a father to three young boys. I am no longer with any order."

"Why, Father?" the question escaped from an unguarded mouth.

"It took more than prayers to heal me after the slaughter," he said with a sadness that he was too distraught to show when I first saw him at the border. "It took holding a pretty and gentle wife and three new lives against my chest. I wept so much when they arrested me. I wept all the time I was in prison. I wept at the border. I wept for everyone who was touched, beaten, or killed. It took a love closer to the earth, closer to my own body, to stop my tears. Perhaps I have lost, but I have also gained an even greater understanding of things both godly and earthly."

39

That night, I watched from my front room as Yves sat under a newer, almost grown traveler's palm, which he had brought there and planted himself in the same spot as the old one that had withered and died. He was reclining on a rocking chair with a bottle of rum in his hand, looking ahead at nothing in particular except maybe the fireflies that lit themselves in unison as they circled him. The slaughter had affected him in certain special ways: He detested the smell of sugarcane (except the way it disappeared in rum) and loathed the taste of parsley; he could not swim in rivers; the sound of Spanish being spoken—even by Haitians—made his eyes widen, his breath quicken, his face cloud with terror, his lips unable to part one from the other and speak.

Over the years, his father's land had grown into more than two dozen acres of bean fields. The more he produced, the more land he bought. His family now owned rice paddies, sorghum and wheat plots, coffee, cacao, and yam lots. He had also built himself a cinder-block workhouse near a creek where he consulted with his workers, ate his midday meals, and took siestas during the late afternoons. The creek itself was surrounded with mango, avocado, and papaya trees,

under which roamed guinea fowls and wild pigeons that
everyone in the area was free to hunt, just as they were to
help themselves to the ripening fruits on all of Yves' trees. In
his mother's old rocker, though, he was simply a poor man
alone, sipping from a bottle of the Gardère family's Réserve
du Domaine and dozing off now and again between glances
at the sky. Before swallowing a mouthful, he would spill the
costly rum on the ground, forming a circle of bubbled dust
for the ones we don't see, the untouchables, the invisibles.

He and I both had chosen a life of work to console us after
the slaughter. We had too many phantoms to crowd those
quiet moments when every ghost could appear in its true
form and refuse to go away.

As I sat on a white plastic bucket and watched him from
my doorway, I regretted that we hadn't found more comfort
in each other. After I realized that Sebastien was not coming
back, I wanted to find someone who would both help me forget him and mourn him with me. Perhaps this was too great
a gift to ask of a man who was in search of the same thing
for himself.

The plastic bucket slipped out from beneath me as I got
up. Yves turned around and watched me stumble, trying to
maintain my balance on my bad knee. By the time he reached
me, I was already on my feet. He let go of my hand and
walked back to the rocking chair, picked up the bottle of
rum, and went into his room.

Once he went, Man Rapadou crossed the yard and came
to my sewing room. She had a cold compress on her forehead and was trying to keep drips of water from sliding
into her eyes. She dropped her wide body down on a long

skirt to which I was adding some last pleats before going to bed.

"Man Rapadou, you are not sleeping well?" I asked.

"It's all this walking in the sun today," she said. "I should not have walked so long in the sun today."

"Are you sick?"

"Not sick, but very tired." She lay back on my bed, which was a plain cotton mattress kept purposely low, close to the ground.

"Amabelle, my life, like yours, has always been rich with dreams," she said. "My head barely touches the pillow at night when I dream that I'm falling."

"Falling?"

"I dream often that I am falling," she said. "And they get bigger, the things I'm falling from. First I am an infant falling out of my mother's body. Then I'm falling off my mother and father's house, a wooden house in the middle of a coffee grove. Then it's the house of Yves' father I'm falling from. Then I'm falling off little hills and cliffs. Then it's mountains; I'm falling off mountains. The next thing to fall from after mountain is the clouds, non?"

"When you fall, where do you come to land?" I asked. Perhaps it was an unnecessary question, but one I needed an answer to, to prepare myself for the time when I would be having these same kinds of dreams myself.

"I always wake up before I come to land," she said, "even if I see myself getting closer to the ground every day."

"What do you make of this type of dream?"

"When I was a girl," she said, searching with her coarse bent fingers for the contour of her own face, now buried under many layers of crow's feet and wrinkles, "my skin was so dry that sometimes it peeled off in scabs pink with blood, like fish scales. I was very clumsy because my feet were weak, but I knew how to slip into a fall, how to not fight the force of the earth pulling me down. When I became a young woman, somehow my feet got stronger and I never thought about falling again, until now."

I tried to gather her into my arms, which was impossible to do, given the breadth of her figure, so I patted the flesh on her back, between her neck and her waist as if burping a growing child.

"It's a hard thing to know that life will go on one day without you," she said.

I too felt and lived my own body's sadness more and more every day. The old and new sorrows were suddenly inconsolable, and I knew that the brief moments of joy would not last forever. When I saw a beautiful young man I tried to pair him up with my younger self. I dreamed of the life without pain that he might have brought me, the tidy parlor and spotless furnishings that our young children would not be allowed to touch, except to dust off on Saturdays.

"Old age is not meant to be survived alone," Man Rapadou said, her voice trailing with her own hidden thoughts. "Death should come gently, slowly, like a man's hand approaching your body. There can be joy in impatience if there is time to find the joy."

"How long has it been, Man Rapadou, since a man touched your big belly?" I asked, to make her laugh.

"Not as long as since one had touched yours," she said,

measuring the length of her own smile with the edge of her fingertips. "From time to time, life takes you by surprise. You sit in your lakou eating mangoes. You let the mango seeds fall where they may, and one day you wake up and there's a mango tree in your yard. "

I knew she meant this as a compliment to me, a kind word for my sudden arrival at her house some years before.

"I have not told this to anyone," she said, her hands patting her too wide hips, "but I believe there are many who suspect, even my son. The Yankis had poisoned Yves' father's mind when he was in their prisons here; he was going to spy on others for Yanki money after he left their jail. Many people who were against the Yankis being here were going to die because of his betrayal. And so I cooked his favorite foods for him and filled them with flour-fine glass and rat poison. I poisoned him. Maybe this is why I am falling in all my dreams. I'm going to him soon and I'm afraid. What will I say to him in the life after? 'Love is only pleasure; honor is duty.' I cannot simply say this thing that I told myself then. It is not enough now. I should not tell you this about me. You might do the same to my son. But then you do not love him like I did Yves' father, but greater than my love for this man was love for my country. I could not let him trade us all, sell us to the Yankis.

"I often hear that silence is holiness, and still I'm not holy," she said, wiping a tear from the side of her face. "I believed then that fortune would favor the brave. How young I was. There are cures for everything except death. I wish the sun had set on my days when I was still a young, happy woman whose man was by her side, with joy in his eyes and honor in his heart. "

The next morning, I left Man Rapadou asleep, with her sorrows, in my bed, to go climb up to the uneven cobblestone road that led to the citadel. There, on the outer galleries, I walked among a group of tourists who were wandering through, photographing the barracks, the stone walls, the rusting artillery, and the vaulted ceilings.

Using broken phrases in various tongues, local boys offered themselves as guides for individual tours through the interior corridors. One of the special guides was a very large Haitian man wearing a long-sleeved white shirt and a black tie. He was leading a group of twelve young white foreigners in beach attire.

With a sweep of his fingers, the man guided his group to the edge of a low wall to show them the ruins of the Palais Sans Souci, the king's old official residence down below.

Pointing to the goat-grazed hills of reddish grass in the direction where my parents' house used to stand, he said, "It was not unusual for people to live here, before the constant earthquakes drove most of them away. You could feel even the smallest earthquake in those hills." I couldn't recognize anymore any place that resembled where our house had been, nor did I want to. Land is something you care about only when you have heirs. All my heirs would be like my ancestors: revenants, shadows, ghosts.

I wasn't certain why I had picked that particular group of white foreigners and Haitian guide to follow until I realized that both the guide's talk and the things that members of the group were whispering to one another were in Spanish. I trailed them to the open courtyard on one of the top tiers of the citadel. It was a place I had always avoided going as a child. In the middle was a raised block of concrete shaped like a coffin, a place sometimes believed to be the grave of Henry I.

As the group circled the concrete block, the guide told the story of Henry I.

"Henry Christophe was at first a foreigner here," he said. "He was born a slave in the Windward Islands and during his life made himself a king here." The large man tugged at the end of his tie as he spoke. Then either to caution his young charges against vainglory—or to be fair to history—he added, "The king was sometimes cruel. He used to march battalions of soldiers off the mountain, ordering them to plunge to their deaths as a disciplinary example to the others. Thousands of our people died constructing what you see here. But this is not singular to him. All monuments of this great size are built with human blood."

To make clear his sentiment, he tapped the mortar pile with his fists, reminding the group of the most unforgivable weaknesses of the dead: their absence and their silence.

"When the king was fifty-three years old," he continued, "he had a sudden apoplexy, which left him paralyzed. His enemies organized a revolt against him, and, rather than surrender, he shot himself with what some say was either a silver or a gold bullet. It is said that he was buried in this palace, many believe in this spot, but there is some mystery as to whether or not he is really under here. He could be anywhere in this palace or nowhere here at all."

As they moved away from the mortar, the man inspected the faces in the group to determine that everyone was still there with him. "Famous men never truly die," he added. "It is only those nameless and faceless who vanish like smoke into the early morning air."

40

This past is more like flesh than air; our stories testimonials like the ones never heard by the justice of the peace or the Generalissimo himself.

His name is Sebastien Onius and his story is like a fish with no tail, a dress with no hem, a drop with no fall, a body in the sunlight with no shadow.

His absence is my shadow; his breath my dreams. New dreams seem a waste, needless annoyances, too much to crowd into the tiny space that remains.

Still I think I want to find new manners of filling up my head, new visions for an old life, waterless rivers to cross and real waterfall caves to slip into over a hundred times each day.

His name is Sebastien Onius. Sometimes this is all I know. My back aches now in all those places that he claimed for himself, arches of bare skin that belonged to him, pockets where the flesh remains fragile, seared like unhealed burns where each fallen scab uncovers a deeper wound.

I wish at least that he was part of the air on this side of the river, a tiny morsel in the breeze that passes through my room in the night. I wish at least that some of the dust of his bones could trail me in the wind.

Men with names never truly die. It is only the nameless and faceless who vanish like smoke into the early morning air.

His name is Sebastien Onius. Seven years before his own death, he saw his father die. Death to Sebastien Onius was as immense as a tree-tossing beast of a raging hurricane. It was an event that split open the sky and cracked the ground, made the heavens wail and the clouds weep. It was not for one person to live alone.

Perhaps there was water to greet his last fall, to fold around him and embrace him like a feather-filled mattress. Perhaps there were ceremonial words recited in his ears: "Ale avèk Bon Dye," "Go with God," "Go in peace," a farewell not so solitary and abrupt, a parting like the dimming of the twilight, darkening the sky for shadows and stars at play.

His name is Sebastien Onius and his spirit must be inside the waterfall cave at the source of the stream where the cane workers bathe, the grotto of wet moss and chalk and luminous green fresco—the dark green of wet papaya leaves.

Sometimes I can make myself dream him out of the void to listen. A handsome, steel-bodied man, he carries a knapsack woven from palm leaves as he walks out of the cave into the room where I sleep.

"Amabelle, it is Sebastien, come to see you," he says. "I have brought remedies for your wounds. I've brought citronella and cedarwood to keep the ants and mosquitoes from biting your skin, camphor, basil, and bitter oranges to reduce your fevers and keep your joints limber. I've brought ginger and celery, aniseed, and cinnamon for your digestion, turmeric for your teeth, and kowosòl tea for pleasant dreams."

He stands over my bed, fills his lungs with the cloud of lint in the room. I reach over and try to touch him, but he scatters with my reach, like a stream of dust caught in a strong beam of noontime sunlight.

I sense that we no longer know the same words, no longer speak the same language. There is water, wind, land, and mountains between us, a shroud of silence, a curtain of fate.

"Tell me, please, Sebastien," I say. "I must know. Did you and Mimi suffer greatly?"

He breathes in more of the cloth dust in my room, as though he wants to inhale me and everything there too.

"Sebastien, the slaughter showed me that life can be a strange gift," I say. "Breath, like glass is always in danger. I chose a living death because I am not brave. It takes patience, you used to say, to raise a setting sun. Two mountains can never meet, but perhaps you and I can meet again. I am coming to your waterfall."

41

At first glance, the Massacre appeared like any of the three or four large rivers in the north of Haiti. On a busy market day, it was simply a lively throughway beneath a concrete bridge, where women sat on boulders at the water's edge to pound their clothes clean, and mules and oxen stopped to diminish their thirst.

The tide was low for October. So low that when the washing women dipped in a bucket, they came up with half of it full of water and the other half full of red-brown sand.

"You see how the river looks now," one of the women said as she threw a handful of sand back into the flow. "When the current rises, the water can kiss the bridge."

On the bridge, young soldiers whose faces looked too youthful to hold a past marched back and forth, patrolling the line marked by a chain that separated our country from theirs. They wore dark green uniforms, carried their rifles on straps on their shoulders, and drummed the ground with their shin-stroking laced boots. Our soldiers stayed farther back, away from the bridge, in the customshouse near an open road, the better to watch for invaders.

The border had lost a number of its trees. Holes were still

too evident where the trees had been plucked out and replaced with poles that held up doubled strands of barbed wire. All along the walls of spiked metal were signs that cautioned travelers not to cross anba fil, beneath the wires.

A tall, bowlegged old man with a tangled gray beard, wearing three layers of clothing padded with straw, walked up behind me. His clothes and hands were covered with dirt, but his face was clean, smelling of vanilla and coconut. His eyes seemed a bright cerise, lush and dense like velvet. The washing women called him "Pwofesè" and cackled as he circled his arms around my waist.

"Where are you going, Pwofesè?" they took turns asking, as though playing a game of chant.

"Grass won't grow where I stand," the professor whispered in my ears, in a voice that I could tell was rarely used, except perhaps on frolicsome occasions like this one. "I'm walking to the dawn."

Before I could drag myself away, the professor planted a damp kiss on my lips. I scrubbed the kiss off, reaching into the river for a fistful of water to cleanse my mouth. The washing women threw their heads back, opening their mouths to the sky to laugh.

"The professor's not been the same since the slaughter," one of them said. "Don't rub it off. Leave his kiss on your lips. Don't you know that if you are kissed by a crazy man, it brings you luck?"

As the professor ran off into the open plains, I walked towards a bare-chested boy who was sitting on the riverbank scribbling in a small drawing book. I had been told that he could help me find someone who could take me across the river. Squatting beside him, I dipped my feet in the water. The current bubbled, gently pulsing beneath my soles, like a baby's fontanel.

"Do you know someone who can help me cross the border without papers?" I asked, keeping my eyes on the water. The boy said nothing until he finished writing a whole phrase in jumbled schoolboy lettering.

"If you want to cross the border without papers, it will have to be at night," he whispered.

"Can it be tonight?"

"Perhaps," he said.

That night, I was met on the road before the bridge by a man in a black jeep. The man, the sole driver and occupant, ran a lottery along the border area—at least that's what the boy had told me. He wore a denim cap on his head and a red bandanna over half his face, starting at his nose.

Stepping out into the night, the man showed me the place he had reserved for me in the back of the car, a small hollow beneath a heavy blanket behind the front seat.

"They know me at the crossing," he mumbled in Kreyòl. "They won't trouble with me."

I squeezed myself into the cramped space, trying hard to ignore the stabs of pain coursing through my knee. Keeping my head down, I reached out and gave him the payment that he and the boy had agreed on. He eased the side door shut and we started on our way.

There was only a brief pause at the first border crossing.

The driver slowed the car at the Haitian customshouse to deliver a bribe to the night guards.

We came to another stop at the Dominican post on the bridge. I heard voices, lifted the sheet, and raised my head to one of the side windows.

"Stay down," the driver commanded.

In spite of what he said, I kept my eyes at the bottom edge of the window. The border guards expressed regret for the wait and quickly opened the car gates for the driver.

"Until tomorrow night," the driver said as he handed the guards more money.

I slept through most of the military checkpoints leading towards Alegría. Sleep had been a comfort to me for the last two decades. It was as close to disappearing as I could come.

The sun had risen when I woke up. The car was speeding along a dirt road between two walls of violet cane. The driver had removed the red bandanna from his face, but still had the cap tilted on one side of his head. He was watching me through the raised mirror in front of him, and I in turn examined his eyes. They were deep set and far apart, the color of clouded amber.

When he saw me looking at him, he removed his cap and turned away. He was a young man, younger than Sebastien when he had disappeared. His hair was braided in long thin plaits, dropping over his ears.

"So it is fitting now," I said in Kreyòl, "for me to look at your face?"

"This is dangerous, what I am doing for you," he said. His

voice was jubilant and loud. "Even with the Generalissimo dead, things are still not tranquil here. There are protests and riots in the capital. I believe there'll be another Yanki invasion soon."

The cane fields stretched for some distance, the stalks all crammed together like a crowd at carnival. He stopped the jeep in the middle of the fields and motioned for me to move to the seat next to him. As I climbed in, he disappeared inside the cane, then came out pulling his pants up by the belt.

"Why are you making this journey?" he asked, speeding down the road again.

"Are you certain you know the road to Alegría?" I asked.

"I will meet you in the square there, to take you back this afternoon," he said.

"And you? What will you do this morning?"

"I will not be in Alegría," he said.

We came out of the cane onto an asphalt road that led to a closed park across from a yellow government edifice.

"Here it is, your joyful land." He stopped in front of a cluster of frangipani with white and yellow blossoms, shading wooden benches at the entrance onto the square. "Wait for me here this afternoon. Try not to arrive early, or you might be mistaken for a beggar."

He climbed back into the jeep and sped down a wide boulevard, keeping one hand out, waving until he turned a corner and disappeared.

The main avenue rose upward towards several narrow streets with rows of palm-shaded sidewalks. Alegría was now a closed town, a group of haciendas behind high walls cemented with metal spikes and broken bottles at the top.

Flamboyants towered over these walls and old men crouching in cane-back chairs guarded the gates. Every house was a fortress, everyone an intruder.

As I walked back and forth along the cloistered cobblestoned streets, in the shadow of these walls, I felt as though I was in a place I had never seen before. There were only a few markers I recognized: three giant kapok trees, which showed their age by their expanse, and the row of almond trees—but perhaps they were newer ones, on perhaps a newer almond road.

I stopped to rest my knees and watched the streets fill with schoolchildren and their parents, pantry maids starting out for fresh food, vendors marching up to the gates to tempt the gatekeepers, and husbands leaving in chauffeured automobiles with curtained back windows. I was lost. The park where the driver had left me was perhaps where Father Vargas and Father Romain's church had been. The cane mills and compounds seemed to have vanished, and even after half a day's wandering, and being too proud (and perhaps too frightened) to inquire about them, I couldn't find either the stream or the waterfall.

I didn't know what Señora Valencia's life situation was, save for what I had heard from a woman I'd sewn a dress for, one who traveled back and forth across the border to peddle her wares, that both the señora and her husband were still alive. Her husband was now an official in the government. He was mostly in the capital, but she stayed in Alegría with her daughter. Though still married, the señora and her husband were living their own lives, the way things had always been. In any case, when I couldn't find the stream and the waterfall, I decided to test the señora's promise to stay in Alegría, near the graves of her mother and son, bound as we are to the places where our dead are lain.

After mistakenly appearing at more than two dozen gates, I finally found a house that looked like the one I'd been told belonged to Señora Valencia now. A large wrought-iron gate had been erected where Juana and Luis' house might once have stood. A cobbled drive wound its way up through a new stone-studded garden towards a pink washed patio.

A little girl in a brown school uniform ran up to the gate as soon as I got there.

"Are you the egg woman?" she asked.

"The egg woman?"

"My mami told me to watch for the egg woman."

"Who is your mami?"

"Mami."

"Who is the egg woman?"

"You are." The girl smiled; she was missing four of her front teeth, two at the top, and two at the bottom. By the time an older boy arrived, she had already lifted the latch and opened the gate for me. The young man rushed forward to undo what she had done, but I had already stepped into the garden.

"She is the egg woman," the girl said, smiling up at him. He tousled her hair and looked me up and down, searching for an egg basket.

"Is Señora Valencia still living here?" I asked. "My name is Amabelle Désir."

After all those years, I was surprised that my Spanish was still understandable.

The young man swayed nervously and shifted his weight from foot to foot. We had four more spectators now: three gardeners and a housemaid with a folded sheet pressed against her chest. The young man lowered his head, then looked to the others as if for help.

"I knew the señora for a very long time before I went away," I tried to assure him.

"They have a new house."

"I will show you." The little girl skipped out before they could stop her. The young man trailed behind her.

The new house was only a few kilometers from the old one, in a more protected area. You had to walk through a guava field before seeing the entrance. It was a large hacienda, four residences joined by a breezeway with a sun parlor and a vast garden on the side. I wrapped my fingers around one of the heart shapes in the grillwork of the gate and peeked at a row of wicker banquettes between the flame trees in the garden, which was filled with twice as many species of orchids as Papi had ever grown.

The girl rattled the gate playfully until a woman walked out on one of the front galleries and peered down at the entrance. The woman had a meaty dimpled face with round shoulders and a fleshy build. She was wearing a sand-colored uniform with a piece of faded matching cloth on her head. She called out for a manservant, but when the manservant did not come, she walked down to us herself, the dust rag still in her hand.

"What do you want?" she asked abruptly in Kreyòl-accented Spanish. Her jaws were tightly drawn, forming a perfect sorrowful ring with the rest of her face. Her voice squeaked one moment and was hoarse the next, as though she risked running out of breath at any time. She gave the girl and older boy a nod of recognition, then kept her eyes on the path behind us, as if waiting for someone to ambush her through the grill in the gate. When she stretched her neck, I saw that she had rope burns above her collarbone. They were even deeper and more pronounced than those on the woman at the border clinic, a deeply furrowed field.

"I would like to see la dueña, Señora Valencia," I said.

"Why?" she asked, pausing for a breath. "What do you want with her?"

"My name is Amabelle Désir," I said. "She will want to see me."

"You can go," she told the girl and the young man.

The young man dragged the girl away. The woman walked up the drive to the patio, with the haste of those afraid to displease at every moment of their day. Working for others, you were always rushing to or away from them.

She was out of breath and visibly uncomfortable when she returned to unlock the gate and motion for me to follow her up the drive, through a rock garden under the guava trees.

As I followed the handmaid down the long corridors inside the house, a surprising feeling of joy took hold of my body. I was beginning to feel glad that I had come, happy that I was going to see the señora again.

The place was airy, spacious, a breeze blowing in from the open terraces. Everything was polished and luminous: from the beveled brass staircase railings, to the old-fashioned chandeliers dangling from the ceilings. The woman led me through the pantry on the way to the parlor. In the center of the pantry stood a marble-topped cooking table. I slid my hand over the cooking table as I went by to wipe the dust and sweat from my palms. The table surface felt pleasantly cold, like the water in the old stream before dawn.

The parlor itself was in the middle of the house, with arches dividing it into several sections, four fans circling from the ceiling, and staircases with metal banisters leading to the top part of the house. The walls were covered with photographs of the señora and her family. I slowed my steps to gaze at them, trying to learn as much as I could before I saw her, in order to avoid any inevitably painful inquiries about those who were no longer in existence or who were no longer considered members of the family. All of her husband's pictures were taken in his uniform. The medals had grown larger and more numerous on his chest. Time had fattened him up, softened his youthful scowl. From frame to gilded frame, he had slowly turned into an old man.

Rosalinda too had a time line of photographs, first darker and taller above a small group of children in apronlike school uniforms, then posing like a beauty queen with a head of thick curly dark hair draping her shoulders as she was surrounded by the thirty youngsters of her court at her quince, and at last one of her leaning into the arms of a young man who carried a sword, attired in a uniform like her father's while she wore a bridal dress.

In Rosalinda's photographs, I could see traces of both her mother and father. She had maintained her father's bronze complexion, had taken his height; but mostly she had her grandfather's, Papi's, worldly and pensive smile, with similar thought lines across her forehead.

The largest image in the room, however, was a painting of a bone-white baby boy, watchful and smiling, in an ivory pearl and satin baptism dress with a matching bonnet framing his water lily–colored cheeks.

Señora Valencia sat facing this portrait as the handmaid and I waited for her to turn around.

When she finally rose, I saw that she was wearing a hibiscus print caftan that reached down to her ankles; the outline of her frame under the dress was narrow, almost gaunt. She used her chair back as a support before starting towards us. She had a few gray streaks in her hair and had taken to Doña Eva's old hairstyle, wearing the heavy lump of a coiled braid on either side of her face.

Once in front of me, she pushed her face at nose length from mine, then turned and marched back to her seat. I remained in my spot while she sat down and raised her coffee cup and sipped it dry, as if in her mind I had simply disappeared. The handmaid grabbed my elbow and tugged at it, encouraging me to leave.

The señora finally spoke. "You are wicked to come here and use Amabelle's name." Like the handmaid's, her voice was hesitant, gasping, nervous. She lowered her empty cup to the table in front of her while still keeping her back to us. "What do you take me for? I spoke to many people who said they watched when she was killed in La Romana, with some others who were hiding in a house by the sea. Pico told me for certain that she must have been killed."

That she did not recognize me made me feel that I had come back to Alegría and found it had never existed at all. But at the same time, without knowing it, she was giving me hope that perhaps all the people who had said that Mimi and Sebastien were dead, they too might have been mistaken.

The handmaid's face was vacant, like mine would have been, had I been standing in her place. She gave me a tolerant nod, but we both knew that she might have to lead me away at any time, if this is what her mistress asked her to do.

I wondered where all the guards were hiding. Where was all the protection that came with her husband's position? Perhaps soldiers would storm the room at any moment, arrest me, and drive me to the border for deportation.

Was I that much older, stouter? Had my face changed so much? How could she not know my voice, which, like hers, might have slowed and become more abrupt with age but was still my own? "I was here—there down the road—in your bedroom when your children were born," I reminded her. "You told no one of your labor pains until the babies were nearly here because you trusted your dead mother to look after you. Your son Rafael, Rafi, named for the Generalissimo, was born first. Your daughter was born second with a caul over her face. You named her Rosalinda Teresa for your mother."

It took some time for her to turn around again. I felt I had to keep talking. "What became of your portrait of the Generalissimo, which was in the parlor in your old house, down the road? Where is Juana? Where is Luis? Did Juana go and live with her hermanas, the nuns?"

"Where did we find Amabelle?" she asked, her voice less certain.

Now it was as if we were doing battle and I knew I must win; she had to recognize me.

"Your father saw me at the side of the Massacre River," I said. "Your father, he asked one of the children by the riverside to question me in Kreyòl, asking who I belonged to, and I answered that I belonged to myself."

I could see a bit of shame and regret in her posture as she took a few steps towards me. The awkwardness of her initial rejection, and what I saw as my coming too late, would allow for no close embrace, no joyful tears.

She took a few more steps in my direction, then hopped back as though I might be dangerous to touch. With a bashful flick of the protruding bone on her slender wrist, she motioned to the wicker sofas around the room, waiting for me to pick one to settle in.

"Sylvie, please leave us." She flicked her wrists once more, signaling for the handmaid to depart.

I too wanted to leave at that moment, but I sat down and stayed, a small part of me rejoicing in having conquered, having gained her full attention.

"We don't have much help anymore," she said once Sylvie was out of sight. "So few have remained loyal over the years."

She looked down at her hands. They were spotless, perfect and soft looking. I too looked down at my own hands, cut and scarred with scissors and needle marks. Why had I never dreamt of her? I wondered. (My dreams were sometimes my way of hoping and not hoping.) Was it because I never truly loved her? All I wanted now was for her to tell me where the waterfall was. What had become of the waterfall and the stream? They couldn't have disappeared. Some wishes sound too foolish when uttered out loud. But this is why I had come back to this place, to see a waterfall.

"Amabelle, I beg your forgiveness for not recognizing you." An odd pained smile never left her face, as though she were thinking of too much to say and could not find the exact words. "We all have changed so much."

"I understand," I said, feeling like an old ghost had slipped back under my skin.

"Where are you living now? Are you here or in Haiti?"

"In Haiti."

"I still paint. Do you see? I painted Rafi." She pointed to the large portrait of the bone-white baby boy in the baptism dress.

Then she told me, "Rosalinda is married."

I felt as though she were speaking to me on behalf of someone else. I couldn't stop thinking that perhaps an older member of her family, a doña with a similar face, similar manners, and a voice similar to hers, had come to keep me company until Valencia herself could talk to me.

When she was younger I could have easily guessed her thoughts, but now I didn't have any idea of what was on her mind.

"You didn't have more children?" I asked.

"Only the two you knew," she said. "I could have no more children. And you? Do you have a husband, children, grandchildren, Amabelle?"

"No."

"After you left, I had some bleeding for a few days. I had perhaps been negligent during my time of risk, after the children were born. Javier was the only doctor I trusted, and perhaps he could have helped me, but he vanished. Even with Doña Eva's connections, she never found him. Pico, he says he did all he could to search for him, but nothing helped. Certain people simply disappeared."

She called for Sylvie, who came running back into the parlor. Sylvie's eyes circled the room to avoid meeting the señora's gaze. Working for others, you are immediately inspected when you enter a room, as if the patrón or the señora is always hoping to catch you with some missing treasure in your hand.

Sylvie waited patiently for her orders in front of a column in the center of the room. She was soon forgotten, left to stand there.

"Papi died before Rosalinda married," the señora explained, pointing to Rosalinda's marriage portrait. "Rosalinda wanted to marry young. She is now in medical school in the capital with her husband. They are doing well, but with the riots in the city, they may come home again with her father this weekend."

"And how is Señor Pico?" I felt now that I could ask.

She joined her hands on her lap and hesitated before answering. "This is an unstable time for our country," she said.

"How did you come to change houses?" I asked.

"Everything must look so different to you now," she said. "Pico bought this house from the family of a colonel who died. They are all in Nueva York now, in North America, like Doña Eva and Beatriz." She breathed out, then slipped into a brisk, animated song—"*Yo tiro la cuchara. Yo tiro el tenedor. Yo tiro to' los platos y me voy pa' Nueva York.*" It was a song of sad and joyous exile, everything lost to Nueva York. "I throw away my spoon. I throw away my fork. I throw away my plates and I'm going to Nueva York."

"When we changed houses," she continued in a more relaxed voice, "Juana and Luis went back to their people. They were getting old and couldn't work anymore. I would have kept them, but they wanted to go."

She leaned forward and squeezed my hand, pressing her fingers down on my knuckles as if trying to leave her hand-prints on my bones.

"Amabelle, I live here still," she said. "If I denounce this country, I denounce myself. I would have had to leave the country if I'd forsaken my husband. Not that I ever asked questions. Not trusting him would have been like declaring that I was against him."

"I understand," I said.

"Do you truly understand?" Her face brightened with a kind of hope I no longer thought I could offer. "During El Corte, though I was bleeding and nearly died, I hid many of your people," she whispered. El Corte—the cutting—was an easy word to say. Just as on our side of the river many called it a kout kouto, a stabbing, like a single knife wound. "I hid a baby who is now a student at the medical school with Rosalinda and her husband. I hid Sylvie and two families in your old room. I hid some of Doña Sabine's people before she and her husband escaped to Haiti. I did what I could in my situation."

What could she have expected me to say? There were no medals to be given. If there were, I didn't know where to tell her to go to claim hers.

"I understand," I said.

"I hid them because I couldn't hide you, Amabelle. I thought you'd been killed, so everything I did, I did in your name."

"I don't see any trace of Don Carlos' mill. Were the people there slaughtered?" I did not want to feel indebted to her.

"None of the people in Don Carlos' mill were touched," she said, confirming what I had suspected, that perhaps if I hadn't told Sebastien to leave the compound and go to the church, he and Mimi might have been saved. "There are no small mills here anymore," she said, "only residences like this one."

Had the stream dried up when these houses were built, the rocks and the sand gathered for mortar, the water for power and lights?

"Amabelle, Pico merely followed the orders he was given," she said, releasing my hand. "I have pondered this so very often. He was told to go and arrest some people who were plotting against the Generalissimo at the church that night, then he was detained by those people who were on the road, that young man Unèl, the one who once rebuilt the latrines for us."

She sat perfectly still for some time, as though Unèl had appeared in front of her and she was examining him with her tearful gaze.

"We lived in a time of massacres." She breathed out loudly. "Before Papi died, all he did was listen on his radio to stories of different kinds of . . . cortes, from all over the world. It is a marvel that some of us are still here, to wait and hope to die a natural death."

All the time I had known her, we had always been dangling between being strangers and being friends. Now we were neither strangers nor friends. We were like two people passing each other on the street, exchanging a lengthy meaningless greeting. And at last I wanted it to end.

"I would like to know what became of the stream," I said.

"What stream?" she asked.

"The one that starts at the waterfall."

"There have been a lot of houses constructed here," she said, "but the houses have not replaced everything. There are many waterfalls still. If you like, I can show you the closest one that remains."

Garaged behind the main house was a wide, two-toned, green and white automobile with a yellow vinyl interior. Sylvie climbed into the back first. Then I took the seat beside the señora's. I saw the señora stifle a gasp as she realized that because of my bad knee, one of my legs now appeared much shorter than the other.

A man came running out from one of the smaller houses when she started up the automobile.

"Señora, you are going out?" he asked, resting his arm on the door on her side.

"I will not be long," she said.

"Should I not go with you?" he asked.

"Please open the gate for us," she said.

The man buttoned the last two buttons of his shirt as he hastened to the gate. Even though he was running as fast as his legs could carry him, the señora's automobile still reached the gate before he did. She waited there for him to open it for her.

"This is my daughter's automobile," she said, driving through the parted gates. "Our Rosalinda, Amabelle, she is so beautiful. She is my whole life. We get along very well, as it might have been with Mami and me. This car was a marriage gift from her father. She taught me to drive so I can move about by myself when I wish. He does not even know, my husband, that I can drive an automobile, isn't that so, Sylvie?"

"That is so, Señora," said Sylvie.

The señora drove her car almost at walking speed through the same streets I had previously traversed, then made a sudden turn that took us beyond all the large houses into wide open meadows, old cane land now filled with wheat and corn fields, the mountain ranges looming over them. We drove past clusters of casitas and small farms where children ran out to chase the car. Finally the señora added some speed, charging through a narrow trail inside a corn field that led abruptly to a long braid of water that grew wider as we climbed to its source.

The señora stopped the automobile with a sudden jolt that sent Sylvie's chin pounding into the back of my seat. We were nearly at the cliff above a giant waterfall, watching the water slide over the ledge into a deep pool, rising and falling with white foam spray. The drop was much longer and the pool deeper than the one I remembered. Perhaps time had destroyed my sense of proportion and possibilities. Or perhaps this was another fall altogether.

We sat there and watched the cascade change colors, from tear-clear to liquid orange.

"Perhaps it's just rained in the mountains, the fall is so strong," she said. "I understand why you would come this very long distance to see it. When we were children, you were always drawn to water, Amabelle, streams, lakes, rivers, waterfalls in all their power; do you remember?"

I did.

"When I didn't see you, I always knew where to find you, peeking into some current, looking for your face. Since then I can't tell you how many streams and rivers and waterfalls I have been to, looking for you."

We watched the pool until it was a perfect mirror of the sky, where the sun was about to set. Sylvie cleared her throat several times, a signal, perhaps, that she thought it was time for us to leave. When we didn't move, the anxious frown became more pronounced on her face; she wiped her sweaty palms on her lap and tried to temper the audible racing of her breath.

"What is it, Sylvie?" asked the señora. "Are you ill?"

Sylvie's upper lip was sweating, turning darker, and for a moment the outline of her face reminded me of Joël's lover, Félice, who'd had a beet-colored birthmark where she would have had a mustache had she been born a man.

"A question," Sylvie said, her voice rising and falling quickly, beyond her control. "If I could ask a question?"

The señora reached for a handkerchief from one of the hidden compartments in the automobile and handed it to Sylvie to wipe her face.

"What is your question, Sylvie?" she asked. "Please, calm yourself."

Sylvie took a few deep long breaths as she used the señora's handkerchief to wipe the perspiration from her upper lip.

"Why parsley?" asked Sylvie.

"What?" responded the señora.

"Why did they choose parsley?"

For some reason, it had escaped me before, I hadn't

noticed, how young Sylvie was. She must have been just a child when the señora borrowed her from the slaughter.

The señora turned to me and raised her eyebrows. She tried to smile, but an uneasy expression kept creeping back into her face. "Do you know, Amabelle, that we have never spoken before of these things, Sylvie and me?"

Sylvie lowered her head, and rocked it back and forth.

"There are many stories. This is only one," the señora said, turning her eyes back to the waterfall. "I've heard that when the Generalissimo was a young man, he worked as a field guard in the cane fields. One day one of his Haitian workers escaped into a nearby field where many things were growing, among them, wheat and parsley. So the Generalissimo would not see him, the Haitian worker crawled through those fields to hide. After the Generalissimo grew tired of chasing him, he called out to the Haitian man, 'If you tell me where you are, I'll let you live, but if you make me find you, I'll take your life.' The man must not have trusted the Generalissimo, so he kept crawling, but he took the Generalissimo seriously enough to cry out the names of the fields as he passed through them. In the wheat, he called out 'twigo' for trigo. And in the parsley he said 'pewegil' for perejil. The Generalissimo had him in plain sight and could have shot him in the parsley, but he did not because the Generalissimo had a realization. Your people did not trill their *r* the way we do, or pronounce the jota. 'You can never hide as long as there is parsley nearby,' the Generalissimo is believed to have said. On this island, you walk too far and people speak a different language. Their own words reveal who belongs on what side."

She concluded almost too abruptly. Sylvie was still shaking

her head, apparently not satisfied with the señora's explanation. Perhaps there was no story that could truly satisfy. I myself didn't know if that story was true or even possible, but as the señora had said, there are many stories. And mine too is only one.

"Come back to the house with us and stay tonight, Amabelle," the señora offered.

Sylvie raised her head and wiped the tears from her eyes. "I have always wished, Madame," she said to me, "for an answer."

"I must go back to the square in town," I said. I didn't want the young man to leave without me.

"Amabelle, can you not stay longer?" the señora asked.

"I cannot stay at all," I said. "Someone is waiting for me."

She drove very quickly back to the square, where the young man was waiting. While he waved his arms over his head, motioning for me to hurry, we sat there unmoving in the silence of the señora's daughter's automobile.

"You will come again, Amabelle?" the señora asked.

I did not want to part with a lie. We left it simply at a clumsy awkward handshake, which, after a moment, she embellished with a fast kiss on my left cheek. I opened the car door and stepped out.

"Amabelle, it was generous of you to visit," the señora said.

"Go in peace, Sylvie, Señora," I said.

The young man offered me his hand to help me into his jeep. The señora stepped out too and leaned on the front door of her daughter's car and waved. With a distant gaze, Sylvie stood devotedly at her side. And in Sylvie's eyes was a longing

I knew very well, from the memory of it as it was once carved into my younger face: I will bear anything, carry any load, suffer any shame, walk with eyes to the ground, if only for the very small chance that one day our fates might come to being somewhat closer and I would be granted for all my years of travail and duty an honestly gained life that in some extremely modest way would begin to resemble hers.

Go in peace, Señora.

The driver started back to the border at great speed. He had a rendezvous and wanted to arrive before morning. He knew how to avoid the military checkpoints, he said, to save time.

I closed my eyes during the whole journey. I could still hear the thunderous waterfall crashing down inside my head, feel the spray against my face, even though we never got out of the car. Sebastien, I didn't find. He didn't come out and show himself. He stayed inside the waterfall.

After some time, the young man tapped my shoulder and asked, "Are you dead there? You can't be dead. It will not be good for me if you are dead."

I could smell Presidente beer and chewing tobacco on his breath. Without opening my eyes, I said, "No son, I am not dead."

"Why do you sleep so much?" he asked. I could tell he desired some conversation, a voice to help keep him awake and in control of the car. "Did you not find the people you went to see?"

We drove in silence for some time until his fingernails drummed my shoulder again.

"It's the middle of the night now," he said. "You can open your eyes and not see anything."

"Are we far from the border?" I asked.

"Not far," he said.

"What work do you do?" I closed my eyes again. "You do more than lottery, do you not?"

"I help bring workers into La Romana for the sugarcane," he said.

"Why do you do this?" I asked.

"The people here need their sugarcane and other things cut," he said, "and people suffer for lack of work in our country."

"Do you know of the big slaughter some years ago?" I asked.

"My mother ran from it with me when I was a baby," he said. "My father died in it."

"So you lived it?"

"If that is what you want to say."

We said nothing more until we were at the bridge crossing. The guards did not even glance at me as we drove through the gate. I tried, in vain, to catch a glimpse of the river, a sliver of moonlight flashing on the surface of the water, a reduced shadow of the sky.

I asked him to let me out before we reached the Haitian customshouse and the open road. He stopped the car and turned off the lights. "Just leave you here? I cannot do that," he said. "I know it's the same time of year as when the kout kouto happened. If you want to stop for a moment, say a prayer, and light a candle, I will wait for you, but not for long because I have an important rendezvous."

"I want you to go now," I said.

"What will you do here?"

"My man is coming for me," I lied. "If he's not waiting at the customshouse now, he will be there soon, and even if he does not come, the guards will let me sleep out front. Besides, it is not long until dawn."

Perhaps pretending to believe me eased his conscience. He was in a hurry and did not want to argue with me any longer. Maybe he was even afraid of ghosts. Every now and then, I'm told, a swimmer finds a set of white spongy bones, a skeleton, thinned by time and being buried too long in the riverbed.

"You are certain you want to stay here all night?" the young man asked.

"Certain," I said.

He spat a clump of chewing tobacco out of the side of his mouth as he considered this. "You are a crazy one," he said.

As he drove off in his car, I walked down to the bank of the river, trying not to trip over my own feet. In the coal black darkness of a night like this, unless you are near it, the river ceases to exist, allowing you to imagine just for a moment that all of them—my mother and father, Wilner, Odette, and the thousands whose graves are here—died natural deaths, peaceful deaths, deaths filled with moments of reflection, with pauses and some regret, the kind of death where there is time to think of what we are leaving behind and what better things may lie ahead.

The day my parents drowned, I watched their faces as they bobbed up and down, in and out of the crest of the river. Together they were both trying to signal a message to me, but the force of the water would not let them. My mother, before she sank, raised her arm high, far above the pinnacle of the flood. The gesture was so desperate that it was hard to tell whether she wanted me to jump in with them or move farther away.

I thought that if I relived the moment often enough, the answer would become clear, that they had wanted either for us all to die together or for me to go on living, even if by myself. I also thought that if I came to the river on the right day, at the right hour, the surface of the water might provide the answer: a clearer sense of the moment, a stronger memory. But nature has no memory. And soon, perhaps, neither will I.

I heard something flap out of the water, like rice rising and falling on a winnowing tray, the tiny husks separating from the grains. A shadow slipped out of the stretch of water before me, a ghost with a smile on his face, his cheeks grainy from the red-brown sand, his eyes bright red like the inside of a flame.

It was the professor, with his three layers of clothing padded with drenched straw, the river dripping from him as he stopped for a moment and stared blankly at my face. He sucked in his breath through his nose, perhaps taking in a few tiny sand grains with the night air as he did. He scratched his tangled beard, then continued down the riverbank, his foam sandals flopping between the sand and the soles of his feet.

I closed my eyes and tried to imagine the fog, the dense mist of sadness inside his head. Would the slaughter—the river—one day surrender to him his sanity the same way it had once snatched it away?

I wanted to call him, but only by his proper name, not by the nickname, Pwofesè, the replacement for "crazy man," that he had been given. I wanted to ask him, please, to gently raise my body and carry me into the river, into Sebastien's cave, my father's laughter, my mother's eternity. But he was gone now, disappeared into the night.

I removed my dress, folding it piece by piece and laying it on a large boulder on the riverbank. Unclothed, I slipped into the current.

The water was warm for October, warm and shallow, so shallow that I could lie on my back in it with my shoulders only half submerged, the current floating over me in a less than gentle caress, the pebbles in the riverbed scouring my back.

I looked to my dreams for softness, for a gentler embrace, for relief from the fear of mudslides and blood bubbling out of the riverbed, where it is said the dead add their tears to the river flow.

The professor returned to look down at me lying there, cradled by the current, paddling like a newborn in a washbasin. He turned around and walked away, his sandals flapping like two large birds fluttering damp wings, not so much to fly as to preen themselves.

He, like me, was looking for the dawn.

Acknowledgements

Mèsi Anpil, Mucho Gracias, Thank You Very Much . . .

This book is a work of fiction based on historical events. Many dates have been changed, some events altered for narrative flow. Most of the inaccuracies or other place and time inconsistencies can be explained in that fashion. As to any others, please forgive the reach of my artistic license.

I am extremely grateful to the Lila Wallace-Reader's Digest Fund for the great honor, and support of its writer's award, which allowed me the time to write. The Barbara Deming Memorial Fund and The Barnard College Alumnae Association for the travel grants that got my research started. To Ledig House International Writer's Colony for a month's shelter. To Julia Alvarez, so generous with time and directions, to Lionel Legros (and SELA) for source suggestions and documents, to Jonathan Demme for the gift of many out-of-print books and papers. And to Archibald Lawless for the ongoing loan of an amazing office and a precious heart, I will always be grateful.

My most heartfelt thanks to Ambassador Bernardo Vega, Madame Jeanne Alexandre, Nicole Aragi, Myriam Augustin, Patricia Benoit, David Berry, Joanne Carris, Angie Cruz, Francis Cruz, Jacqueline Celestin-Fils-Aimé, the late Jean Desquiron, Junot Diaz, Pierre Domond, Lionel Eliel, Jean Paul Fils-Aimé, Melanie Fleishman, Laura Hruska, Juris Jurjevics, Michéle Marcelin, Caroline Marshall, Sheila Murphy, Kareen Obydol, pigeon voyageur, and Dr. Michel-Rolph Trouillot.

To my manman, my muse, who taught me all about pèsi and other mysteries. Yes, I do always remember that these stories—and all the others—are yours to tell and not mine. To Jacques Stephen Alexis, for Compére Général Soleil. Oné. Always.

The following works were also helpful in my research: Suzy Castor's *Le Massacre de 1937 et les Relations Haitiano-Dominicaines,* Bernard Diederich's *Trujillo, the Death of the Dictator,* Rita Dove's wonderful poem, "Parsley," *Blood in the Streets* by Albert C. Hicks, His Excellency Bernardo Vega's *Trujillo y Haiti,* as well as the pamphlet "Beyond the Bateyes: Haitian Immigrants in the Dominican Republic," written by Patrick Gavigan and published by the National Coalition of Haitian Rights. President Sténio Vincent's letter, which appears on the endpapers, was found among the papers of Sumner Welles in the Franklin Delano Roosevelt Library by Ambassador Bernardo Vega. The words of Rafael Trujillo's speeches were quoted and paraphrased from Chapter 21 of the book *President Truijllo, His Work and the Dominican Republic,* written by Lawrence De Besault and published in Santiago in the Dominican Republic by Editorial El Diario in 1941.

And the very last words, last on the page but always first in my memory, must be offered to those who died in the massacre of 1937, to those who survived to testify, and to the constant struggle of those who still toil in the cane fields.